NANSHE CHRONICLES 2

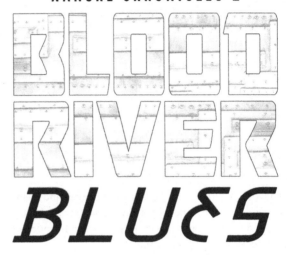

BLOOD RIVER

# BLUES

# JESSIE KWAK

First edition July 2022

Cover elements by diversepixel, CGPitbull, and Daniel Zadorozny

Cover design by Jessie Kwak and Robert Kittilson

Edited by Kyra Freestar

www.jessiekwak.com

# THERE'S MORE TO THE STORY!

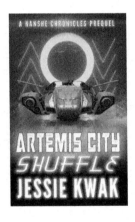

... in *Artemis City Shuffle*.

Raj and Lasadi may both be down on their luck. But as a series of near misses and close calls spin their futures into a collision course, that's about to change.

Get the free Nanshe Chronicles prequel novella!
jessiekwak.com/nanshe

# BLOOD RIVER BLUES

## NANSHE CHRONICLES 2

*Saint's path to you.*

# CHAPTER 1
## RAJ

THE PLANET INDIRA FILLS THE VIEWSCREEN WITH DEEP BLUE seas and emerald forests, delicate streaks of white clouds. The New Manilan continent is front and center with its frosted, jagged peaks and lush jungle carpets and coastline glittering with cities; the Teguçan archipelago stretches offscreen into the southwest corner of the Thúella Sea, partially obscured by the spiral arms of a gathering hurricane.

Raj Demetriou hadn't thought he'd ever be this close to home again. The home he's from, at least; he still hasn't quite redefined the word for himself in exile, and the last five days trapped in a tiny transport with Jay and Ruby and Alex is the closest he's felt in three years.

His home country, Arquelle, is comfortably on the opposite side of the planet. Thank the gods.

"Is everything where you left it?" Jay Kamiya asks.

"Pardon?"

"On your planet." Jay lifts his chin to the screen in front of them, where Indira is drawing the *Nanshe*'s tiny shuttle inexorably down out of orbit. Jay's at the controls, with Raj in the co-pilot's chair; Ruby and Alex Quiñones are strapped into the passenger cabin behind them. "All the continents and rivers and whatever you've got down there."

"Looks about the same," Raj says.

"You worried about going back?"

Anyone else, Raj would shrug out an easy *No*. But after five days getting to know Jay better, Raj has come to realize the other man doesn't ask idle questions, and he doesn't mind waiting for a true answer. So Raj takes his time.

"No," he finally says. "It's a big planet, we'll keep a low profile. Are you worried?"

"About Las, yeah." Jay says it without hesitation.

Raj wants to say something comforting: *She'll be fine, everything will be okay.* But Jay's not looking for unfounded reassurance — they have no idea what they'll find when they track Lasadi down. Raj turns back to the screen and studies the rapidly approaching surface of Indira, trading worry for calm, breath by breath.

It's been over a week since Lasadi Cazinho took off from Ironfall in the *Nanshe* by herself, without a word to anyone. Jay'd spent two days worrying before he broke into her messages to figure out where she'd gone. And when Jay called Raj, it took all of two seconds for Raj to volunteer to help Jay go after her.

Raj has worked a lot of odd jobs with makeshift teams over the years, but something clicked for him when he shipped out with Lasadi and Jay to Auburn Station just a couple of weeks ago. Throw in Ruby and

Alex Quiñones, and it almost — *almost* — feels like they're a real crew.

Before that job, Raj hadn't thought he'd ever feel this sense of camaraderie again. He'd spent the last three years paralyzed by the fear someone would uncover his past, which made real friendship out of the question. But when Lasadi and Jay found out what was in his sealed military records, they'd simply believed him when he said he was innocent.

He'd been waiting, terrified, for the mask to slip, only to find that when it did, it wasn't a catastrophe. Instead, he could breathe freely once more.

He'd found his people, he thought. Then Lasadi had disappeared on them all.

They'd paid for transport to Indira and found the *Nanshe* in orbit, but Lasadi had taken one of the two shuttles down to the surface. The flight plan gave them a set of coordinates in the heart of New Manila, and there was only one settlement for fifty kilometers, so it hadn't been hard to figure out where she was headed. In the days since she landed, though — Lasadi could be anywhere by now.

The one thing they know for sure is she was lured to New Manila under false pretenses. She'd received a message supposedly from an old comrade, yet Jay had discovered the person actually behind the message: Anton Kato, their old commander, the ex-leader of the Coruscan Liberation Army. Lasadi's former lover.

Jay hasn't told them much about Kato except that he was a good leader but bad for Lasadi. Raj can guess what he's insinuating: Raj's parents ran in powerful circles. He's seen firsthand the way some powerful men burn brighter by absorbing the flames of those around them. Lasadi is strong and fiery and capable, but even in the brief time they spent together during their last job, Raj could see how hard she was working to rebuild a psyche that something — some*one* — had systematically broken into pieces.

"You sure we're doing the right thing?" Raj asks Jay.

Jay gives him a wry smile. "Eighty-five percent at least."

"And the other fifteen percent?"

"Ten percent is Las blows a gasket that we thought she needed rescuing." His mouth flattens. "Five percent is she knew it was Anton and came anyway."

"You worried about seeing him?" Raj asks. He's been debating asking the question all day, but there's something about reentry that peels back layers of vulnerability. The way the view from your ship shifts from black to gentle pink to incandescent orange and blazing red, the atmosphere sparking against the windows, the ship shivering around you — it convinces the animal part of your psyche you're about to die.

Jay shakes his head. "Nope."

"No?" It's not the answer Raj expected to hear. "He basically accused you of committing a war crime."

"Yeah, but no, you know what I mean?" Jay takes a deep breath, dark brows drawing together in concentration. He blows out, huffing a lock of shaggy black hair out of his eyes. "I mean, he didn't do it to fuck with me and Las — or anyone else in Mercury Squadron. He did it because the Alliance needed a scapegoat, and Corusca needed peace, and he thought we were all dead."

"But your memories — your families . . ." Raj trails

off, waving a hand — he has the vaguest idea of how the Coruscan ancestral spiritual traditions work, and what it means to have your memory erased from the family altar.

"We were all willing to die for a free Corusca, Anton knew that." And Jay grins at him, hands firm on the shuttle's controls. "I've always wanted to try flying in atmo."

The shuttle shudders in the increasing atmosphere, the windows glowing with the friction of entry. Raj glances back through the open door to the passenger cabin. Alex gives him an excited thumbs-up; Ruby's eyes are squeezed closed, her fingers tapping rhythmically in prayer.

"Welcome to Indira," Raj says over the open channel. "Can't wait to show you all around."

The coordinates they found on the *Nanshe* lead them to a tiny clearing in the heart of the jungle that sprawls through central New Manila, the canopy swallowing their shuttle as they descend, the light mellowing from brilliant morning sun to dappled green and soft shadows. After five days of travel, the planet's gravity drags at Raj's limbs, his muscles remembering this specific weight — the weight of his youth — even though it's been more than three years since he's felt it.

Jay cuts the engine. It's a moment before anyone speaks.

"Well," Ruby says from the back. She unbuckles

with a click. "Shall we go see what this fuss is all about?"

"Do you have a read on the *Nanshe*'s other shuttle?" Raj asks.

Ruby's chin bobs in a distracted nod as she studies her tablet. "It's nearby," she says. "We'll start there, will we? Then head into town?"

"Bring everything you'll need with you," Raj says to the group. "If she's traveled on, we can probably follow her in the shuttle. But we may need to take local transport. Jay, you do the talking if we meet any locals."

"Copy that," Jay says; they've discussed this already. This deep in New Manila, the locals are more likely to be sympathetic to the guerrillas and the independence movement, and hostile to the Alliance. Raj can tone down his Arquellian accent, but he'd rather not risk the trouble.

"Did you pack snake spray?" Alex asks his older sister.

Her eyebrows shoot high. "The what?"

"Snake spray," says Alex. "It's the only thing that keeps the elephant boas from attacking you. They're as big around as one of those tree trunks."

"There are not snakes," Ruby says. She shoves her tablet into her pack. "You haven't the faintest."

"Tell her, Raj."

"There are snakes," Raj concedes; he doesn't know much about the jungle, but he does know that. "Probably not that big, though. Anyway, Alex will go first and let us know if he finds one by screaming his lungs out."

"Typical," grumbles Alex. "Send the kid out to

spring all the boobytraps. What would you do without me?"

"Don't get me started on a wonderful daydream," Ruby says. She blows him a kiss and palms open the door. "Off with you, then. Go find us some snakes."

After the stale, recycled air of the shuttle, the jungle's aroma hits them in full force: rich and humid, lush with fertile decay, and tinged bright green with freshly growing things. Ruby lets out a little gasp. Beside her, Jay takes a sharp breath. Alex grins, breathing deep.

Raj fills his lungs — it's not the air of his homeland, not the sharp tang of salt wind. But it's real atmosphere that's been filtered through the forests of a planet and freshened by its storms rather than recycled through the lungs of everyone else living in the same box as you in the middle of the black.

"That's good," he says. "That's really good."

"What's that noise?" Alex asks, and Raj looks up, listening to the deep-throated *whuff-hff-whuff* coming from high above them.

"There are a lot of primates that live up in the canopy." Raj had read it somewhere in school. "It's probably one of them."

"Probably?" Ruby asks.

"We're quickly reaching my limits of knowledge of the jungle," Raj says. "My parents used to take me to this replica reserve in Arquelle, but I was a kid."

"Best assume everything out here is going to eat you," Alex says cheerfully. "I'll protect you, sis."

"You watch your own self," Ruby says, checking the pistol strapped to her thigh. She tightens the straps of her pack, frowning at the slice of jungle through the shuttle door.

Jay hasn't joined in the banter; he's standing apart, lines of worry sketched between his dark brows. "What was out here for you, Las?" Jay murmurs, and the others fall silent a beat; no one answers. Finally Jay sighs. "C'mon. We gotta find her."

Jay hoists his pack onto his shoulder and hops out of the shuttle, boots thudding softly in the clearing. Alex hops out after him, stumbling a touch in the unfamiliar gravity; Ruby follows more carefully. Raj brings up the rear, palming the shuttle closed and locking it.

"Which way's the other shuttle?" he asks Ruby. She points to the east, and Alex sets out in that direction, heading towards the edge of the clearing and vaulting a fallen log.

"Here, snakeys," the kid calls. "Ruby wants to say hello."

"Alex, hold on," Raj says before he even knows he's going to. His hand falls to his sidearm, loosening it from the holster automatically while his conscious brain tries to parse what his subconscious is telling him.

Something's wrong.

Something about the sudden stillness of the birds, maybe. Or he'd heard a strange crack of a twig, scented some bitter, sulphuric aroma under the redolence of the jungle. Whatever it is, Raj is too slow to put his finger on what — as he opens his mouth to order Alex back, the quiet *phap* of a stun carbine cuts through the rustling of a breeze high above them. Alex hits his knees with a yelp.

Raj's pistol is in his hands and Ruby at his back

almost immediately; Jay's taken cover with his pulse rifle. But a half-dozen guerrillas in jungle-green fatigues shimmer like mirages at the edge of the clearing. One has their rifle aimed at Alex's head.

"You're now prisoners of the NMLF," the guerrilla says, voice muffled by a bandana. "Drop your weapons or we kill the boy."

# CHAPTER 2
## LASADI

FROM THE BRIDGE AT THE EDGE OF THE VAST BLUFF, jumping to freedom looks like it should be easy, the landing so soft on lush jungle that sweeps out beyond the edge of the cliff like carpeting for as far as the eye can see. Nothing is holding her back.

Nothing but logic. The drop is over two kilometers, Lasadi reminds herself.

If she could sprout or build a pair of wings, though, get a running start down the packed red-earth road to the cliff and launch herself over the edge, she'd soar on the thermals like that majestic bird gliding towards them from the west. She'd sail over the scar of the gold-mine scratched halfway down the verdant face of the bluff, away from the red dirt roads and red metal roofs of the town of Icaba, south along the seam where the savannah highlands jut out of the jungle to roll gentle and flat for a hundred kilometers before pitching up once more into the rugged Liluri mountain range. The peaks of the Liluri Mountains are silvery and calm in the distance.

When Lasadi was a child, she used to study the planet Indira overhead through the glass domes of its moon, Corusca. She'd thought the continent New Manila resembled a sleeping bear: verdant green surrounded by blue seas, so vast she never could see the entire bear at once. Now she's somewhere near the bear's heart, far from the glittering chain of cities lining New Manila's southern coast.

Far from *anything*. Far from freedom.

While the remote beauty of the plateau is stunning, the town of Icaba is nothing to write home about. It consists of three short streets scratched into the dirt at the edge of the bluff. Squat, do-it-yourself printed houses are tumbled among buildings constructed of lumber roughly hewn from the jungle below.

The village is shaded by scrub palms and ceiba and some kind of towering, thick-trunked tree with spiked leaves and red fruits that attract chattering birds. And, of course, the ubiquitous moa palms that trace the path of the Icaba River as it wanders lazy and silt-rich through the savannah before the floor falls away and the river cascades in a frenzied freefall into the jungle.

Maybe five hundred people live in the area, most employed in the mine scarring the bluff below; in the morning, buses and transports fill with clean workers, and in the evenings they all come back the same muddy red-earth brown as the streets.

There's no security, no fences. Some of the homes don't even have doors, let alone walls on the first floor:

their kitchens open to the street with the bedrooms on the upper level.

The lack of walls doesn't keep her from feeling like a prisoner.

The bird is gliding closer; its shadow blocks out the hot sun for a brief moment as it passes overhead, and Lasadi's eyes widen at how massive it is up close. Its hooked beak is blood red, its vicious talons an inky black. It doesn't make a sound.

She didn't think she swore out loud, but she must have, because one of her guards — the sister — laughs.

"It's a Liu's condor," Qacha Batbayar says. "Scary-looking bastards, but they're carrion birds. Nothing you have to worry about unless you're already dead."

Lasadi tries to find that comforting. "It's bigger than I am," she says, and Qacha's twin brother, Temu, grins.

"Lots of things out here are bigger than you are," he says.

He's teasing, not threatening. Lasadi's been thinking of the pair of New Manila Liberation Front guerrillas as her guards, but they introduced themselves as her *guides*, and nothing about the barely twenty-year-olds is threatening. They're both shorter than she is, with wiry muscles, sun-bronzed skin, and thick black hair, Qacha's coiled in a military bun and Temu's shorn to the scalp. Qacha's laugh is infectious, Temu is disarmingly sincere about absolutely everything: the local flora and fauna, the mining operation, the unfamiliar food, NMLF doctrine, the fact she's not a prisoner.

It's not like she's under lock and key, not even at night. Instead of a cell, she's been given a hammock strung up in the common area of the school where children learn history during the day and the New Manila Liberation Front trains locals to fight in the evenings. Qacha and Temu sleep in hammocks nearby, as do a dozen other NMLF soldiers — but when she got up in the middle of the night to use the bathroom, no one even stirred.

In fact, she's been given a hero's welcome. She's here as Anton Kato's guest, after all, and rumor swept quick through the village: Lasadi Cazinho fought in Anton's Coruscan Liberation Army, she was the captain of the elite Mercury Squadron of fighter pilots, she was Anton's lover. His inspiration. *Muse.* The NMLF guerrillas have been treating Anton like a font of insurgent wisdom, and they're hanging on her every word now, too. Like she and Anton will be the key to helping the NMLF's fledgling movement succeed in driving out the Indiran Alliance where the CLA failed.

And Lasadi would have enjoyed helping them, if it weren't for Anton tricking her into coming.

She's not a prisoner, he's told her. If Lasadi wasn't a prisoner, though, Anton wouldn't have hidden her shuttle away in the jungle and taken her comm so she can't tell Jay where to find her.

A chorus of howls knocks her from her thoughts, and Lasadi glances over her shoulder, unable to pinpoint where the racket is coming from.

"What the hell is that?" she asks.

Qacha and Temu share a grin.

"Oyi howlers," says Temu. He points into the jungle. "They're similar to monkeys. A troop of them swings through the edge of the jungle every few days, but you don't have to worry, because they never come up here."

Lasadi shoots him a look; she hadn't realized she needed to worry about monkeys, of all things. She's seen nature vids, they always seem friendly. "Are they dangerous?"

"No, just annoying," says Qacha. She turns and her face lights up. "Oh, hey!"

Lasadi follows her gaze; the other woman is reaching out a hand to a beetle the size of her palm, iridescent green and gold, a sharp horn protruding from what Lasadi assumes is its forehead. It gives a violent rattle of its wings, then reaches a tentative foreleg to step onto Qacha's fingertips.

"These little guys are harmless," she says. "The rattling noise is to warn you off — but it mimics the sound a golden drummer makes, so if you hear it, be careful until you know what you're dealing with."

"Golden drummer?"

"A type of viper," says Temu. "They're not so common."

"What's your definition of 'not so common'?"

Temu laughs. "Don't worry," he reassures her. "Not everything in the jungle is dangerous — most things just want to be left alone."

Sure. Like the enormous spider Las'd seen first thing when she opened her eyes this morning. She'd nearly screamed before realizing it was outside the fine layer of bug netting fitted to her hammock.

She peels the neck of her shirt away from her throat, a bead of sweat trickling down her ribs. Besides the towering trees, the enormous raptors, the constant cacophony of birds and monkeys and insects, the biggest difference between here and Corusca is that on

Corusca, you're always the right temperature. Lasadi wonders if she'll ever stop itching. Or ditch the feeling something's crawling on the back of her neck.

"Where does the river go?" Lasadi asks, peering over the edge of the bridge.

"The water falls so far it never touches the ground," Temu says. "It vaporizes before then and waters the jungle in mist."

Fantastic — that means no landmark to be had there. Las was blindfolded when they left her shuttle, and the faint cleared patch she'd been instructed to land in had been difficult enough to spot when she had the coordinates and was directly above it, let alone from this angle. But she can see where the road that snakes down the face of the bluff enters the edge of the jungle. If she can follow it out — and can steal back her comm — she'll be able to find the shuttle.

"How do you navigate?"

Temu smiles. "It's easy once you learn."

"And you won't have to worry about it," adds Qacha. "One of us will always be with you."

"Of course." Lasadi smiles easy, but that's exactly the problem, isn't it?

Qacha seems about to speak again when her expression shifts to serious, her spine straightening as though listening to someone through her earpiece. "Yes, Commander," she says. "We'll be right there."

"Vasavada?" Lasadi asks. Commander Vasavada, the commanding officer of this local NMLF column, had hinted this morning she wanted them to stay close. Of course, "Stay close" is a bit of a joke in this tiny town. There are two restaurants and one bar, three stores. The NMLF-run clinic marks this end of town, the school building bookends the other side. It's a five-minute walk between them.

"Vasavada's ready for us," Qacha says. She's going for a stiff, serious, military aura, but youthful excitement is tugging at the corners of her mouth. Lasadi can't help but see herself in that expression — she'd been twenty, a touch older than Qacha, when she'd joined her own country's fight for independence. It was a heady time, full of passion for the cause, for the nation of Corusca. For Anton.

Though there's something more than patriotic passion in the glance Qacha and Temu exchange with each other — there's genuine excitement. Whatever Anton tricked her into coming to New Manila for, Lasadi can't help but be reluctantly intrigued.

Bitter resentment curls under her ribcage; olds, how different things would be if she were here under any other circumstances.

The twins shepherd Lasadi the few hundred yards back into Icaba proper, to the small shack outside the NMLF clinic that serves as Commander Vasavada's office. Except for a brief audience when she arrived in camp, Lasadi hasn't had much contact with the woman. She seems levelheaded and pragmatic, with none of the visionary mystique Anton had worn around his shoulders like a mantle. But, of course, having vision isn't Vasavada's role; she's only the commander of the Icaba column. The true leaders of the NMLF keep a low profile, unlike Anton.

"Speak a devil's name and sharpen your knife," Lasadi's grandmother always said — and before Temu even opens the door to the office, Lasadi can hear Anton's voice. Lasadi forces her shoulders to relax, ignores the numbness spreading below her sternum. Forces herself to soften her expression when she follows Qacha and Temu through the door.

Anton Kato is perched on a stool to one side of Vasavada's office; Commander Vasavada appears to have been pacing. The office is simply furnished: two stools and a table in the corner with a portable desk rolled out, schematics for a new community hall hovering above, the remains of Vasavada's lunch pushed to the side. Running an NMLF column seems mostly to consist of overseeing public works projects.

Commander Vasavada is dressed neat in military fatigues, wearing an NMLF armband with no visible rank. Her sleeves are rolled up over dark, muscled fore-arms, black hair in a series of braids coiled into a bun at the nape of her neck. Anton, on the other hand, is dressed in a lightweight suit that's open at the collar, a nod to Icaba's scorching heat.

"Lasadi." Anton gives her his most winning smile — the one that used to melt her heart. "How's the tour going? I trust Qacha and Temu are giving you the lay of the land? I can't think of anyone better for the job."

Qacha beams at Anton like stars are born in his foot-steps, and Lasadi can understand why. He's easy to like, and the intense focus of his pale blue eyes makes you feel like you're the most important thing in the world. Once you've felt that attention, his approval is gold; it gets addicting. And Anton knows full well how to use it.

"Qacha and Temu have been great," Lasadi says.

Railing against Anton on the first few days didn't get her anywhere, so she's experimenting with getting along. She smiles at Vasavada. "Thank you for your hospitality, Commander."

Vasavada nods, curt. "And we appreciate your patience. Take a seat."

The only other chair is a second stool next to Anton's; Lasadi tugs it as far away as she dares in the guise of leveling it. Vasavada props a hip on the corner of her desk.

"We've asked you here for a unique mission," Vasavada says, and Lasadi keeps her expression pleasant. "Asked" is one way to put tricking her here under false pretenses and keeping her against her will. But Lasadi suspects that part was all Anton. Blaming it on the NMLF isn't going to help her get back to the *Nanshe* any faster.

Vasavada lifts an eyebrow at Qacha. She hasn't cracked a smile once since Lasadi arrived. Now, though, the commander doesn't bother to hold back amusement at Qacha's excitement. "Would you like to do the honors, Private?"

Qacha's spine straightens. "We're going to race in the Liluri Star Run," she says; it comes out in an enthusiastic tumble. "You as captain, me as navigator — it'll be a good community-building effort for the NMLF, and excellent publicity if we win." She grins at Lasadi. "You know the Star Run, right?"

"The Star Run," Lasadi repeats, numb. She's lost track of the rhythm of Indira's seasons while living the last three years out in Durga's Belt, but it's the right time of year, isn't it? The Star Run is part of the Outland

Tour, a rugged circuit of three extreme aerial races that take place in remote areas of Indira each year. The part of Lasadi who's still a kid piling in front of the live feeds with her family every week during race season sits up in delight. "You're serious?"

"We're serious," says Anton. He's smiling at her, too, now, and it's all Lasadi can do to keep from smiling back. He knows, of course. Watching the Liluri Star Run in person has been a wish since she was a child memorizing the stats of every plane, the histories of every pilot. Racing it would be a dream.

"Qacha will be an excellent navigator," Temu says, earnest. Maybe he's mistaking her shocked silence for disapproval of the choice in navigation partner. "We both grew up flying with our father, but Qacha caught the love of it. She's amazing."

"Surely the NMLF has pilots who know the region better than me," Lasadi says. What she wants to say is, *You didn't have to trick me into this. You didn't have to lie to get me to help the NMLF* — and obviously not to enter the Liluri Star Run.

And yet. Even if she'd known about the plan, she still never would have come if Anton had contacted her under his own name.

"It sends a message of solidarity between our two countries to have a joint Coruscan and New Manilan team," Anton says.

Lasadi lifts an eyebrow to him. "You know I'm supposed to be dead, right?" Not to mention the fact that he tore her name to shreds after the Battle of Tannis. The NMLF might still respect her, but they'll be in the minority.

"You'll use a pseudonym," Anton says. "Though the race is only a small part of the mission."

"Senator Kato will brief you on the rest while you're flying to Moie for the race start," Vasavada says. "And Private Batbayar will acquaint you with the terrain and your ship."

"It'll be tricky terrain," says Qacha. "But I learned to navigate in my father's rust heap with computer nav systems you couldn't trust. These mountains are etched in my blood. It will be an honor to fly with you."

"I'm — yes." Lasadi shakes her head. "Likewise. When is the race?"

"Two days from now. You leave for Moie this afternoon."

And they're just telling her *now*? Lasadi bites back the objection — it's irrelevant, and from another world entirely. She's spent three years getting used to civilian life. Even when the *Nanshe* — and her time — belonged to Nico Garnet, she'd had a great deal of autonomy. Here, she's just another soldier taking orders on a need-to-know basis. And Anton hadn't trusted her to know before this moment.

Vasavada stands, dismissing the meeting. "Let Private Batbayar know what additional supplies you need."

"Actually." Lasadi turns to Anton, heart pounding in her throat; she knows full well how he can react to being crossed in public. It's a risk she's willing to take, though. Maybe the old Las was fine taking orders in the dark; that's no longer how Lasadi Cazinho operates. "What I need is some more information. Why don't you brief me on the rest of the mission now, so Qacha can focus on acquainting me with the ship and terrain once we're in the air."

Anton's practiced politician's smile sharpens, so fast the others won't have caught it; they won't know to watch for it.

"Of course," Anton says, easy once more. He stands, tossing a salute to Vasavada and buttoning his suit jacket. "We'll go grab a quick drink."

Lasadi gives her best smile to Vasavada and the Batbayar twins. "Thank you," she says again. "I'll see you all in a few."

Anton gestures Lasadi to walk ahead of him, fingers brushing her arm as he guides her through the door. Her skin flushes cold in the heat of the day, but she'll be damned if she lets him see her flinch.

# CHAPTER 3
## LASADI

SHE'D BEEN IN LOVE WITH ANTON KATO BEFORE SHE EVER met him in person.

She'd collected his writings in secret for almost two years. She'd watched his illicit broadcasts late at night, imagination caught as much by his lofty calls for resistance as by the golden tones of his voice, the curve of his smile.

She might have stayed an admirer from afar were it not for that final fight with her grandmother. The Senate had narrowly agreed that Corusca should join the Indiran Alliance, and Lasadi's grandmother had been one of the deciding votes. With the benefit of age and hindsight, Lasadi can understand her grandmother's decision, but as a twenty-year-old, she'd been incensed. She'd called her grandmother a traitor and slipped out of the house that night to seek out the man with the golden voice and incendiary ideas.

When she found him, she'd met his eye with chin held high, met his hand with a firm shake, hid her nerves behind practiced confidence. She was accustomed to meeting famous people through her grandmother, but Anton Kato had been the first who'd knotted her gut with anticipation. The way he looked at her slid through her soul like a blade; as the world knocked sideways, she knew at the very core of her being she'd made the right decision.

There are two parts of her life Lasadi would do over, if given the chance. She would apologize to her grandmother before she left, and she would believe Anton when he told her the only thing he would ever truly love was the cause.

After the disastrous Battle of Tannis, Anton had managed to spin the CLA's defeat into peace — and a political victory for himself. He won — and has held onto — a seat in the Senate because although not enough Coruscans had an appetite for the fighting, most are still wary of the Alliance. They support Anton to make a statement: *We fought you once and we'll do it again.*

Is that why Anton is in New Manila, making plans with the local insurgent movement? To send the Alliance a message? She hasn't been following Coruscan politics, but she has a vague sense they're nearing an election cycle. Maybe Anton needs to build up some political clout. Or maybe he's preparing for another round of warfare with the Alliance.

Lasadi tamps down the spark of hope. Whatever greater movement Anton's planning, she wants no part of it.

"Lasadi." Anton says her name soft as they walk; reverence and attention in every syllable. If the

Batbayar twins appreciate the small rays of attention they've gotten from Anton, they have no idea what it's like to stand in the full sun of his devotion. To be worshipped like a goddess by the man everyone else worships like a god.

It's intoxicating, and Anton knows it.

Lasadi takes a deep breath, locking pieces of her armor in place with fierce determination. She holds up a finger when he starts to speak.

"I need a drink," she says. "And I need some answers."

He pauses, one foot on the raised wooden deck of the bar. She searches his face for the changes. He's going prematurely gray, but the silver in his dark hair and dappling his rugged, light-tanned jawline suits him. Fine lines are etched around his blue eyes and the corners of his mouth, and a faint scar ghosts his chin; she wonders where that came from.

"Vasavada wasn't sure we could trust you," he finally says. "Especially after your reaction the first day. But she's made her decision now, and it's time you knew the real reason you're here." He smiles at her like it's a favor he's offering, rather than him acquiescing to her demand for information. "Come on, it's quiet here."

Icaba's single bar is an open patio shielded from the sun and rain by a sloping metal roof on poles. A pair of hand-carved dice boards sit at the far end, and the rest of the patio is populated by wooden benches and rusted metal tables. The bar is a slab of polished wood set on a pair of barrels, the glassware and liquor kept in a storage unit behind the bar that padlocks shut when no one's around to tend it.

Lasadi follows Anton to the bar, smoothing her hand over the satiny wood grain; a bartop like this on Corusca would cost a fortune. Anton orders a pair of beers from the bartender, a woman with a shaved head and well-muscled forearms, then picks a table far from the foot traffic on the road and hands Lasadi one of the beers, his fingers leaving prints in the frost on the glass that she tries not to touch. The beer tastes like slightly bitter, aromatic water, but it's refreshing and cold in the heat of the day.

Anton sets his bottle down and leans back in his chair, regarding her. "I'm sorry, Lasadi," he finally says.

Lasadi is too startled to answer. He's apologized before, but he's always come at it sideways, and she can't think of a time he used those actual words. Maybe he's growing; olds know the last few years haven't been kind to either of them. Or maybe he's simply got a new trick up his sleeve.

"I brought you here under false pretenses," he continues. "You have every right to be angry with me, but I need your help, and I didn't think you'd respond if *I* asked."

"So you forged a message with Henri's name."

He'd known it would get her attention, of course. Henri had been under her command in Mercury Squadron. Lasadi had believed he, Tania, Anna Mara — everyone but her and Jay — had been killed in the final battle, and she would have done anything for that not to be true.

"I'm sorry," he says again.

"You used *Henri*," she says. "Who's dead, like all the others. Do you even care?"

He leans forward, voice low. "I miss them, too," he says, words raw with real grief. She sits back in surprise. The Anton she remembers never would have let her see the mix of anguish and regret flooding his face. "I miss them every day."

She traces a finger through the condensation on the side of her beer bottle and studies the cold droplet of water clinging to her fingertip, fighting back her own sudden barrage of grief. *They're gone,* she tells herself. She knows, now, that it wasn't her fault, but in the end that hardly matters. When she meets Anton's gaze again, the grief has been replaced by something softer.

"I've missed you, too. I know — " He cuts himself off with a sharp breath. Another first for Anton, not knowing what to say. War does leave its marks. "I'm not asking anything of you for myself, Lasadi. But we accomplished great things together. We could do great things again. For Corusca."

The beer bottle scuffs against the rusted metal table when Lasadi sets it down. "You have no right to ask me anything."

There's that flash of irritation on his face. Even this new, softer Anton is used to getting his own way — and Lasadi doesn't intend to give in to him so easy.

"I did what I had to," Anton says, quiet. "For the cause. You weren't there — I made difficult decisions and concessions to save as many of the rest of our fighters as I could. To save as much of our *cause* as I could."

"I wasn't there because I was too busy being scraped out of the wreckage of my ship." Her fingertips brush her abdomen, over the ridge of scar tissue under the fabric of her shirt, still unfamiliar even three years later.

"You don't think I would have come after you if I knew you were alive?" Anton's voice splinters on the words; the shrapnel pierces Lasadi's heart. "I would have done anything for you. But by the time you got in touch it was too late to change course. I'd already made the announcement."

"Did you know you were lying when you said Mercury Squadron destroyed that medical transport?" Lasadi has been dreaming of confronting him about this ever since she found out the truth, but now she just feels exhausted.

"I believed what the Alliance told me," Anton says. "They had evidence, and we needed to make peace."

"You believed my team would fire on an unarmed neutral ship."

"I believe accidents happen in battle, especially when you let feelings get in the way of what has to be done." There's a blade buried in those words, Lasadi has pushed him far enough. "And I believe no one person is better than the cause."

For Lasadi, the fight had always been specific. She fought for her family. For her friends. For her comrades. But Anton had always fought for the *cause*. The fate of an individual person — no matter how close they'd been — didn't matter. Lasadi used to find his single-minded dedication admirable. Maybe some part of her still does. She considers telling him the truth: that what happened to the medical transport was simply an accident. A tragic, ill-timed failure on the ship itself — but it won't matter to him. The truth won't further the cause.

She takes a long pull on her beer. It's already warming in the heat of the day.

"And this?" she asks, circling her bottle to indicate the bar, Icaba, the NMLF — all of it. "Is it part of the cause?"

Anton takes a drink, setting his own bottle back down in the exact same ring of condensation on the metal table. His gaze drops to her wrist, and Lasadi realizes she's fingering the bracelet she's wearing. It's a simple thing, a well-worn, twisted cittern string Raj had left on the dash of the *Nanshe* when they'd docked in Ironfall after the job on Auburn Station. Lasadi had slipped it on her own wrist before taking the shuttle down to New Manila without quite knowing why.

She lets her hand drop into her lap, out of sight below the table, a trickle of adrenaline ticking up her heart rate. She's bracing for questions, she realizes: *Where did you get that? Who gave it to you? Did you sleep with him?*

But Anton doesn't ask.

"We have a chance to weight the scales in favor of the NMLF," Anton says. "And maybe even revisit our own bid for independence. Do you want that?"

"Of course."

That tilt of a smile; he knows she does. "There's a bill in the Senate right now, the Limitations Act. If passed, it would place restrictions on Alliance authority in Corusca. We're close on votes, but we also need Alliance cooperation."

"And working with the NMLF is going to get you that?"

Anton leans in. "Do you know the story of Theodor Usoro?"

Lasadi frowns at the shift. "The pilot?" And at Anton's encouraging nod: "Of course. He was only the most famous Coruscan to fly the Star Run. He made that huge statement, what was it, four years ago? In support of the independence movement."

"The Alliance talked the organizers of the Outland Tour into banning him the year after. Do you remember?"

"I missed that one," Lasadi says, keeping her voice light. "I was spending a lot of time in regen tanks at the time."

Anton's eyes flicker shut as he realizes what she means; he reaches for her hand and squeezes her fingers. "I'm sorry," he says, the third time this conversation — maybe the third time she's ever heard him say it. "I wish I'd known. I wish I could have come to you."

"It's all right," she finds herself saying, but she knows he never would have come, not when Corusca needed him. She extracts her hand, but gives him an encouraging smile. "Tell me about Usoro."

"He and I corresponded quite a bit after he made his statement," Anton says. "Until he disappeared before last year's Star Run. He was favored to win it, which would have made him only the third person to win all three Outland Tour races in one year."

"He crashed on a training run?" Lasadi guesses. The Liluri Mountains eat pilots, and training run crashes happen all too regularly, even to the best.

Anton shakes his head. "He came back from a run and sent me a message saying he'd found something in the jungle that would help Corusca. I replied, asking for more details, but he didn't respond. He flew out the next morning and never returned. His body was never recovered."

"Sounds familiar." Lasadi hasn't exactly been avoiding coverage of the Outland Tour these past few years, but she hasn't sought it out. Even the glimpses she sometimes caught in bars brought back a painful flood of memories of a home and family she can't return to.

"He was officially declared dead a few months ago," Anton says. "Which means his lawyers released a parcel no one but Theo knew they'd been holding. He'd addressed it to me, with a note claiming what was inside would help Corusca achieve independence."

Lasadi can't help the spark of curiosity. "What was it?"

"Theo's journal. He claims to have come across a crashed experimental Arquellian plane at one of his secret layover spots, deep in the mountains. He says they were testing some sort of stealth technology, and he flew back to Moie to get the tools to collect it. I believe that's where he was heading when he disappeared."

"Does this journal say where he found it?"

"In a way." Anton gives her a grim look. "Theo was whimsical — and obviously secretive."

"About his layover spots? Of course he was." Most Star Run pilots plan their route to overnight at one of the five checkpoints; experienced Star Run pilots have their arsenal of secret layovers in the mountains, scant few places where it's safe enough to land for the night.

No one is foolish enough to continue their run after dark. "Every pilot keeps that close to the heart."

"Theo described the crashed Arquellian plane as being 'at the end of the River of Blood,'" Anton says. "He left coded notations in his journal, but we need his maps to decipher them."

"And his maps went down with the ship," Lasadi guesses.

"We're actually in luck," Anton says with a smile she knows well: He knows something no one else does. Lasadi finds herself leaning forward without realizing. "We can get to the maps. And then you, Lasadi, will go down in history as the person who changed the tide of war. Imagine what the NMLF could do against the Alliance with Arquellian stealth technology. Imagine what we could have done — what we could do yet."

Imagine how proud her family would be, to learn she's not only alive, but that she's redeemed herself from the atrocity everyone believes she was responsible for. That flicker of hope dies quick, though. Raj is the only one who could tell the world the truth of what happened, and no one in the system will ever believe him.

"I'm in," Lasadi says, and catches herself with a start. She probes at the armor she thought she'd put in place against Anton; it's still there, she thinks. She asked for intel and he gave it to her, and she doesn't think she let him cross any boundaries. She still doesn't have a choice, not really, but at least she knows what she's getting into. And Anton's always been good at making you think the decision was yours in the end.

"There's one more thing," Anton says, and she

tenses. She should have known; there's always one more thing, with Anton. "Henri. I don't think he died in the battle."

Lasadi's lips part; she doesn't dare nurture the tiny seed of hope growing in her chest. "Where is he?"

"I have people searching," Anton says. "We'll find him together, when this is all over."

"Thank you." She means it this time.

Anton smiles, and olds be damned if it doesn't slip past her armor to coil warm and narcotic around the base of her spine. "Of course," he says, then frowns past her.

Someone's coming over the bridge from the bluff road, the same bridge she'd been standing on with the Batbayar twins earlier. The revving of an engine, the rattling of a truck down the pitted dirt road, men shouting. Three men are in the back, one lying between two others.

"Someone must be hurt," Anton says, but the truck doesn't stop at the clinic. It bounces its way down the road, and as it passes by the bar, it's clear the man who's lying down isn't a miner. He's cleaner than the others and his arms are tied behind him. When he thrashes against his captors, Lasadi gets a look at his face.

Shoulder-length black hair tied back, strands plastered onto his sweat-drenched forehead. Laughing dark eyes hooded with pain. Lips that always seem ready to smile, now flecked with blood.

A jolt of shocked recognition shoots through her.

Raj.

# CHAPTER 4
## RAJ

BY THE GRADUAL FLATTENING OF THE ROAD AND THE shouting of the men holding him, they must have reached the village on the top of the bluff — which means at least this hellish ride will soon be over. Though gods alone know what's coming next.

Another bump in the road slams Raj's ribcage into whatever rock or lump of hard-packed clay has been rattling around the back of the flatbed truck with him, spiking pain through an already tender bruise. He tries to shift again and gets a knee in the small of his back. A lot of pent-up aggression over who controls mineral rights in the Liluri Mountains is getting worked out on Raj's kidneys, and he can't even blame them. New Manila got the raw end of a deal, and the more Raj is learning about the history, the more he'd like to punch anyone with an Arquellian accent, too.

He doesn't know where they took the others. He doesn't know why they split them up — but he assumes the NMLF guerrillas who captured them heard his Arquellian accent and have something special in mind.

The truck finally rumbles to a stop and Raj is hauled out, shouted at to move. His ankle turns on a rock that blended into the sawtoothed grass, shorn almost to bare earth in this field fringed by scrub trees and tattered palm. Raj might assume it was a ball field if he weren't being prodded across it by rifles, his hands bound behind his back.

It's a killing yard. Even out in Durga's Belt, even trying to wean himself off a constant diet of Alliance politics, Raj has heard the squawking protests of Alliance officials who think New Manila isn't taking their insurrection problem seriously enough. Grisly details of executions of Arquellian citizens, New Manilan villages razed or starved out — Raj had assumed it was hyperbole until this very moment.

He can imagine the headlines around his death: *Grieving Admiral Demetriou Demands Reprisals Against NMLF After Son's Murder.*

There are a lot of reasons Raj wants to live. But making sure his father doesn't get an excuse to rain fire down on the Liluri Mountains like he did on the people of Tannis is pretty high up on that list.

He lets himself stumble again. When the soldier on his left grabs his arm, Raj rolls, pulling the man off-balance and taking out the legs of the second soldier at the same time. He kicks out, catching the first in the thigh with the heel of his boot, then forcing himself unsteadily to his feet, cursing the rope around his wrists.

He's fifty meters from the line of scrub, but he's got

a head start. He breaks left, darts right, trying to keep his path erratic.

A rifle's report cracks through the afternoon, the bullet scoring into the turf and sending flecks of dirt and gravel flying a couple of meters off to Raj's left. His guards are yelling for backup, and a trio of new NMLF soldiers have emerged from the low building at the far end of the field. Two begin racing after him, but Raj is nearly to the scrub — which probably won't help him much with his hands still tied behind his back, but at least they'll have a harder time shooting him, and he'll have some cover to slip the knife out of his boot.

He changes direction again as another rifle report sounds, this one hitting even farther off course, and the part of his mind that isn't entirely focused on closing the last ten meters with the scrub pings for his attention.

The third newcomer has kneeled down at the edge of the field, lifting a massive rifle — no, a drone launcher — to his shoulder.

Ah, shit.

Raj lunges for the scrub as the hollow *thunk* of a shell fires, the report quickly replaced by the high-pitched whine of a half-dozen drones. The first zips between him and the scrub when he's a scant few strides from freedom, trailing glimmering strands of sticky filaments. Raj's momentum carries him forward and drags the drones along with him, but his legs tangle in the netting and he crashes to the turf with a thud.

Where the *hell* did the NMLF get a weapon like that?

Rough hands pull him to his feet, detangle him from

the netting, and Raj braces himself, chest heaving with the effort of the sprint. He's meters from the scrub now, but instead of his original two guards, he's staring down four rifle barrels.

"Do I get a last request?" Raj asks.

A rifle digs into his back once more.

"Move."

It slowly dawns on Raj that they're not going to kill him — at least not at the moment. Instead of shooting him right here at the edge of the murder shrubs, they push him back across the field to the building. With the sun behind it, it's hard to tell, but it could be some sort of civic building, or maybe a school. Squat and utilitarian, with rows of identical doors and windows. A mural on the side of the building confirms his suspicion: scenes from New Manilan history, interspersed with the alphabet.

The soldier who'd fired the drone shell at him opens a door, and Raj is shoved inside without ceremony. The door slams and locks behind him; it takes a moment for his eyes to adjust to the inside of the classroom.

"Well, fuck," he says.

The rest of the *Nanshe*'s crew are here, Jay, Ruby, and Alex perched around the room on chairs clearly sized for children.

Ruby lifts an eyebrow. "Saints in hell, Raj. You look awful."

"You're a doll." Raj shifts, presenting her his bound hands. "Are you going to help me, or throw shade? There's a knife in my right boot."

"Have you seen Las?" Jay asks.

"No. You?"

The mechanic swears under his breath and screws his eyes shut, pinching the bridge of his nose.

"We heard gunshots," Alex says. His lips press into a bloodless line. "We thought they'd — "

"They were shooting *at* me, not shooting me," Raj says. The kid relaxes slightly.

"Lemme guess," Ruby says. She slices through the final strands and Raj's hands come free. He stretches them in front of him, massaging life back into his fingers. "They were bringing you here and you tried to run. The grass stains on you, you look like you were playing sweeps."

"More like a bunch of sweeps players were using him as the ball," Alex says helpfully.

"I may have gotten tackled by a drone net. What's plan B?"

"Escape," says Alex. "Which should be easy enough. We're in a *classroom*, not a prison."

He's right — the room is ten paces by ten, with a high ceiling, a stack of chairs against one wall, and an open cabinet full of school supplies Raj assumes Alex already picked the lock on.

"A classroom surrounded by guerrillas with guns and drone launchers," points out Ruby. She turns back to Raj, real concern on her face. "You hurt for real? Good. Then go help Alex." She pulls a teaching tablet, stamped Hypatia Educational Facilities, out from beneath her red leather jacket and starts fiddling with it. "I got through the child lock on this thing, but they're just connected to a local network. Gimme a minute."

"To get a message out?" Alex asks her. "Spot me," he says to Raj, then scrambles onto the chair he's stacked on the teacher's desk and starts unscrewing the ceiling panels. The chair wobbles a hair closer to the edge of the desk with every turn of his utility knife.

"Who to?" Ruby shoots back. "Anyone I know who could help us is on Ironfall."

Alex drops a screw into Raj's outstretched hand. "Heya Raj, would your dad — "

"He would absolutely not."

"That's too bad." Alex drops another handful of screws, then glides the panel aside and grips the edge of the hole he made, chin-upping his lanky seventeen-year-old frame like a gymnast to see what's above. In this planet's gravity, the kid's strength-to-weight ratio is impressive.

"It's tight," Alex says, dropping back onto the chair and dusting off his hands. One of the chair's feet scoots precariously close to the edge of the desk; Raj catches it before it goes over and takes Alex down with it. "But there's no separations. We could get up into the ceiling and drop out in another room."

"I found a floor plan," Ruby says. "There's basically two rows of rooms back-to-back. They might not be watching the other side." And she smiles. "Got it. I'm in the wider network."

Jay leans over Ruby's shoulder. "Get me into the *Nanshe*'s remote system and — "

Footsteps stop in front of their door, the window darkening in shadow. The handle turns. Ruby slides the tablet back behind her. Alex hops down from the desk, casual-like.

In stalks a tall, well-muscled woman with dark skin, a coil of black braids, and a mouth that probably doesn't waste time smiling. She's got a sidearm on her hip, and the pair of guards flanking her hold rifles at the ready. All three are wearing military fatigues and NMLF armbands, and though Raj can't make out any symbols of rank, it's clear the tall woman in front is in charge.

Jay straightens and Raj tenses, ready to fight. Alex steps in front of his sister; she gives his back a look that's part charmed surprise, part worry, then slips Raj's knife out of her sleeve. They're going to have to teach the kid to fight if they're going to keep dragging him into scraps. Raj files away a mental note to talk with him once this is over.

The tall woman's gaze shifts to the hole in the ceiling above. "No need to dismantle our school building, young man," she says mildly. "You're not prisoners."

"The door was locked, wasn't it," Ruby points out.

"A precaution, until we figured out who you are and why you're here." The woman regards each of them grimly, one by one. "Let's start with who you are."

Raj nods at Jay's questioning glance, and Jay steps forward with an outstretched hand the woman doesn't take.

"I'm Jay Kamiya. Formerly of the CLA. I'm here looking for Lasadi Cazinho."

That little flash of recognition, though the woman's expression doesn't shift much; Raj's hope soars. She knows about Lasadi. After a long moment, the woman takes Jay's hand.

"Commander Vasavada," she says. "Head of the

NMLF's Icaba column. Who are you to Captain Cazinho?"

"I flew with her in the CLA," Jay says. He thumbs over his shoulder to Raj, Ruby, and Alex. "We all fly with her now."

"She flies with an Arquellian." Vasavada's talking to Jay, though her gaze flicks to Raj. So they did notice his accent.

"She does," Jay says. "When she left without a word I was worried. So we followed her."

"How'd you find her?"

"We traced her ship and found the shuttle coordinates," Jay says. "I have credentials to get that information — no one else would be on her trail."

"We just want to talk to her," Raj says. They've already pegged him as Arquellian, no need to keep his accent toned down. "That's all we're here for."

Vasavada's nostrils flare as she thinks. "She's here," she finally says. "You're just in time."

"Just in time for what?" Jay asks.

But Vasavada doesn't answer. She lifts her chin to the soldier on her right. "Go find Captain Cazinh— ah." She tilts her head, listening. She doesn't exactly smile, but she seems vaguely amused. "Small town," she says as though in explanation.

And then Raj hears it, too: footsteps getting louder, and Lasadi's voice cutting through the rest. After five days of worry, relief washes through him like water. They've found her.

The two NMLF soldiers step aside as Lasadi bursts into the classroom. Vasavada's watching her with interest, probably gauging by her reaction whether or not Jay and Raj have been telling the truth.

Lasadi appears uninjured. Healthy, even — the olive tones of her fair skin have been drinking up the sun and warmth, her dusky blond hair is threaded with gold. Strands have escaped her utilitarian braid to curl around her cheeks in the humidity.

Lasadi's stunned gaze sweeps over them. "Olds bless," she finally says. "What the hell are you all doing here?"

# CHAPTER 5
## LASADI

LASADI ALMOST HADN'T BELIEVED HER EYES WHEN SHE caught a glimpse of Raj in the back of that truck. It had been wishful thinking, maybe — she'd been toying with his bracelet on her wrist and primed to see a familiar face in the black-haired, tawny-skinned prisoner. She'd been expecting to find a stranger in this schoolroom, but, no. Raj is here in the flesh, along with Jay and — even more inexplicably — Ruby and Alex.

Ruby's got one hip cocked against a table, arms crossed under her chest. Her curly black hair is pulled into a bouncy ponytail, and she's wearing a sleeveless top that shows off the gold-ink tattoos of the Pearls glittering on her dark collarbones. Her red leather jacket is draped over the back of one child-sized chair. Her brother, Alex, is wearing a crew jumpsuit with no logo, sides of his head shaved fresh and not a hair of his pompadour out of place. He grins at her through a spray of freckles.

Jay's expression is one of pure relief, but Lasadi simply does not understand what's going on.

Jay, she gets; she knew he'd be worried when she didn't get in touch, but she hadn't expected him to actually track her down. The others, though? Did Jay hire them?

"Olds bless," she says again; in her shock she's channeling her grandmother.

"Good to see you, too, Cap," Ruby says.

"You left without a word," Jay says, reproach in his tone. "I figured it was trouble, and I'm always going to come after you if you're in trouble. You know that, Las."

"I know," she says. "But — " She cuts herself off, still not certain how to address the presence of Ruby, Alex, and a very grass-stained, disheveled Raj. "Are you all right?" she asks Raj.

He gives her that easy, exasperating smile. "All good," he says, but the gentle relief in his gaze turns troubled as it shifts over her shoulder; Anton has caught up with her.

"What's going on here?" Anton asks. His eyebrows lift when he spots Jay. "Kamiya?"

"Commander." Jay steps forward with a smile, hand outstretched. "Wouldn't have expected to find you here."

Ruby and Raj share a complicated look, probably wondering what Jay's gotten them into and wishing they hadn't agreed to come — olds, what did Jay tell them? Anton doesn't seem to notice. He waves away Jay's formality and steps forward to bring Jay into an embrace. "No titles here," he says. "And she wasn't in trouble, she was with me."

"What a fucking relief," Jay says, clapping Anton on the shoulder. "All this time without a word, we expected the worst." He inclines his head to Vasavada. "No offense, Commander, we didn't know what the situation was."

"I'm sorry," Lasadi says. "I should have said something." The apology is out before she means to say it, never mind she'd been told not to tell anyone where she was going, never mind that her comm had been taken away "for safety" as soon as she landed and realized Anton had tricked her into coming.

"It's fine, Las." There's a flash in Jay's eyes, brief but intense, like he's trying to tell her something important. "We're here now. Wanna fill us in?"

"Of course." She takes a deep breath. "Introductions, I suppose. This is Ruby, her brother, Alex. And Raj — folks, this is Anton Kato. He's working with the NMLF, and they've got a job for me." She turns to Anton and Vasavada. "For us."

"I'm not sure that's wise," Anton says. "This isn't their business."

"If you want this job done right, I need my crew. I vouch for them."

Vasavada's nostrils flare, but she doesn't speak. Anton's lips part, his relaxed politician's smile turning serious. "You're sure."

"With my life. Commander Vasavada, Anton. If you trust me with this, you can trust them."

She knows the risks Vasavada and Anton are calculating right now. A single moment of trust poorly given can destroy lives, plans, entire movements. It's often a far smarter move to eliminate the source of potential betrayal rather than give them the chance to bring everything you've worked so hard for crashing to the ground.

In the CLA, Lasadi had only ever vouched for someone she trusted with every fiber of her being. She likes Raj, Ruby, and Alex — she definitely doesn't know them well enough to vouch her life for their actions.

But Jay brought them, which means he trusts them. And she trusts Jay.

Of course, the alternative is letting Vasavada and Anton believe they're a risk that needs dealt with. They came all the way out here to find her. She owes them a chance to get out of this alive, at least.

Vasavada levels a searching look on Lasadi; seconds tick excruciating into the heat of the day while she makes her decision. Finally, Vasavada nods. "I'll defer to your judgement," she says to Anton. "We agreed to provide the resources you need, and if you think you need a larger crew, that's your call."

"Then consider yourselves hired," Anton says. He settles a warm hand on Lasadi's shoulder, gives it a friendly squeeze. "Anyone who's earned Lasadi's trust has earned mine."

Ruby raises a hand. "And what is this job?" She lifts an eyebrow at Lasadi; she understands the stakes here, but isn't ready to get in over her head.

Anton settles onto the edge of a child's desk, hands in his lap, relaxed. "Ruby, right?" He's all charm once more. "Good question. Have you heard the name Theodor Usoro?"

Ruby's nose wrinkles in *No*; beside her, Alex straightens.

"Usoro?" he asks. "Isn't he the one who got abducted by aliens?"

Ruby elbows him. "What are you on about?"

"He was a pilot who crashed in the mountains a few years back," says Alex, tone like everyone knows this story. "Apparently he went out into the jungle looking for a crashed alien ship, and everyone says he was abducted by aliens."

"It wasn't aliens, Alex," Anton says, giving the younger man an amused smile. "He may have been an international celebrity, but he was also Coruscan, and a supporter of the CLA. He found a crashed experimental plane from an Arquellian test program on one of his practice runs, and we believe he died trying to find it again. We're attempting to recover it."

"The job is to race the Liluri Star Run as a cover to search for the covert Arquellian tech," Lasadi says. She turns to Anton. "Only, you said we still needed to get access to Usoro's maps."

"They're on his ship," Anton says.

"The one he crashed in the jungle?" Lasadi says. "That won't help us."

"No, on his racing ship. The *Figment of the North*. Theodor's benefactor still owns it and he's put it on display for this Star Run, in honor of Theo's legacy."

"So we break onto the ship?" Alex asks. "Easy."

"Not so easy," Anton says, smooth as silk. "The ship will be surrounded by people and top security. We'll need to convince Theodor's benefactor to let us on."

"Us?" Lasadi asks.

Anton winks at her; unease creeps through her gut. "Of course. You think I'd miss out on the fun?"

"However you decide to get on the ship, you'll need to talk about it on the ride there," Vasavada cuts in, saving Lasadi from having to feign delight at Anton's bombshell. "We've had enough delay. Moie is still hours away, and the pilot's orientation starts after dinner."

"Understood, Commander."

"Getting on the *Figment* will be the least of your worries," Vasavada says. "With Qacha at your side you'll have an advantage, but the Liluri Mountains swallow pilots regardless of skill. If you'll come with me, I'll show you to the ship you'll be flying in the race. Tell me what you need from your shuttle and I'll have it brought right away."

Lasadi stands back as the others file out behind Vasavada; Ruby and Alex are already giving her the laundry list of tech they'll need brought from their shuttle, while Jay's ribbing Raj with some inside joke she's unfamiliar with. It hits her that the four of them have spent almost a week traveling from Ironfall to Indira together, trading stories, telling jokes, bonding. And after her initial shock at having them here, she's surprised to find a seed of comfortable anticipation growing below her ribcage. Ruby's banter, Alex's jokes, Raj's patient calm — she's actually looking forward to this.

She's about to follow when Anton catches her wrist.

"You vouch for them," he says, quiet. A spark flicks between them in the now-empty classroom; his charm has vanished and his tone is dark and dangerous. The tentative warmth that had been blooming in Lasadi's chest washes ice cold.

"I do," she says. The voices of the others are fading, faint echoes down the school building's arcade. "As does Jay."

"You vouch for an *Arquellian*."

She tries to pull her hand back, but Anton's grip doesn't break. "I trust Raj."

"With my life? With the fate of New Manila?" Anton's grip is verging on painful. "With the *cause*?"

"I know what it means to vouch for someone."

"And I know you sometimes let your feelings cloud your judgement, Lasadi. This isn't about one person, or even several. This is about the freedom of *every* person in this system."

"I understand that." She shifts, trying to lessen his grip. "Anton — "

"I want to trust you, but you're making this difficult. Swear to me."

"I vouch — "

"No." Bones grind in her wrist, Lasadi bites her lip to keep from crying out. "I don't want you to swear on your life. I want to know that if one of them betrays us, you'll pull the trigger yourself. I don't care if they're your friends."

"They're not my friends," she snaps. "Anton, that fucking hurts."

Anton's grip doesn't change. "Not your friends?"

"They're my crew." She's been angry with him before; what she feels now is something beyond frustration, beyond rage. Her fury is so white-hot it's almost cold. She ignores the grinding agony in her wrist, and when she speaks again her tone is as frosty as his has ever been. "And I know what it means to take responsibility for them. Let me go."

Surprise glints in his eye; she's never dared fight back.

"Let me go," she whispers, and this time he does. She snatches her hand back, massaging her bruised wrist.

He glances down, frowning. "Your wrist," he says. "Did that hurt? I didn't realize."

"It's okay," she says; it's automatic. "It's fine."

"You're sure? Lasadi — "

"It's fine." Her wrist is throbbing, but he didn't break anything. She just needs him not to lose his temper before they can get to Moie. One step at a time, she thinks, and they'll be on the other side of this. She smiles at him, smooths her good hand down his arm. "We're fine."

"Hey, Las?" Jay's voice sounds from outside the schoolroom, he pops his head through the doorway. "Ah, great, Anton. Like old times," he says with a grin. "Feels good, yeah? Having a purpose?"

"It feels good," Lasadi agrees.

Anton's all charm and dazzle once again as he claps Jay on the shoulder, and Lasadi takes a deep breath of relief. "You were always one of the best of us, Kamiya."

"Means a lot, coming from you, sir. Vasavada said she needed to run something by you."

Anton nods at them both before heading out the door. Lasadi follows, but Jay's touch is light on her arm as they walk, slowing her down to lag behind as Anton strides away from the building. It's lunchtime, maybe — the sun is high overhead, the heat hitting Lasadi's shoulders with palpable pressure when she and Jay step out of the shady arcade. Children trickle out of the other classrooms, screams and laughter echoing down the arcade.

"You aren't supposed to be here, Jay," Lasadi says. "You're supposed to be nesting with Chiara."

"Yeah, well, that didn't quite work out."

"Oh, shit, I'm sorry. What happened?"

"We'll talk about it later," Jay says. "Let's just say it wasn't going to work."

Lasadi gives him a sideways look, but she knows that set of his mouth. She can pry later. "At least tell me how you talked the others into coming."

"I called Raj when I couldn't find you. I hoped maybe you'd . . ." He shrugs.

"Gone on a wild sex bender with a man I'd just met?" Lasadi's grateful the heat of the day will hide the flush in her cheeks; she actually had been minutes away from calling Raj when she got the message from "Henri."

"A friend can hope you learned to live a little," Jay says. "Anyway, Raj said he'd been trying to get in touch with you, too, he's got this idea of us pulling some more jobs together — I'll let him tell you about it later. Just. You sure about this, Las?" He's pitched his voice low, now, a stitch sketched between his brows.

"About the race?"

"About working with Anton."

She studies him, surprised. "You seemed pretty thrilled to find him here."

"I knew he was here," Jay says.

"What?"

"When you stopped answering my calls and the *Nanshe* was gone, I got into your messages and figured out Anton had tricked you. I got here as soon as I could, and I figured it would be best to play along once he and the NMLF got the drop on us. Did he hurt you?"

"Of course not," Lasadi says. Her wrist still throbs, but it's ebbing quick — and despite Anton's frustrating single-minded obsession with the cause, he's never been violent. She casts her mind back through the years, trying to understand why Jay would even ask that question.

"Do you trust Vasavada?" he asks, and there, she's back on solid ground with a question she can actually answer.

"I do. And you'll meet our navigator, Qacha — she's earnest and sharp. They're both committed."

"Good." Jay squeezes her elbow, the corners of his mouth tightening as his gaze flicks down. To her wrist, maybe, though she can't quite tell. "Remember I'm here for you, Las," Jay says. "Especially if it's just like old times."

# CHAPTER 6
## RAJ

THEY'RE CROSSING THE MURDER FIELD ONCE AGAIN, although it's much less ominous now that it's starting to fill with clusters of children carrying satchels and chasing each other through the shorn grass. No one's guarding them anymore, though the pair of NMLF soldiers accompanying them still have their Teguçan-made pulse rifles slung over their shoulders.

"Heya," Ruby murmurs, nudging Raj with her elbow.

"What's up?" he asks. They're heading to the hangar where the plane Commander Vasavada promised them is kept. Given the state of the hangar itself, Raj is preparing to be unimpressed.

"Two questions," Ruby says. "What's the Liluri Star Run, and how do we feel about this job?"

"It's one of the three races in the Outland Tour series. Pilots come from all over Indira — throughout the Durga System — to race in it. You've seriously never heard of it?"

"Raj, love. I look like I follow sports, do I?"

"It's only hugely famous." He shrugs. "And the job? Somebody's hired us to bring back something tricky. This is probably a better cause than working for Tora and Nico Garnet. You worried about the NMLF?"

"Doesn't bother me. There's a bit too much drama, only. She doesn't want him to come with, and I don't want to get burned by a lover's spat."

So Ruby had noticed that, too. The way Anton and Lasadi had reacted to each other in the schoolroom had the feel of a rich and complicated history, intimate yet strewn with hidden, jagged threat. She hadn't been happy to hear he was coming with them, but she also hadn't objected.

Jay'd said Anton was a good leader, but bad for Lasadi, and Jay truly seems to believe that. Raj would hazard Lasadi believes that, too. Raj's parents' friends probably thought the same of his father. But good leaders don't twist tragic accidents into excuses to bomb innocent civilians. Good leaders don't try to assassinate the people who try to hold them accountable. Good leaders don't abuse their spouses.

Sure, Jay didn't come out and say that, not exactly. But the moment Anton Kato walked into the room, Lasadi's body language had been tuned to him like a prey animal to a predator. Like Raj's mother had been with his father.

"I need you to find out everything you can on Kato," Raj says quietly. "Why's he really working with the New Manilans?"

Ruby cocks an eyebrow at him. "You think himself has his own agenda? Jay said he trusted him."

"So? I don't. Do you?"

"Course not. I trust you and the ayas, only. Alex is barely on the list."

Raj glances at her in surprise. "You trust me?"

"Am I not here on this planet with all its spiders and snakes?"

"Just, you told me I had a death wish and you never wanted to work with me again."

"And I stand by that. If you were going to keep trying to get yourself killed, I wasn't about to stick around to see it, only." Ruby sighs. "But, Raj. The NMLF? A Coruscan senator? Arquellian military tech? We don't know this world, and I've got a brother to bring home alive. Don't go stirring up trouble."

"If Lasadi needs anything — "

"If she needs anything she'll ask — like she would have asked Jay."

Raj frowns at her. "You don't think we should have come?"

"I'm saying don't go assuming you know what's best for her." Ruby comes to a stop, holding his gaze until Raj finally nods.

"I won't go stirring up trouble."

"Thank you." She starts walking again. "I'll dig for dirt on Anton, you know I'll dig anyway. Can't help being such a nosy one."

"That's one of my favorite things about you."

"Toss your flattery, I already said I'd look. Saints in hell, this heat, yeah?" That last a touch brighter, louder — they've nearly reached the hangar and Anton, Lasadi, and Jay have caught up with them. Ruby smiles at them. "I don't know about Corusca, but only time it gets this hot in the Pearls is when something's about to blow."

"Of course you're from the Pearls, with your charming accent," Anton says, seizing the chance to turn the full force of his charisma on Ruby. "Let me guess. Artemis City?"

"Born and raised," laughs Ruby, and soon they're exchanging stories while Raj hangs back, watching with skepticism. Anton is empathetic, charming, attentive. Well-spoken and genuinely interested in the conversation — Raj can see why people followed him into battle and elected him to the Senate. As a fellow grifter, though, Raj can admire the man's technique while seeing straight through the mask.

Vasavada and the others have already reached the hangar; the commander hits a switch and the massive, rusted doors slide open with a grating shriek until they settle into a groove. There's a collection of planes inside. A few crop dusters, a couple of agricultural and cargo drones, but if the NMLF are amassing an air force, it's not out of Icaba or whatever this scratch in the dirt is called. The biggest plane in the hangar is a squat, rusty bucket of bolts about twice the size of the shuttle they flew down from the *Nanshe* on. The words *Green Lightning* are painted on the side.

Lasadi's eyes go wide. "Is that it?" she asks Vasavada, brushing her fingers over the wingtip.

Ruby elbows Raj. "I hope that's not it," she murmurs.

"There's your ship," Vasavada says, and Raj cannot believe the amount of pride in her voice over this death trap.

"It's a Misaki VTL-313 Garuda bush plane," Lasadi says to the others, and for the first time since they reunited, her face is lit up with genuine joy. Raj can't help but smile as he turns back to examine the plane with fresh eyes; he'll bring her rusted buckets of bolts every day for the rest of their lives if that's what it takes to make her this happy.

Ruby gives it a suspicious once-over. "It runs, does it?"

"The engine and all the systems are fully restored," says a new voice — a wiry, dark young woman in NMLF fatigues has emerged from the ramp in the plane's side. She's short but tough-looking, her black hair coiled in a military bun. "And it flies like a dream. I did most of the work myself."

"Then I look forward to flying it," Lasadi says. "Everyone, this is Qacha Batbayar, our navigator."

Qacha greets everyone with a serious handshake as Lasadi makes introductions.

"You didn't tell me we were flying a Garuda," Lasadi says to Qacha when they've finished. She turns back to the rest of the crew. "This is the same plane Theodor Usoro flew — these things are legendary. Originally designed for short-distance cargo hauling in places where the landing is tricky, but they turned out to be surprisingly fast and agile, which makes them perfect for racers and drug runners." Her lips quirk to the side. "And Mila Jacks."

"Oh!" Alex straightens, apparently far more interested in the plane than before. "I loved Mila Jacks vids. You're right, she flew a Garuda." He starts humming the theme song to the action adventure series. "'There's danger in the air, and peril everywhere. But Mila Jacks is here — *da-da-daaa!'"*

When he catches Qacha's shy smile at his antics, Alex adds another few bars of humming and executes a complicated dance move. Ruby rolls her eyes.

"Plus they're tough as nails," Qacha says. "They can fly away from almost any crash landing. I would know — this is the same model our father had. But his wasn't in near as good of shape as this one," she finishes quickly.

"Jay?" Lasadi turns to the mechanic, who's studying the plane with arms crossed. "You ever work on a Garuda?"

"Never met a ship I couldn't keep running, and I'm sure Qacha can show me the ropes. You just focus on keeping her in the air."

"Then let's get you loaded up," Vasavada says. "Then saints' path to you all." An ORV has arrived, packed with soldiers and the gear from the *Nanshe*'s shuttle. Or, Raj assumes, from wherever the soldiers had stashed their gear after salvaging it, since it should have taken them much longer to get to the shuttle and back.

He searches out Lasadi, hoping to speak with her privately before they take flight, but he can hear her voice from inside the plane, talking with Qacha.

"Not used to picking up your own luggage, Arquellian?" Anton Kato calls loudly from the ORV. He grins like he's joking; some of the NMLF soldiers join in a laugh.

Raj tosses an easy smile back. "You caught me daydreaming."

Anton beckons him over to pick up the other end of a crate. "Give me a hand with this."

Raj obliges, wrestling one end of the crate backwards up the ramp into the *Green Lightning*. Anton releases his end too early as they lower it into place, throwing Raj off-balance. Anton gives him a rueful grin. "Sorry, mate."

"No worries." Raj eases his jarred shoulder with a wince. "It was heavy."

Anton's smile sharpens at the dig. "Tell me something," Anton says; he's made no move to get out of the way and let Raj out of the corner he's been backed into. "What's the line you're using to get Lasadi and Jay to trust you?"

"Just my natural charm." Honestly, if Raj knew why Lasadi and Jay had decided to trust him, it would make *him* feel a whole hell of a lot better. As it is, he can't shake the thought that he's unintentionally grifting them — but doesn't even know the game he's playing, or how not to lose.

"They'll see through you in a heartbeat if they haven't already."

"Then let them." Raj returns Anton's smile, easy, like the thought isn't on a constant loop in his mind. Of course Lasadi and Jay will see through him — it's a matter of time. And lately, he's starting to think about how he can be the best version of himself when they do finally see through the layers and masks.

"Charm may work on them, but I'm sure we'll see soon if you're a man of substance, too." He claps Raj on the shoulder. This close, in this heat, Raj can practically taste the other man's cologne. "Welcome to the team."

# CHAPTER 7
## LASADI

THE CLIFFS DROP AWAY BENEATH THEM, AND IT'S EXACTLY as Lasadi had imagined: wings spread and soaring over the lush green carpet of the jungle far below. She'd been imagining this flight alone, in the *Nanshe*'s shuttle. Not in a restored VTL-313 Garuda bush plane called the *Green Lightning*, with Qacha Batbayar in the co-pilot's seat and the rest of the crew — her crew? — in the back.

She can hear their voices, indistinct beneath the hum of the engines. Laughter and conversation with a comfortable warmth developed over their last week together. Jay's part of the in-jokes, now, she could see it when they loaded up the plane. Teasing Alex like a big brother would, trading jokes with Ruby, falling into an easy work rhythm with Raj.

Anton's charming his way into their little cadre, of course, with much more natural ease than Lasadi — despite the fact that she already pulled a job with them. He's always been able to do both: be the easy friend in the barracks and the single-minded commander making the hard decisions when he needed to. Every fighter in the CLA had been ready to die for Anton and his cause. And every one of them knew he would ask it of them without hesitation — or regard for their friendship — when the time came.

He'd tried to train her to do the same, but she'd never been able to stop letting her feelings for people cloud her judgement.

Like Raj — olds, she's grateful she hadn't actually called him after the Auburn Station job. Sleeping with a crew member would have been a terrible mistake, especially if they're going to keep working together. She's not Anton, who can perfectly compartmentalize bedroom and war room. The cittern-string bracelet — the one Raj left on the *Nanshe* that she'd been wearing for good luck — is safely out of sight in her pocket. She couldn't bear the mortification of him spotting it.

Always a hopeless romantic, Anton had called her, sometimes affectionately, mostly critically. Her grandmother, too: "Think with your head, Lala, not your heart. That's what it's for."

She'll get that tattooed on her arm, someday.

"Setting our course for Moie," Qacha says, reaching for the nav panel and shaking Lasadi out of her thoughts.

"Let's do it manually," Lasadi says. "That's part of the race, right? No computer navigation? You said you were good at that."

The corner of Qacha's mouth tugs into a smile, and she hits the switch to kill the nav panel. "My dad's Garuda's nav system was broken before I was born," she says, pulling a binder of yellowing papers out from under her seat and peering out the window. She studies the compass in her hand, then makes a notation on the map. "Three degrees starboard," she says. "And we'll maintain for five minutes."

Lasadi loses herself in the flight, in establishing a rhythm with Qacha as she guides them north to trace the edge of the plateau separating the Liluri Mountains to their right from the jungle to their left. The plateau narrows as they fly, the barrier between mountain and jungle slowly erased.

Lasadi grew up idolizing the VTL-313 Garuda because of the Mila Jacks action vids she watched as a kid; she and her younger siblings had taken turns pretending to be the dashing pilot zipping around Indira from one adventure to the next, imagining amazing places that she at least hoped she'd one day visit. And, of course, she'd dreamed of racing one in the Outland Tour series.

"Have you ever seen the Run in person?" Lasadi asks Qacha. "You must have, growing up here."

"The village we grew up in is pretty remote, but one year the route went by us. We sat out with Dad all day watching the planes go by."

"Is your dad still around?"

Qacha shakes her head. "Just me and Temu, now."

"I bet he'd be proud of you right now."

She laughs. "He'd be thrilled." Qacha checks her clock and compass, then makes another mark on the map in her lap. "Twelve degrees port, and hold this heading for now. We've got about an hour of smooth flying before we need to do anything tricky."

"How tricky will we need to get?"

"Not very, taking the usual route." Qacha holds up the map, sweeping a finger around a jutting mountain. "We skirt all the way around Mount Madsha and come in from the north. It takes about an hour."

"And what's the not-usual route?" Lasadi points to a gap on the eastern flank of Mount Madsha, which opens up direct into the town of Moie. "Can we go through here instead?"

"No one goes through there. Look." Qacha lifts the map, stabbing a finger at the ravine. "It's called the Leopard's Maw. It's literally marked with a skull."

"But is it impossible?"

Qacha gives the map a worried frown, but doesn't answer.

"You don't think you could lead me through it?" Lasadi says, teasing, and Qacha finally breaks into a tentative smile.

"I could."

"Sounds fun." Lasadi hits the button to patch them in to the rest of the team's comms. The cockpit's open to the back of the plane, but she can't hear much over the racket. "Heads up we'll be in Moie in about two hours, and things are likely to get interesting in the last hour. We'll want to come up with our plan to get on Theo Usoro's ship by then."

"I've been reading up on Theo's sponsor," Ruby says. "Guy named Francis Edan. He's New Manilan. Real playboy billionaire type, he runs some international shipping and logistics company that sponsors part of the Star Race."

"Star Run," Lasadi says; Ruby shrugs.

"Francis Edan likes to throw his money around,"

Raj says. "He owns a couple of sports teams, does flashy charity work — anything that gets him positive press."

"He must have loved sponsoring Theodor Usoro, then," says Lasadi.

"He's still trying to ride that wave," says Ruby.

"So how do we get on Theo's old ship?" Lasadi asks. "Is Edan doing tours?"

"Not until after the race," Ruby says. "He's having another pilot race it as a publicity stunt, so he's not letting anyone close until after."

"Who's the pilot?"

"Guy named Sevi Bryant. Lots of hits on him — he was a controversial pick."

"Edan sponsored *Bryant*?" Qacha asks. "He's got a bit of a . . . reputation."

"As a cheater," Lasadi says. Qacha may be trying to be delicate, but she doesn't need to be. "I remember hearing about him. He's an amazing pilot, but he's also an asshole with an image problem. And a few years back a couple people accused him of sabotaging their ships so he could win the Run."

"I guess Edan's looking past it," Ruby says. "He was on a winning streak with Theodor Usoro when Usoro disappeared, and the pilot he backed for the first two of this season's Outland Tour races didn't even finish. Lots of bad press about whether Edan's going to come back from this. Bryant seems a sure winner, if a little rough around the edges."

"So we give him another sure winner," Lasadi says. "One without the image problems his current pilot comes with."

"Another hotshot Coruscan pilot, like Theo Usoro," says Jay with a grin.

"Hold on," Anton says, tone reasonable. "We don't need to race for him, we just need to get onto Theo's plane."

"And what better way than being asked to fly it?" Lasadi says. "Yes, Alex could probably break onto the *Figment of the North*, Jay could pose as one of the mechanics. But if Theodor Usoro was as secretive as most pilots are, we'll need some time to find what we're looking for."

"I like it," Raj says before Anton can answer. "We give this banker second thoughts about the bad press his current pilot could cause, and dangle a perfect replacement right under his nose. Ruby, can you create a new identity for Lasadi with lots of wins under her belt?"

"Absolutely. One tempting pilot with no sponsor coming right up."

"It would be pretty unlikely for a pilot to show up to the race with no sponsor," Lasadi points out. "But not uncommon for one sponsor to make another a last-minute deal for a pilot."

"Got it," Ruby says. "One tempting pilot with a shitty, down-on-his-luck sponsor coming right up." She glances at Raj. "That'll be you, will it?"

"Perfect," Raj answers. "I'll work Edan to make sure she's on his radar. Where's he staying?"

Ruby makes an appreciative sound. "Some place called the Golden Macaw. Real flash."

"Any rooms available?"

She hums another minute. "There are now. I got us four near each other."

"Qacha?" Lasadi asks. "Be my roomie?" She doesn't want Anton making any assumptions.

Raj's voice cuts through the comms. "You and me, Jay?"

"Sure, leave me stuck with Alex," Ruby says.

Anton hasn't gotten into the little fray; no one assumes he's the sharing type.

Jay clears his throat. "While Ruby's seeding rumors about you on the net and Raj is talking you up in person, I'll talk to the people whose opinion really matters. The mechanics."

"Perfect," Lasadi says.

The landscape has been changing subtly as they've flown north, the jungle and the mountains starting to blur. First, the plateau started to break up, jagged ravines snaking into the tabletop. Then, the flat surface of the table began to ripple and rise, hills jutting out of the jungle until now there's no distinction. Knife-sharp mountains scrape the sky, ridges falling away, all covered valley to peak in the emerald green of the jungle.

Lasadi cranes her neck to catch a glimpse of the mountain peak high above; no wonder they ground racers after dark. She wouldn't want to be caught out here trying to navigate.

"Is this Mount Madsha?" Lasadi asks Qacha. The mountain looms in front of them, sloping gentle down to the west and jagged down to the east, to where the Leopard's Maw awaits.

"That's it," Qacha says. Her lips press tight, like

she's considering talking Lasadi out of this madness. She doesn't.

"Since you all are supposed to be talking me up, let me give you something to brag about," Lasadi says. "Strap in, we're taking a detour."

Qacha shoots her a wild-eyed grin and Lasadi banks to the right, aiming for the gaping cleft in the emerald mountainside.

Lasadi can immediately see why this route isn't popular. Whereas the valleys she was already navigating were reasonably wide, the Leopard's Maw is closed in and narrow. Like the Tourmaline Range Lasadi learned to fly in on Corusca. Of course, navigating a racing ship in Corusca's much lower gravity is different than here. But she's had some time to get used to the controls and she settles into the turns and banks, listening to Qacha's instruction.

The kid's good under pressure. Despite her objections to taking this route, she seems excited, calling out turns and distances as they soar past spires and crags.

"This is easy," Lasadi says. "Let's have some fun. Increasing speed by five percent."

Qacha makes a little noise of surprise, but reacts quick to redo her calculations. "Five degrees starboard in five, four, three, two — okay. We're getting to the end. This is the obstacle we'll want to fly over."

"What's our elevation."

"Three thousand four hundred and seventeen meters. But — "

"Can't break thirty-five hundred in the race, right?"

"We're not racing," Qacha points out.

"Guide me through."

Qacha takes a sharp breath, and Lasadi loses herself in the controls and the younger woman's commands as the ravine narrows even further, the jungle canopy reaching up from the floor, vines trailing down the rocky cliff walls.

"Hard to port," Qacha yells, and Lasadi takes them on knife's edge to sweep past a spectacular waterfall, the sunlight catching rainbows in the spray, through the last of the closing-in ravine walls of the Leopard's Maw, and through into the Moie Valley.

Lasadi rights the *Green Lightning* with a whoop. Beside her, Qacha is grinning.

"That was amazing!"

"Couldn't've done it without you," Lasadi says. "That oughta catch Edan's attention."

"And everyone else's," Qacha says, almost breathless with the excitement. And she's right; the Leopard's Maw put them out right at the end of town, where everyone could see them slashing on knife's edge out of the ravine.

Lasadi relaxes, soaring back over Moie to get a better view while Qacha calls in their arrival to the landing pad. The Moie Valley is really more a ravine itself: steep and verdant and barely two kilometers across at its widest point. The town is nestled in the bottom like it spilled there, a tumble of houses built climbing up the ravine on both sides. A river cascades like molten silver through the middle of town.

It's still hours from sunset, but the sun has sunk behind the tall mountains and already visibility is starting to get poor. Clouds are piling up around Mount Madsha and catching vivid orange fire, the last rays of sun slanting in gold swaths through the clouds to strike the jungle hillside above Moie, lighting up the foliage in a green glow.

The town itself is decked out in banners and flags and lanterns for the festivities surrounding the Liluri Star Run; the other five points of the star are different every year, but Moie is always the race's starting and ending point.

Lasadi maneuvers the *Green Lightning* to the landing pad on the north side of the river and sets it down gentle, then follows the controller's instructions to their reserved dock. She pats a fond hand on the control panel when it's become still.

"So that's what it's like to fly a Garuda," Lasadi says.

"Not bad for your first try," says Qacha.

"Thanks for having faith."

"Consider me impressed."

"That was *wild*," Alex says; the kid's grinning at Qacha. "You were great. You too, Cap," he adds quick, to Lasadi.

"Thanks, Alex," Las says, wry. She glances at Raj, who's got a gray undertone to his warm, tawny skin. "You're looking a little green," Lasadi teases him.

"Could've used a little warning before the sideways flying," Raj says.

Jay laughs and claps the other man on the arm. "You'll get used to it, brother."

Anton is sitting back as the others jostle their way out of the plane, but when he catches her eye he inclines his head in respect. "Impressive as always," he murmurs, and the compliment seeps golden through her soul. She can't help but return his smile.

A small swarm of kids have gathered around the *Green Lightning*, yelling offers of lodging at hotels, restaurants. A tall blond woman wearing a faded jumpsuit wades through them, yelling for the kids to stay off of the dock.

She shakes her head. "They always see opportunity. Captain?"

"That's me," Lasadi says. "I'm, ah . . ." She trails off with a quick flush of panic as the woman crushes her hand in a shake.

Ruby's voice sounds through her earpiece. "Tita James."

"Tita James," Lasadi says. "And my navigator, Qacha Batbayar."

"Pleasure. I'm dockmaster here. Any one of those kids can help you with your bags to your hotel before pilot's orientation."

"Thank you. We were trying to make good time."

"No kidding." The dockmaster leans in. "You came through Leopard's Maw?"

"That's right."

"Damn, girl." The dockmaster grins, then touches her ear, listening. She turns back and flags down a man in a matching jumpsuit on the other side of the dock. "Incoming in five!" she shouts, then turns back to the others. "Busiest day of the year. Welcome to Moie!"

# CHAPTER 8
## RAJ

THE HOTEL RUBY SNAGGED THEM ROOMS IN IS AT THE TOP of a street that climbs straight up from the east bank of the river, so steep it's less a road, more a series of wide steps through a kaleidoscopic explosion of colorful buildings, race pennants, and flickering street signs advertising food, trinkets, lodging, guide services. It hasn't rained on them yet, but the town's architecture is clearly designed for downpours. Every shop is accessed by a stone bridge across one of the wide, paved gutters on either side of the street, and the river promenade is covered with awnings.

Every building on this main road is aimed at tourists, though when Raj sneaks peeks down the narrow alleys, they're strung with laundry. Living in Moie must be a bit like living in one of the neighborhood hubs of Ironfall, Raj thinks. Pods stacked haphazardly up the walls so one family's roof is another's terrace.

The smell is incredible. Earthy, humid, fresh —

grilling meat from street carts, baking bread from open restaurant doors, the sweet steam of a distillery. The whole town is filled with the white noise of the river, though the farther they hike up the road, the more it becomes a quiet background static.

It's been a while since Raj felt Indira's gravity. His thighs are aching by the time they reach the top of the street to find the softly lit archway announcing the name of the hotel: the Golden Macaw. Lasadi's a bit out of breath, but she hasn't complained. Qacha, on the other hand, looks like she could have jogged up the road with her heavy backpack without effort.

Ruby and Alex are here at the hotel already, having slipped ahead while Lasadi was registering the *Green Lightning*. Jay stayed with the ship, and Anton and his multiple suitcases were waiting on a porter. He'll be lying low in Moie, pretending to be simply a spectator should anyone spot him and start asking questions. One of the downsides of having your face plastered all over the news feeds.

Of course, there's the off chance Raj might be recognized, too. Some of his parents' wealthy friends might be staying at a place like the Golden Macaw, or a head-hunter could recognize him from the job boards. Ruby's been keeping an eye out, though; the odds his father has managed to put up a bounty Ruby hasn't taken down are slim.

The others don't have much to worry about, though Lasadi's face has a chance of making it on the feeds. She's got her long, dusky blond hair coiled up under a hat and is wearing wide, yellow-lensed glasses.

Qacha is staring at the arch, wide-eyed. "This place is amazing."

"All part of the job," Raj says. He gestures for her and Lasadi to go ahead. "Shall we?"

Raj has stayed at a lot of nice places by virtue of his family's money, and he's stayed in a lot of dives since deserting from the Arquellian navy. Frankly, from the looks of Moie he'd expected a dive — but the Golden Macaw is shockingly lovely.

A blessedly flat path leads from the archway into a swath of perfectly manicured jungle, with witch lights floating in the foliage and birds calling from the branches above them. The path opens up to the hotel's lobby, where poles and interlocking branches arch overhead to create an airy woven dome. Circular glass-topped rattan tables are surrounded by sunken leather benches, each covered in blue silk cushions. Potted fan palms and screens of trailing vines give each table a sense of privacy.

The telltale shimmer of an environment shield keeps insects out while letting fresh air in; it shivers faintly against Raj's skin as he walks through, dodging white-clad waiters carrying trays of drinks and picture-perfect New Manilan delicacies. Raj's stomach growls audibly, and Lasadi shoots him a look. Qacha laughs.

"Probably a good thing I didn't have much to eat before the flight," Raj says. "Given how you two like to fly."

"Checking in?" The concierge, a tall bald man with pale skin and a broad smile, has crossed the lobby to herd their little group of gawkers out of the dining area.

"Yes, thank you," Raj says. Anywhere else, Raj

would feel underdressed. But Moie attracts adventure tourists more than posh resort types, and the clientele dining in the Golden Macaw's lobby are dressed casually enough. Raj's mother would be having a heart attack. "The name on the reservation is Colman."

"Excellent." The concierge taps something into his gauntlet, the lens in his left eye glimmering as information flickers over it.

"Edan is at the bar," Lasadi murmurs, and Raj turns his attention to the sparse crowd of pre-dinner drinkers. Edan is sitting by himself, nondescript yet clearly wealthy. Brown skin a few shades darker than Raj's and a neatly trimmed beard, thick black hair going pure white at the corners of his mouth and his temples. He's the nicest dressed person in the lobby, wearing a casual lightweight gray suit. He's holding a book and sipping a coffee, the fingers on both hands crusted with rings.

"Alex," Raj murmurs. "You around?"

"On it."

The credentials Raj gave the concierge must have gone through without triggering any red flags, because the man's eye flickers silver, then goes clear as he turns back to Raj. "If you'll — "

"Holy saints," Alex exclaims, crossing to Lasadi. "Are you Tita James? You flew the Leopard's Maw — I was down on the river when you came out. Can I get your autograph?"

Lasadi takes Alex's proffered pen with a perfect blend of surprise and embarrassment, and Alex turns back to the concierge. "It was incredible. You should have seen it." He grins at Qacha and hands her the pen next. "I admire an excellent navigator."

Qacha ducks her head with a shy smile that doesn't seem feigned in the slightest. Lasadi catches Raj's eye over the young woman's head, eyebrow quirked in amusement.

At the bar, Francis Edan has halfway turned in his seat to study the newcomers.

"You flew the Leopard's Maw?" the concierge says. "Very impressive. Best of luck in the run, Ms. James, and I'll have someone show you to your rooms. Is there anything else I can do for you?"

"No, thank you," Raj says. "You two go on ahead," he says to Lasadi and Qacha. "I need to make some calls."

He hands off his bag to the porter and swipes them a handful of credits for a tip, then finds a spot at the bar not too far from Francis Edan. The bartop is polished stone, refreshingly cool to the touch in the waning heat of the day. The barstools are real leather, the glasses heavy tumblers instead of the bulbs he's gotten accustomed to drinking out of in zero G. Raj recognizes ornate bottles on the shelves with a pang of fondness for friends he hasn't seen in years.

He's going to enjoy being back on Indira.

He slumps onto the stool and lets his body language shift: shoulders slouching, mouth tightening, fingers drumming restlessly on his knee. He runs a hand through his hair and signals the bartender, gives Edan a wry smile when he catches the other man evaluating him, then orders a shot of trendy, overpriced brandy.

"How are you, sir?" the bartender asks politely, pouring with a practiced flick of the wrist.

"Been better," Raj says, downing the shot and

pushing his glass forward for a refill. "Bit of a wild ride getting here, but we're all in one piece, yeah?" Raj taps at his cuff, touching his ear. "Hello?" he says to no one. The bartender retreats. Francis Edan goes back to pretending not to pay him any attention, his ring-encrusted fingers still on the pages of the book.

"Yeah, good to hear from you," Raj says, faking suave confidence again for his pretend conversation partner. "Tita and I just arrived in Moie, we're all set for the race. No, I — " he lowers his voice with a glance at Edan; the other man is staring at his book, but he hasn't turned the page since Raj sat beside him. "I don't have the money *now*, I told you. I'll have it once she wins the race. Yeah, I *know* what I said, but — "

Raj lets his fingers drum in agitation again as he pretends to listen.

"I'll get you the money," he hisses, and swipes the fake call closed. He glares at his glass of trendy brandy, the warm buzz of the first glass already a comfortable glow in his veins. And hides a smile at the sound of a book closing, its cover scuffing on the polished stone bartop.

"Bad day?"

Francis Edan has a velvety voice, smooth and cultured to match his casually rich wardrobe and brilliant white teeth. Raj looks up like Edan caught him deep in brooding, plasters cool confidence on his face once more.

"No day's bad when you're sitting in a place like this, am I right?" Raj grins. "Anyway, my luck's about to change, I can feel it." Raj downs the second shot and pushes the glass away. "Put it on the room tab," he calls to the bartender. "Name's Luke Colman."

Edan doesn't pick up his book after Raj walks away; he pulls out his comm. And if Raj were a betting man, he'd put down a hundred credits Edan's looking up the names Luke Colman and Tita James. When he finds a rising star pilot currently being sponsored by a cash-strapped businessman on a clear downward spiral, he'll see the business opportunity.

Now to give him the push he needs to let his current pilot go and snatch up a new prospect.

# CHAPTER 9
## LASADI

THE VENUE FOR THE PILOT'S ORIENTATION IS NOT GRAND —
a small open-air amphitheater next to the dockyard,
rough-hewn stone steps set in a semicircle overlooking
the river. It's humble, yet Lasadi steps into it with awe.
Some of her biggest childhood heroes sat on those steps.
Are sitting on them now, even.

The other pilots and their crews are milling about,
some holding themselves off to the side, but others
mingling like the old friends they probably are.
Growing up, Lasadi saw the same names over and over
in the competitors lists, and even though it's been a few
years since she followed the racing circuit, she still
recognizes a few of the older faces.

"That's Noura Samson," she says to Jay and Qacha.
"*The* Noura Samson. Casually talking to Li Damian."

"They were both racing the year my father took us
to watch," Qacha says; her voice is barely a whisper. "I
saw their planes!"

"They looked over." Lasadi's cheeks blaze, though

Samson and Li are all the way across the plaza and can't possibly have heard her. She lifts a hand in what she hopes comes across as a casual, normal greeting. The other two pilots incline their heads, then go back to their conversation.

"Li smiled at you," says Qacha.

Jay laughs. "We'll get you two some signatures later. But remember what we're *actually* here for." He lifts his chin — Theodor Usoro's ship, the *Figment of the North*, is on display in the pedestrian plaza beyond the amphitheater, next to a banner that reads Registration. "Let's get you checked in," Jay says. "And get a closer look at that ship."

As they approach the registration table, it's clear how heavily guarded the *Figment* is. Black velvet ropes — backed by a faintly shimmering shield — keep visitors from getting too close, and if getting zapped by a shield isn't enough deterrent, armed guards are stationed around the ship. Lasadi counts at least four, smiling polite yet firm at the gawkers.

The registration line affords her a chance to admire the ship. It's a Misaki VTL, though a few models newer than the 313 Garuda they flew here on. Misaki refined the engine pivots on this model to make the transition from liftoff to flight smoother, and the wings are redesigned for better maneuverability, but the basic operation of the ship should be the same as the *Green Lightning*.

"I can't wait to fly that thing," Lasadi says.

"Then you better get to charming," Jay says. "Because we're definitely not stealing it. Francis Edan has guards on it all night, and that red light blinking on the door? A Far-Xiao system — a couple of steps up from what we've got on the *Nanshe*, even."

"I can charm people," Lasadi says.

Jay's cheek dimples in a smile. "I'll believe it when I see it. You're up."

Lasadi steps up to the registration table and palms the scanner; the alias "Tita James" pops up on the desk. The harried young man is about to swipe over her orientation packet when he does a double take. Lasadi's heart skips a beat — is something wrong with her ident card?

"You're the one who flew the Leopard's Maw this afternoon," the young man says. "Right?"

A few nearby heads turn at his words, and Lasadi feels heat rising in her cheeks. *You're charming, Las. You can charm people.* "That's right."

"Everyone's talking about it." The young man glances again at her file. "Of course. You're not from Indira. The offworld pilots are always daredevils."

"Are there any other offworlders racing this year?" Lasadi asks.

"Peter Fangio's crew." The young man gestures towards a tall man standing at the edge of the amphitheater. "They're from somewhere in Durga's Belt. Orientation will start in a minute or two, good luck in the Run." He turns to the group standing behind her. "Hi there. Name?"

The man from Durga's Belt, Peter Fangio, is watching when Lasadi steps away from the table. He's tall and broad, muscles he seems proud of straining under his suit. Dark skin, wavy black hair slicked back. She lifts her chin in greeting and he does the same.

"Do you recognize Fangio?" she asks Jay. If Peter Fangio is from Durga's Belt, there's a nonzero chance he might recognize them, even though they both kept a fairly low profile when working for Nico Garnet in the Pearls.

Jay shakes his head and touches his ear. "Ruby? What do you have for us on Peter Fangio?"

"His ship's registered in Artemis City, but it hasn't been in home port for almost three years," Ruby says. "Spends most of his time on the race circuit. Fangio and his crew have competed in the Star Run every year for the last six — almost won it last year, too. Ended up third."

"He's the guy to beat, huh?"

"Him and Sevi Bryant, but if we play our cards right, you won't be racing against Bryant. He's on your nine."

Lasadi glances over to find another man approaching Fangio. Lanky and fit, with a confident swagger that borders on aggressive. His thick brown hair is cut close and expensive, rugged handsome face perfectly tanned, dark glasses perched on an aquiline nose. Lasadi recognizes him from past races; he's from somewhere on Arquelle's north coast, a longtime fixture in the racing circuits, renowned for his skill as well as his hair-trigger temper. And plagued by rumors that he won his last few races through cheating and sabotage — though anyone who's been bold enough to say it aloud has found themselves spinning in gale-force lawsuits.

If they're going to find anything that sticks on Bryant, they'll have to be smart about it.

"Go see what the word is from the other mechanics," Lasadi says to Jay. "Qacha and I will meet the competition." She puts on a smile and heads over to the two men. "Peter Fangio?" She holds out a hand. "Tita James. I hear you're a man to watch out for. This is my navigator, Qacha Batbayar."

"And I hear you flew the Leopard's Maw this afternoon," Fangio says. "Didn't know you were Coruscan, though." He inclines his head to the *Figment of the North*. "Some sort of quota needs filled, is there? Now Usoro went sailing the stars."

"They say you only got on the podium because he went missing."

Fangio studies her a moment, then smiles. "Best blasted pilot I ever saw fly," he finally says. "Outland Tour's not the same without him, is it."

"Maybe it's time for a new competitive element," cuts in Bryant; he doesn't enjoy being ignored. "Show you offworlders how things are done on Indira." He gives Lasadi an evaluating look, smile cocked to the side. He's not studying her skill.

"Oh, sorry," Lasadi says, blinking at him in surprise. She's obviously supposed to recognize him. "Are you one of the mechanics?"

Bryant's dark eyes flash angry; beside him, Peter Fangio's lips twitch in amusement.

"This is Sevi Bryant," Fangio says, wry. "He won the Shalima Circuit this spring."

"Okay." Lasadi shares a look with Qacha, who shrugs like she's never heard of him either. "Well, it's nice to meet you."

"Mr. Fangio?"

Ruby's here, right on cue. She changed at the

hotel, into a close-fitting dress splashed with tropical flowers she must have bought here in town. It's cut low, displaying the gold tattoo of the Pearls etched into her dark collarbones. Her hair is loose and tousled, the perfect image of a tourist from Durga's Belt enjoying the jungle heat. She steps right past Bryant. "Mr. Fangio! You'll be a love and autograph my scarf?"

At her accent — pure Pearls — Fangio grins and signs away. Ruby bats her lashes in thanks, then seems to notice Lasadi. "Oh! And you're Tita James?" She holds out the pen and scarf. "The nerves on you flying like that, I can't wait to watch you race!"

"Excuse me," Bryant snaps, but he's not talking to Ruby. Alex has slipped past them, jostling Bryant with a tossed "Sorry!" over his shoulder, and, presumably, Bryant's hotel card now in his pocket.

When Lasadi hands Ruby's scarf back, Bryant starts to reach for it. Ruby frowns at him, brow drawing in and the corners of her mouth tightening in the perfect facsimile of polite confusion.

"Oh!" she says. "And you are?"

"Sevi Bryant," Lasadi tells her. "He's won a race or two himself."

Irritation scrawls across Bryant's face. "I've already won the Shalima Circuit, just this year alone." He takes Ruby's proffered pen and signs in a gnarled scribble. When he hands it back, he leans in to Lasadi with teeth bared. "One thing you learn about flying out here: The Liluri Mountains eat alive cocky pilots."

"Is that a threat?" Lasadi asks.

"Do you want to find out?" Bryant gives Fangio a

sharp nod, then turns his back and stalks away, all hint of his earlier swagger stitched up tight with fury.

Ruby whistles, low. "Touchy, is he," she says. She smooths a hand down Peter Fangio's arm. "Good luck, you! I've put a few credits down on watching you come in on top." She winks at him, then sashays away. Fangio's attention follows her through the crowd.

"Good meeting you," Lasadi says as a woman in a neon green suit jacket calls for everyone to take a seat; Fangio's attention snaps back. "And good luck."

The returning pilots seem to be gathering in their usual groups. Noura Samson, Li Damian, and some of the older pilots are sitting in the back. Fangio has joined his crew somewhere near the middle. Bryant's getting plenty of polite nods, but no one has welcomed him to join them — and no one invites Lasadi over, either. This is the thirty-seventh Star Run, which means legendary pilots have been winning this race since almost a decade before Lasadi was born. She may have pulled an impressive stunt, but she's still new blood.

She and Qacha join Jay on a step near the entrance and settle in to listen. Lasadi has heard this welcoming speech so many times over the years she could probably give it herself, but still she hangs on every word the woman in the green jacket says. She has to shake off the strange sense of deja vu, all those years elbowing her younger siblings to get a closer view of the feeds, imagining she was among the crowd sitting on the steps, waiting nervous for their chance in the spotlight.

She shakes herself out of memories; she can't keep letting herself go down that road. She never thought of home much when she was working for Nico. Probably because she'd assumed she could never go back, but Anton has hinted that if things go well here, she might even be considered a hero again.

She shakes off the dream and turns her attention to the explanation of the race.

The Star Run begins and ends in Moie, with five secret checkpoints that will be revealed moments before the racers leave. Racers can hit the checkpoints in any order, which means winning is as much about a navigator's skill as a pilot's prowess. Of course, Lasadi's crew has a secret sixth checkpoint they'll learn about once they get the coordinates from the *Figment of the North*. There's a slight chance they'll be able to hit all six and still make it back competitively, but there won't be any way to know until the race begins.

Choosing the checkpoint you'll overnight at is a critical part of the race. Stop too early and you lose precious hours of flight time. Stop too late and you'll be caught flying after dark. The more experienced veterans definitely have their secret spots in the jungle where it's safe to land; Theodor Usoro did. Lasadi hopes once they get access to his maps they'll be able to decipher them.

Every ship will be checked before the race to make sure the navigation system is locked, and checked afterwards to find out whether it was used. Altitude data will be checked after the race, too — going over thirty-five hundred meters disqualifies you. This forces pilots to actually fly the ravines and valleys of the Liluri Mountains, rather than hopping over them to get to the next checkpoint. Over the years, laser grids have been installed along some of the more popular routes to make doubly sure no one cheats.

The orientation finishes up with a reminder to enjoy the sendoff party tomorrow night, and the racers and their crews begin milling around the amphitheater once more. Quite a few have drifted over to admire the *Figment of the North*, and Lasadi catches Theo Usoro's name floating through more than a few snippets of conversation.

Lasadi sits a moment longer, enjoying the buzz of energy and anticipation flowing through her veins. She's sat in this amphitheater in her imagination so many times, but it couldn't compare with the reality. The sharp bite of engine oil and grill smoke spiking through the lush aroma of the jungle, the muffled roar of the Moie River tumbling through the steep valley, even the rough, sun-warmed stone step beneath her palm as she smooths her hand over it, trying to ground herself.

She's in Moie. And she's about to compete in the Liluri Star Run.

Something dark and restless edges at her attention beneath the rush of excitement, and Lasadi scans the crowd, trying to put her finger on whatever's bothering her subconscious.

Jay's shoulder is warm against hers when he nudges her. He lifts his chin at Sevi Bryant, who's still seated on the other side of the amphitheater. Bryant's watching Lasadi like a tiger considering his prey.

"Looks like we got under his skin," Lasadi says.

"Looks like," Jay says. "Don't go anywhere without your gun."

# CHAPTER 10
## RAJ

"Wow, small towns," Ruby says. She's back with Raj at the Golden Macaw, waiting for Alex to return from breaking into Sevi Bryant's hotel, and for Lasadi, Jay, and Qacha to return from the pilot's orientation.

"What about small towns?" Raj asks.

"Everything is drama," says Ruby. "There is literally a three-hundred-message chain about how the owner of Moie Dreams Adventure Company hasn't fixed a pothole on the riverfront, and only five of the messages are about potholes."

"What are the rest of the posts about?" Raj asks.

Ruby hums a moment, reading. "Fragile male egos," she finally says. "More or less. Ooh, wait, here it is. One of the Moie Dreams guides is apparently sleeping with six — no, *seven* — women. Well done, you. They all found out about it in this thread." She tilts her tablet to him. "It's brilliant, look — "

"Is this going to help us get on Theodor Usoro's ship?" Raj cuts in.

"Ah . . . no. But I'm saving this thread to make you read later."

"I can't wait."

Raj stretches out, making himself comfortable on the couch beside her while she taps against her tablet. Their rooms are a circle of dome-shaped cottages standing apart on the far end of the property, with a private sitting area between them. Low rattan tables and couches covered in silk cushions, faux torches providing mood lighting as the sun sets. There's even a rain-repelling shield that can be activated at the touch of a button, covering the entire clearing.

After the cramped transport they'd shipped from Dima to Indira on, the cottages are practically palatial. Raj's pod in Ironfall is smaller than the one he's sharing with Jay, never mind the massive, comfortable bed. There's a soaking tub. A real shower. Raj is in heaven.

Or would be, if it was just their little crew here. Anton hasn't left his room since they arrived this afternoon, though he's having the occasional conversation in low tones. Even absent from view, his presence is a dark pulse in the corner of an otherwise lovely moment.

At the *kriit-kriiiiit* of some jungle bird in the canopy above, Raj realizes Ruby's gone still beside him. She's frowning at her tablet, lower lip caught in her teeth.

Raj leans over. "What is it?"

"What's what." Ruby swipes away the message before he can read it, but he catches the sender: Ayalasi Kateri. The head aya of the Aymaya Apostles, the group that raised Ruby and Alex in Artemis City. Ruby begins typing again. "More gossip, only."

"Is everything okay?"

Ruby's nostrils flare. "Why wouldn't it be?"

It's not, though, Raj knows her well enough to recognize the telltale spike of anxiety under Ruby's mask of irritation. Raj will press later; she's not going to tell him anything right now.

Raj cuts his gaze to Anton's room. "Have you found anything on . . ."

"No joy — I haven't had much time," she says, gnawing her lip. But her shoulders relaxed when Raj steered the conversation away from the personal. "I took a stab at his messages, but the encryption's flash. Nothing I can't get through, obviously, not with a bit of time."

"Have you looked into his Senate campaign?"

"Of course, haven't I. Not sure if this means anything, but he's had a few massive donations lately from the same anonymous donor."

"The NMLF? Might be why he's working with them."

"I couldn't guess. There's a lot of news about this Limitations Act they're debating in Corusca now. It'd put a bit of a muzzle on the Alliance there — countries like New Manila have got their eye on what happens. Anton's a key vote, so I could see the NMLF wanting to make sure he stayed in power. But there's nothing illegal about anonymous campaign donations, love."

"Humor me and keep digging." Raj glances over his shoulder. The constant murmur of Anton's voice in conversation — muffled to an unintelligible blur by a privacy screen he must have brought with him — has gone quiet. "I'd love to find out who he's talking with, too."

Ruby sighs pointedly, but doesn't say no. She's always preferred to take the safer line than Raj likes to, but her instincts will be humming, same as his. Anton Kato isn't telling them everything. He doesn't need to, but he also didn't need to come with them. Maybe he doesn't trust them to do the job right, maybe he's here to keep watch on Lasadi. Or maybe he just likes to keep a tight hold on his plans.

Either way, Anton's a snake, and Raj isn't going to let his crew get bit.

Familiar voices on the path from the main part of the hotel pull him out of his concentration. Lasadi steps into the little clearing along with Jay, Qacha, and Alex.

"All good?" Raj calls.

"It's perfect," she says. "We're registered, Bryant hates me, and Alex had an extremely successful burglary session."

"Hey!" Alex holds a hand to his chest in mock outrage. "I'm not a burglar. I'm an exceptional thief."

Lasadi's laughter catches Raj off guard, and he breaks out in a smile. It's the first time he's seen her this relaxed since before the Auburn Station job — but it doesn't last. Anton's cottage door opens, his polished politician's voice slicing through her levity like a blade.

"Glad you've all been having fun," Anton says. "I look forward to hearing about it over dinner." He crosses to Lasadi and smooths a hand down her arm. Her smile stays on her face but vanishes from her eyes.

"I think I'll go get cleaned up," she says, stepping past him.

"A shower sounds good to me, too," Jay says. "You leave us any hot water, Raj?"

"Nothing but hot water out here," Raj says. He gets to his feet. "We'll pull some chairs together. Gimme a hand, Alex."

Dinner arrives while Jay and Lasadi are gone, a big family-style meal of local delicacies, some of which Raj recognizes from the New Manilan restaurants he used to frequent in Arquelle as a young man. His stomach growls in delighted anticipation. There's a few New Manilan food stands in Ironfall, and even one in his neighborhood hub, but nothing that holds a candle to what he remembers. And this array is phenomenal. Grilled bird, fish roasted in thick green leaves and served over rice, a sour orange soup — Raj's favorite — and a round of tiny beer bottles with a picture of a snow leopard on the label.

Lasadi emerges a few minutes later, hair still damp and pulled back into her usual braid. Raj has yet to see her hair down, but based on the few strands he's noticed escaping her braids, he suspects her hair has a touch of natural waviness. He can picture the full, soft curls Lasadi would have if she let her hair dry in that braid, silken strands glimmering dark gold in the light of the faux torches. It would soften the severe set to her jaw, the smoldering undercurrent in her smoky brown eyes.

She lifts an eyebrow at him and heat flushes under Raj's collar. He grabs two of the tiny beer bottles and cracks them open, handing one to Lasadi. "Good to be working with you again, Captain," he says. She's his captain. That's all.

"You too." Does her smile linger a touch longer than it needs to? Or is it Raj's reckless imagination? He settles back on the couch beside Ruby; Lasadi sits in the chair Anton has beckoned her to and begins filling a plate. "Raj, how did things go with Francis Edan earlier?"

Raj spears a bite of roast fish; it melts on his tongue. "He definitely was curious about me," he says. "The 'Luke Colman, investor at the end of his rope' act seemed to go over well."

"He went digging around for news on you as soon as you left," Ruby says, then inclines her head to Lasadi. "On Tita James, too. He found Colman plagued by impatient creditors, and some unsubstantiated rumors that Tita James has been looking for new sponsors for next year."

"She is," agrees Jay. "At least, that's what I've been hinting to the other crew I've met so far."

"Bryant's been scouring the race boards for information, too — he used a throwaway account, but it's pretty obvious." Ruby swipes open her tablet. "Moie has a simply gorgeous gossip network. A thriving ecosystem of messy drama, all the busybodies stirred up with the race in town. I posted a rumor about Edan signing Lasadi and dumping Bryant."

She grins down at her tablet. "Here we go. Maria42 responded 'who's Tita James' and tagged three people into the thread — ooh, including the race hospitality coordinator. He's a champion gossip, isn't he." She takes a sip of her beer. "'Everyone knows Tita James,' he says. 'She's the one who ran Leopard's Maw.'"

"'Everyone knows Tita James,'" Lasadi repeats, a faint, complicated smile on her lips. She reaches for her soup, stirring in a spoonful of the charred red sauce from a tiny bowl in the middle of the table. "This food is amazing. It's going to be hard to go back to living off what we can whip up in the *Nanshe*'s kitchen." She picks up the bowl of hot sauce. "Alex?"

He reaches for it with a grin. Beside him, Qacha gives him a warning look. Lasadi waits until Alex has stirred in the hot sauce before taking a deliberate spoonful of her own soup. Alex matches her, then coughs. Reaches for his water, a sheen of sweat breaking out on his dark brow, a flush of color deepening the rich brown of his cheeks.

"I warned you," says Qacha. She turns to Lasadi, who seems completely unaffected. "Do you need some water?"

"She's the queen of fire." Alex coughs into his sleeve, then takes another gulp of water. "She's not even fazed."

Lasadi winks at him. "So," she says. "Francis Edan is interested, and Bryant's temper is rising. Even if we can goad Bryant into doing something stupid, it might not be enough to get Edan to switch pilots right before the race. Alex?"

He coughs once more, then straightens to give his report. "I broke into Bryant's hotel room," he says. "I didn't find anything out of the usual, but he'd left the login open on his desk. I cloned his messages." He slips a data stick out of his pocket, waving it at his sister.

"Ah, give us a look," Ruby says, and Alex flips it across the table to her. Ruby plugs it into her tablet with a smile. "Bryant, for sweetness' sake," she says, shaking her head. "If you're going to set up clandestine meetings with race officials, do it in code."

"Where are they meeting?"

"In an hour, some dive bar on the south end of town," Ruby says.

"I could shadow them," Alex offers.

"I'll do you one better," Ruby answers. "We've a nosy reporter on the boards, one Joli Sainz, she's hungry to break something interesting this race." Her fingernails click against the tablet's screen. "There you go, love. Enjoy the tip."

"Perfect," Lasadi says. "You're the best, Ruby. Alex, you should still shadow him — take Raj. Bryant won't have seen either of you yet. If the reporter doesn't bite, we still need to know what they're planning."

"Got it."

"Thank you. Jay — "

"Is all this necessary?" Anton cuts in; not unkindly, his tone is simply curious. But something's shifted about his manner in the last few hours. On the ride here this afternoon he'd been jocular and friendly, worming his way into everyone's affection with calculated precision. During the meal, though, he's been listening quietly, almost preoccupied.

Lasadi frowns at him. "If we're going to race this ship — "

"Which is also not strictly necessary. We could get onto it another way."

"Jay and I saw the security today," Lasadi says. "It's impressive. Not to mention we need prolonged access."

"And we've already got this plan in motion," Raj says. He lets a touch of a blade slip into his own tone; Anton's nostrils flare. Ruby nudges him under the table, but Raj doesn't break his gaze. He may not know what

Anton Kato's end game is with this job, but he knows exactly what program the other man is running on Lasadi. Is it any of Raj's business? Maybe not. But she's his captain, and he doesn't need Anton taking a scalpel to her sense of self-confidence.

"In the CLA we taught our fighters to pivot." Anton leans back in his chair, relaxed like he's holding court. He *has* set himself up at the head of the table. "Sometimes when you see the lay of the land, you make a different decision. We've seen the lay of the land. We've tried your little feints. I'm suggesting we consider other options."

"If we could get the coordinates by breaking into the ship, we'd do it," says Lasadi. She tears off a piece of flatbread and scoops up a bite of chicken and rice. "We agreed — "

"You *agreed* to work this job for me." Anton holds up his hands as though to calm Lasadi, though she's gone blank as ice, fingers perfectly still on her plate. "I have no problem with you having fun, but if you're putting the cause in jeopardy because of some whimsy — "

"No one's putting the cause in jeopardy," Raj says. Ruby clears her throat pointedly; Raj ignores her, ignores Anton. "It's your call, Captain."

"I've made my decision," Lasadi says.

"You're sure you can even fly it?" Anton asks.

"Of course she can," Jay says. "I've never met a pilot better able to keep a plane in the air."

"Well, almost always," Anton says mildly, and the color drains from Lasadi's face. She and Jay went down in the Battle of Tannis, Raj knows that much, and Anton obviously knows it, too; the gleam in his eyes says he chose exactly the words to bring Lasadi to heel right now.

Ruby's hand on Raj's knee under the table is about the only thing keeping him from launching himself across the table and grabbing Anton Kato by the throat, throwing him and his fine suit down on the leaf-strewn patio floor and seeing who comes out on top of that fight.

Ruby squeezes Raj's knee, gentle but firm.

"Any one you walk away from," Jay says, with a laugh like what Anton said was meant as a joke. "Right, Las?" He winks at Qacha, who's been following the whole conversation with a deepening frown. "Sounds like you've got a few stories to tell yourself about going down with the ship, yeah?"

And Jay coaxes Qacha into a story, so seamlessly it feels like a pattern. It probably is, Raj realizes; he'd done it himself with his parents, distracting them with a story to ease the tension and get the day back on track. It never worked for long, though.

"You hired Lasadi to make this decision," Raj says quietly, leaning in to Anton while the others laugh at Qacha's story. Lasadi's gaze snaps to his, eyes flaming bright with warning. "And she's made it."

"And I'm presenting alternatives," Anton says, tone reasonable. "You may have your own concerns about Lasadi, but believe me, she's been through more than you can imagine. She can handle a little constructive pushback against her plans."

"That's not what I said."

Anton continues like he hadn't spoken. "The ability to share and entertain other positions is necessary for leadership. Maybe things were different in the Alliance. Or maybe deserters don't know much about working in a team. But you have to be flexible when you don't have the full might of the Arquellian navy behind you."

Before Raj can answer, Lasadi pushes back, snatching her empty beer bottle off the table. "I'm going to grab another beer," she says, bright and fierce. Qacha stutters out midstory and Lasadi sweeps her gaze over the table, ending on Anton. "The plan isn't changing, and you all have your orders. Good night."

Raj starts to rise, ready to apologize, but Ruby pats him on the arm and gets to her feet.

"Enjoy your meal," Ruby says, and he knows that brilliant steel gleam in her voice; she's just this side of murdering him. "I've got this one."

# CHAPTER 11
## LASADI

LASADI SINKS ONTO ONE OF THE BARSTOOLS, PUSHING HER empty bottle forward and nodding when the bartender points at it with a raised eyebrow.

It's hard to think around Anton — he makes it *so* fucking hard. She knows he just wants what's best for the cause. She knows he's particular about how things are done, and it can't be easy for him to sit back and let others take lead in the planning. Maybe if she was a stronger leader she'd be able to hear his cross-examination without taking it personally; their shared history has her reacting emotionally.

All she knows is she needed to get her head together before she broke down in front of her crew and they lost what little confidence they might have in her. She scans back through their faces in her mind, searching for signs the seeds of doubt are already sown. Jay had been worried, Qacha obviously uncomfortable. And Raj —

Apparently doesn't think she can stand up to a little pressure.

Uneasy nausea settles in her gut, turning the delicious meal she just finished sour and heavy. To finish this job, she needs to be strong, the crew needs her to be strong. But she can't help thinking the others may be right to worry. Is she even the right person to lead them?

The bartender slides a fresh bottle across the bar.

"And two shots of jienja," says a voice over Lasadi's shoulder. Ruby slips onto the stool beside her.

"Right," Lasadi says; her tone's too bitter but she doesn't really care. "Are you here to check on my fragile mental health, too?"

"Fuck those two." Ruby smiles, then tips her beer bottle against Lasadi's. "No, I had to get away, only. I couldn't decide which of the men I wanted to punch more — Anton for being insufferable, Raj for his chest-puffing, or my little brother for trying to show off for Qacha." She takes a long drink. "Which of the cis men, I guess. Unless Jay's done something obnoxious I haven't heard about."

"Jay's been great."

"Glad to hear it. What's on your mind, Cap?"

"Thinking about the race."

"Bullshit," says Ruby, amicable. "You don't have to talk to me — I know we barely know each other. But I thought you could use a drink with someone who doesn't want anything from you."

The bartender returns with a pair of shot glasses filled with clear liquid. The jienja smells of fresh herbs and makrut lime. "Can I ask you a question?"

Ruby lifts one bare shoulder. "Sure."

"Why did you come here. To New Manila."

"Because Jay said you needed help."

"So you dropped everything and flew halfway across the system for someone you barely knew."

"If I'm honest, I didn't do it for you." There's something troubling the surface of Ruby's effortless cool facade when she clinks her glass against Lasadi's and drains the shot. She jerks a nod when the bartender lifts the bottle to ask if they want more. Once he's left them again, Ruby traces a finger around the rim of her glass, deep in thought.

"I don't know how to raise a kid," she finally says. "I mean, I know Alex is basically a grown adult, but he's spent his whole life with the ayas in the convent. I'm the one who's supposed to introduce him to the rest of the world, and almost everyone I work for are people I'd rather keep him away from, you know?"

"Sure." Lasadi and Ruby'd had a few conversations on the Auburn Station job, but nothing that scratched below the surface. It was one of the things Lasadi had found comforting about Ruby, honestly — she was bubbly and chatty without creating any pressure to share personal details. Now Lasadi watches the other woman struggle to chip away her own walls in fascination

"You seem like a good person," Ruby finally says. "You, and Jay. And I know Raj is, even if he doesn't know when to leave well enough alone. I suppose that's part of what makes him good."

Ruby sips her jienja and turns to frown over the bar. "I want to be a good person, too," she says. "For Alex, at least. That's why I came."

"I don't know if I'm a good role model for Alex,"

Lasadi says. "Just today I've asked him to pickpocket someone, break into his hotel room, and now eavesdrop on him."

Ruby waves a hand, laughing. "Bryant's trash, isn't he, so it doesn't count. All I'm saying is, you and Jay, you're different than other people I've worked for. You gave a shit what happens to Alex even when you'd barely met him. You give a shit about everyone. I didn't think I could afford to care about anyone else, not if I wanted to keep Alex safe. But I kind of want to try."

"Thank you," Lasadi says. "For telling me."

"Yeah." Ruby clears her throat uncomfortably. "Tell me to toss it if it's not my business, but you and Anton. You met in the CLA?"

"We did." Lasadi considers leaving it at that — it's not any of Ruby's business — but the jienja is warming her blood. "I'd been obsessed with him for years before, though. I read everything he wrote, I listened to all his speeches. I guess I joined the CLA as much for the man as for the cause."

Ruby props her cheek on her fist, smiling. "Our stone-cold captain's a hopeless romantic?"

"I've learned my lesson."

"What's the fun in that?" Ruby's dark eyes catch the light, mischievous. "My ex-girlfriend, Kitty, we broke up at least three times because I'm a hopeless romantic, too. One time? She let me know we were done by shoving all my stuff into a bag and flinging it over the balcony. She didn't tie the bag shut, only, and it all came tumbling out as it fell. One of my favorite bras was hanging off the top of the market for three weeks like a lacy yellow flag." She laughs at the image, and Lasadi can't help but smile with her. "I was so pissed at the time, but it's at least funny looking back."

"What did you do to make her so mad?" Lasadi asks.

"I don't even remember." Ruby's still laughing; she wipes a hand over her eyes. "She was an artist, she was always mad at me for something. The worst bit is that wasn't even the last time we broke up."

"You know how I learned Anton and I were done?" Lasadi says — it's not what she means to say, she hadn't meant to talk about Anton at all. But Ruby's vulnerability was a gift, one Lasadi suddenly feels compelled to respond to

Ruby lifts an eyebrow. "No, but I hate him already for whatever it was."

"He — olds. I haven't told anyone this." Not even Jay. When it happened, Lasadi didn't even know Jay was still alive, that he'd been watching over her while she healed, that he'd fought Nico Garnet's mercs not to let her die, that he'd been trading jobs for Nico to buy Lasadi the time in the crime boss's regen tanks.

"I almost died in the Battle of Tannis," Lasadi says. "Our ship was hit, and Jay was able to get a distress call out. Some of Nico Garnet's mercenaries picked us up and took us back to Ironfall. I woke up there after a few weeks in a regen tank."

"So that's how you got started working for Nico?"

Lasadi lifts her left shoulder, feels the tight stretch of scar tissue. "Basically, yeah." She clears her throat. "When I could finally stay awake for more than a few minutes, I made them bring me a terminal. I found out I was presumed dead. I should have reached out to my family, but the first person I messaged was Anton. We were — I thought he would be worried about me. I thought we were . . ."

No way in hell is she going to say *in love*. She finishes the shot of jienja instead.

"What did he say?" Ruby asks.

"Nothing, at first. But I saw the press conference he'd held during peace negotiations with the Alliance and the Coruscan government, where he'd claimed my squadron was responsible for that medical transport being destroyed. He blamed it on an inexperienced captain, and took responsibility for promoting someone who obviously wasn't ready."

"It wasn't your people," Ruby points out. "And he can fuck off."

Lasadi's hand is shaking as she takes another drink. Ruby lifts the empty bottle to the bartender for another round of tiny beers.

"He was doing what was best for the cause," Lasadi says. "But when he finally did respond, he said I should never come back to Corusca. That my family had held banishing." And at Ruby's puzzled expression, "It's basically disowning a dead relative — you're not allowed to speak their name, there's no place for them at the family shrine."

"And did they?"

"I — " Anton had told her they had; would he be mistaken? "I don't actually know."

"They'd be only delighted to find out you're alive, I'd think."

"Maybe." Anton gains allies fast. Her own grand-mother supports him in the Senate now, Lasadi has seen them smiling together at press conferences. If her grandmother believes Anton's version of events, she may not be happy to have Lasadi back in her life.

"I'd give anything to find out I had family alive," Ruby says. "Listen. I told Raj if you need help with Anton you'll ask for it. To me it seems you've got him handled, but I'm here if you need anything."

"Why would I need help with Anton?"

"Because he's an abusive bastard," Ruby says.

Lasadi shakes her head, caught off guard. "He never laid a hand on me."

"Doesn't mean he didn't leave scars." Ruby reaches a long brown finger to tap over Lasadi's heart; warmth rushes through her body, radiating out from that spot on her sternum. "Right there. He's our client," Ruby continues, voice low. "We're all professionals. We can pretend nice if it's part of the job. But every single one of us has got your back if you need us."

"Thank you." The words feel wrong; Lasadi isn't entirely sure whether it's because she doesn't mean them, or she doesn't know how to believe Ruby. But before she can parse that, Ruby winks and throws her arm around Lasadi's shoulder, squeezing her in for a hug. It's brief, Ruby must notice how she tenses.

No one touches her any more. Jay gives her the occasional hug, but Lasadi grew up tumbling in a pile with her siblings and cousins to watch vids; she remembers walking arm in arm with her sister through a mall, talking with girlfriends with their legs thrown over each other. Even in the CLA there had been a level of fraternal touch: sleeping in close quarters, throwing arms over one another's shoulders, finding oneself at the middle of a group hug when celebrating those little victories.

"Lotta testosterone around here." Ruby's tone is teasing once more; Las is back on firm ground. "We've got to stick together."

"There's Qacha. Though she's probably a lost cause, fooling around with your little brother."

Ruby sighs. "We're going to have some broken hearts on our hands, aren't we."

"Should we try to stop them?"

Ruby laughs and lifts her beer. "You think either of them would listen?"

"Not in the slightest." Lasadi clinks. "To making stupid decisions in love."

"And to coming out stronger on the other side."

Lasadi's shoulder still tingles where the other woman's arm had rested, and she almost reaches out for a real hug — Ruby would let her, she thinks — but a familiar voice from the entrance to the restaurant stops her.

Francis Edan has entered the restaurant, in pointed argument with a young woman with flame-red hair. She's wearing a green silk jacket over a smart black pantsuit, her lips and fingernails the same deep maroon. She's dressed to be memorable — and it works. Lasadi spotted her during the pilot's orientation, pressing in on the more popular racers with her camera drone in tow.

"I'm not going to comment on any rumors," Edan says to her, polite yet firm. "As I've told you repeatedly today, Ms. Sainz."

"Is that your reporter?" Lasadi asks, and Ruby turns

to look. She breaks into a grin.

"So she is — Joli Sainz took our tip and ran with it."

"I have something more than a rumor," Sainz says to Edan. "Can I get a comment on how your pilot, Bryant, met this evening with one of the race organizers to ask for the coordinates?"

"I'm not going to — " Edan frowns at her. "He did what?"

Sainz swipes up a vid from her cuff; Lasadi can't make out the image, but she can hear the murmur of Bryant's voice. From the stiff set of Edan's jaw, the way he smooths a hand over his neat-trimmed black beard, Joli Sainz has the evidence to back up her claim.

"This is the story I'm running as soon as I leave this hotel," Sainz says. "So, Mr. Edan. Do you have any comment?"

"I'm appalled, and will immediately investigate these allegations," Edan says.

"Will you be firing Bryant?"

"I obviously won't tolerate any attempts to cheat." Edan straightens his shoulders. "But I also don't make decisions on camera. Good night, Ms. Sainz."

Ruby grins at Lasadi as Joli Sainz finally takes her leave. "Sounds like my cue," she murmurs. Then, bright and bubbly as she slips off the barstool: "It was such an honor to meet you, Tita! Good luck in the race!"

She's not over loud, but the restaurant is quiet, and Ruby's voice catches Francis Edan's attention. He seems to notice Lasadi sitting at the bar for the first time. Lasadi waves after Ruby, ignoring Edan as he straightens the cuffs of his suit and makes his way towards her. She does surprised when he clears his throat over her shoulder.

"Excuse me," he says, holding out a trim brown hand encrusted with rings. "I've been meaning to introduce myself. Francis Edan."

"Of course," Lasadi says. "I'm Tita James."

"I know who you are. I've heard quite a bit about you today."

"You have?"

The bartender's hovering, but Edan waves him politely away. He makes no move to sit, leaving Lasadi a comfortable amount of space.

"You made quite the impressive entrance." Edan smooths the snow-white patches in the corners of his mouth, clearly thinking through his words. "Your sponsor, on the other hand, is . . . less impressive. I wonder. Are you happy in your current arrangement?"

Lasadi presses her lips together, pretending to think it over. "I used to be," she says. "But lately I'm not really getting the resources I need, you know?"

Edan smiles. "I do know. Ms. James, it turns out I might need to hire a new pilot to fly the *Figment of the North* in this race. Are you interested?"

"My contract with Colman — "

"I'll speak with your sponsor. I would be honored if you agreed to race for me."

Lasadi's been trying to play the part of a young, new racer to the best of her ability, but she doesn't have to fake the grin spreading across her face.

"Absolutely," she says. A shiver of excitement runs down her spine.

The *Figment of the North* is theirs.

# CHAPTER 12
## RAJ

RAJ HAS LOST HIM.

Somewhere in Moie's tumble of alleys and stairways and promenades and miniature pedestrian plazas, Raj lost track of Anton Kato.

Anton left the Golden Macaw before breakfast like a man on a mission, and on a whim, Raj decided to tail him. He's not sure what he was expecting to find. A clandestine rendezvous with the NMLF? A romantic tryst? A secret meeting with Francis Edan? All Raj knows is that while the rest of them have been working their parts of the plan to get the coordinates they need for this job for the NMLF, Anton has been sequestered in his room, alternating between silence and calls he takes in low tones.

It's unsettling, but Raj prefers it when the man stays in his room — especially since Anton's other hobby seems to be seeking out hairline cracks in other people's psyches and putting surgical pressure on them until they fracture.

Raj melts into the shadow of a doorway, trying to suss out any clue as to where Anton might have gone. Either Anton took a sharp left to double back down another alley, a soft left to take the steep stairs through a community vegetable garden, or he veered lightly right and downhill past a row of expensive-looking townhouses.

Raj opens up a connection request.

"He's gone," he says when Ruby answers; she curses. "Unless you can give me any help."

"I don't have a tracker on him, love."

"Maybe he's meeting with more campaign donors," Raj says. "Were you ever able to trace that deposit to his account?"

"Working on it. You missed the most epic temper tantrum this morning. Bryant stormed into the restaurant at breakfast to confront Edan about rumors he'd hired Las, and threw a fit when Edan fired him for cheating. Coffee and shattered plates everywhere, it was stunningly juvenile." She sounds delighted.

"You loved it," Raj says with a smile.

"I did. Sorry you missed it."

"Thanks, Ruby. Keep me updated — I'm heading down to the docks to give Jay a hand with the *Lightning*."

And, honestly, to make sure he and Jay are still okay after the tense dinner last night. Lasadi's certainly still pissed at him, and rightly so. Maybe Raj shouldn't have confronted Anton — he knows she can fight her own battles. But what kind of friend would he have been to watch the bullshit Anton was pulling with her and not say something?

He's not just worried about Lasadi, though. Anton's clearly a master when it comes to manipulation — most leaders with his levels of charisma are. Anton's trying to keep Lasadi unbalanced so he can control her, but he can multitask. He's also been making subtle digs at Raj, constant reminders to the others that he's Arquellian and an outsider. The enemy.

Which Raj gets. He had gone to war thinking he was protecting innocent people from radicals like Lasadi and Jay and Qacha. He'd believed the Alliance was a good thing, and couldn't understand why the CLA would fight against collectively raising the bar for everyone.

He'd been sold that dream since he was a child. Arquelle had eradicated poverty, he'd been told. Instead of barring people from jobs because they couldn't pay for the education, they'd made education free. Of course, the teachers weren't going to work for free — so an indenture system made sense. Employers could foot the bill, and workers could be trained based on the demand. If Sulila forecasted a need for an increase in doctors in the next five years, they could fund the education of a corresponding number of students. If Francis Edan's logistics company was going to open a new shipping route to Bixia Yuanjin, he could fund the right number of students from engineers to pilots.

Yes, you'd be contracted to work a certain number of years to pay off your indenture, but then you could do whatever you wanted.

From the indenture system to the mandatory military and volunteer service, Raj had believed Arquelle's system created a cohesive fabric, everyone working together to make their society a better place. So why wouldn't Arquellians want that for everyone else in the system? Why would other countries resist being part of the Alliance?

He sees the cracks now, though.

His comm chimes: Jay.

Where are you? Am at the *Lightning* with the two most adorable young lovebirds in the system. Save me.

Raj laughs. Almost there.

There are a few more planes in the dockyard than when they landed with the *Green Lightning* yesterday afternoon, and the yard seems to be at capacity. Raj finds the *Lightning* parked where they left it, the door folded down and voices drifting out over the rhythmic beat of Coruscan kafusa. Mostly Alex's voice. Raj grins as he gets closer and can start making out the words.

"So *then* the captain and Tora got kidnapped by pirates," Alex says. "And I said, 'What if we sneak in and grab a couple of the pirates, and then take their suits and pretend to be them?'"

"Seriously?" Qacha asks.

"It was a great idea, Alex," Raj calls as he climbs aboard. The kid shoots him a slightly guilty look, but Qacha doesn't notice and Raj doesn't care. Let the kid take the credit and enjoy his few days with his guerrilla girlfriend. Maybe some of Qacha's levelheaded calm will rub off on him.

Qacha and Alex are in the cockpit — she's wedged under the dash sorting through a tangle of wires while Alex helps, or at least entertains her. Jay is messing with the starboard thruster, an array of tools set within easy reach.

"Thank the old ones," Jay says, reaching over to turn down his music. "Hand me that spanner."

Raj grabs the spanner the other man is pointing at. "I didn't expect to find the plane in pieces."

"A little faith," Jay answers. "I'm just smoothing out the rotation on this guy — he's a little sticky. And Qacha's sorting out a glitch in the landing lights. Might as well keep our hands busy while we wait to get on the *Figment*. Never know when you need a backup plane."

"Never hurts," Raj agrees.

"Plans get moxed in the best of times," Jay says, returning his attention to his work. "Hold this. Perfect."

"Question for you. Do you know where Anton went this morning? I thought I heard you talking to him before he took off."

"He said he was going for a walk."

"You don't think that's suspicious?"

Jay grunts, tightening a bolt. "Walking?"

"All his behavior."

Jay frowns at Raj, thinking carefully before he speaks. "Anton's hard to work with, but his heart is for the cause."

"You think I'm being paranoid."

"You don't know him like I do. He always keeps his plans close, unless you need to know them."

Raj sighs. "Maybe you're right. His leadership style, it reminds me too much of my father, I think. And my father did try to have me murdered."

Jay works silently a minute. Then, "You and your father. Did you ever get along?"

Raj shakes his head. "You know how parents are, they decide ahead of time who they want you to be, and nothing you do can get them to change their minds."

"Doesn't have to be," Jay says. "My parents always dreamed of having a little girl, but that didn't stop them from loving and supporting me when I told them I was their son." He hands the spanner back to Raj. "If they didn't believe you when you showed them who you were, that's on them. What you do now is on you. But real family loves you for who you are. Hand me that bolt."

Raj hands over the bolt, Jay's words running over in his mind. He's spent his entire life trying to conform to someone else's expectations of himself. Even once he washed up on Ironfall, he'd had to hide his identity. He'd lived every day with the fear that as soon as someone realized the truth about his past, the desertion, the fact that he'd been court-martialled for supposedly destroying the medical transport, they'd turn on him. He'd never have believed someone would trust him.

But then the AI on Rashida Auburn's haunted station had accessed Ruby's records and torn open the truth to the entire crew. Raj had figured they were done, except that apparently Ruby had always known and still believed in him. And Jay and Lasadi and Alex had accepted his version of events.

Raj isn't sure what to make of it all, still. But he's going to work like hell to make sure he doesn't destroy the chance he's been given.

"You ever gonna make a pass at her?" Jay asks, and Raj blinks at the change of subject.

"What?"

"At Las."

"You don't think she'd murder me?"

"I can't read her mind."

Jay knows Lasadi better than anyone, though, and a hint of a dimple ghosts Jay's cheek. The other man would warn Raj off if he thought Lasadi wasn't interested.

A tentative thrill blooms beneath Raj's ribcage. In their first meeting — their tussle in Sumilang's museum — he'd felt an instant flicker of fire between them. But then she hired him for the Auburn Station job, and she's been nothing but professional ever since. Aside from his initial subtle inquiries with Jay at the beginning, Raj thinks he's been carefully neutral, too. The way she reacted when she caught him staring last night, though, maybe it wasn't all in Raj's imagination.

"If you do," Jay says, "do us all a favor. I'm starting to like this crew we've got going, and I'd hate to have to kill you if you screwed it up."

Raj laughs. "Understood." It's a joke, but underneath is a reality: Crews get torn apart by romance gone bad, and Raj misreading the situation and propositioning his uninterested captain is a good definition of gone bad.

"You've got a girl back in Ironfall, right?"

Jay's lips purse as he tightens the final bolt. "Probably not at this point."

"No?"

"No." He holds out his hand for help back to his feet. "Her name's Chiara. Ironfall born and raised, from a big family who've also never left the Pearls. We were going to move in together, before the Auburn Station job, but she hated I was gone so much. For a while I thought maybe it sounded nice to stop flying. And then . . ." Jay shrugs.

"And then you went after Lasadi," Raj guesses.

"Chiara hinted maybe if I was gonna go after Las I shouldn't come back." Jay sighs. "But that's not it at all. In the end, I'm not ready to stop moving."

"I get that."

"So here I am, about to go on a wild ride in one of the most iconic racing planes in the Durga System. You don't get to work on the *Figment of the North* if you never leave Ironfall."

"No regrets then?"

The complicated flicker in Jay's eyes is the only answer Raj gets. Jay claps him on the shoulder as he moves past to peer into the cockpit. "You getting any work done in here, Qacha? Or do I need to put a gag on Alex?"

Before Qacha can answer, the ship's comms crackle to life. Lasadi's voice cuts through; she sounds breathless. "Jay? Raj? Where are you?"

Raj straightens. "On the *Lightning*. Where — "

But she's talking over him like she couldn't hear. "If you're near the *Figment*, I need help."

Her voice fizzles out; Jay is already on his feet, Alex steps to the ramp, scanning what little they can see from their parking spot.

"Lasadi?" Raj asks. But she's not answering. In the distance, he can hear shouting, and a grunt of pain comes through the comms.

Something's burning, he realizes, that acrid smell of smoke curling through the air.

Fire, and close.

# CHAPTER 13
## LASADI

WHEN LASADI ARRIVES AT THE DOCKYARD THE GATE IS wide open to the amphitheater and the rest of the town; members of the various crews seem to be coming and going at will. She reaches for her credentials when a young man in Moie Dockyards overalls walks her way, but he just waves her past and continues on his own way to the shop.

The dockmaster had told them there was state-of-the-art security here — but "state of the art" for Moie must not be what it is in Ironfall. This isn't a busy through-port like Ironfall, it's a destination, and even now that the town has probably doubled in size with race contestants and tourists, there must still be less than six or seven thousand people in town.

The dockyard — like the rest of the town — is a testament to how keeping the jungle out of Moie must be a full-time job. Step past the edge of the docking pad and there's no soft transition from the edge of town into the jungle itself, just a sharp line where humans press into the jungle and the jungle presses back twice as hard. The air is rich with earthy rot and ozone, last night's rain evaporating into a heady engine oil–tinged perfume in the morning's sun. The packed earth is solid under her boots, the heat of the day starting to rise, the humidity of the morning thickening the air.

This is the first time Lasadi's been back to the dock-yard since she landed, and she finds herself relaxing. The rapid-fire staccato of an air compressor, mallet-on-metal thumps coming from the workshops. It smells earthier than the dockyard she'd called home in Iron-fall, but it still feels like home.

She hadn't been the only one crashing on her ship in Ironfall — and like Ironfall's port, Moie's dockyard has its own amenities for pilots who are sleeping on board their ships. A pair of shop buildings sit inside the gate to the left — both big enough to park a plane inside for repairs — followed by an open structure with a dozen planes parked underneath. The rest of the planes in the dock are parked in four neat rows stretching away from town, along the river. At the end of the covered parking is a smaller open building, a ramada designed as a makeshift common area for the pilots staying in their ships.

A half-dozen battered tables are set up in the ramada, along with a pair of cookstoves sizzling with late breakfasts, the crews mingling and giving each other good-natured ribbings while blue-black scav-enging birds — zanates, Qacha had called them — hop along the outskirts searching for scraps and chirping an annoyed cacophony. Las catches a whiff of incense; there's a shrine to some local saint on the side of the ramada closest to the gate, well tended and full of offerings.

It sparks a strange yearning in her, the easy way they're bantering over breakfast. She always liked the work she and Jay did for Nico Garnet, even if she didn't love who they were working for. Now the *Nanshe* is theirs, what's to stop them from flashing around the Durga System like Peter Fangio, working the odd job and dropping in to race the Liluri Star Run every year?

She and Jay have a crew now, after all. Don't they?

Peter Fangio's there under the ramada, lounging at a table with two other people. His own crew, she guesses. He'd dressed sharp for the pilot's orientation, but Lasadi gets the impression he's most comfortable like this: work trousers and boots, tight shirt showcasing dark muscles, black hair swept loosely back from his proud forehead in lazy curls. Fangio raises a hand when he sees her looking their way and drops his boot from the chair it's kicked up on, shoving it towards her in invitation.

Lasadi checks her comm. She's supposed to be meeting Francis Edan at the *Figment of the North* in a few minutes, but he hasn't pinged her that he's here.

"Morning," she says, taking the chair Fangio offered. "Is it always this hot here?"

"Most years it's worse," says Fangio. He sweeps a lazy hand at the others at the table. "Nia Amani, she's our mechanic. And Finley Ryan — they're my co-pilot."

"L — Tita James," Lasadi says; she'd gotten so

comfortable she nearly forgot she's still playing a part. "Good to meet you both."

Both Amani and Ryan are dressed like Belt drifters in jumpsuits and boots, though Amani's jumpsuit is unzipped and tied at the waist in deference to the heat. Her pale forearms are marked with the mechanic's expected collection of nicks and scars, and her curly red-brown hair is cut close in the back and left unruly on top. Her honey-gold eyes are edged with laugh lines. Ryan's fit for how slender they are, head shaved to reveal intricate tattoos etched into the warm brown skin of their neck and scalp.

"Your ship?" Lasadi asks, hooking her thumb at the nearby early-model CG Taipan, a light cargo hauler designed for deft maneuvers despite its size, like its namesake. The paint is weatherworn but clean, the pale blue chipping along the seams to reveal metal beneath.

"That's our baby," Fangio answers. "*Kalliope's Wager.* I hear you're getting an upgrade."

Finley Ryan leans forward, curious. "So are the rumors true?" Ryan asks. "You'll be flying Theo's ship, will you?"

"Gossip chain moves fast in Moie," laughs Amani when Lasadi looks surprised. "Everyone knows Edan gave that idiot Bryant the boot."

"And everyone knows Edan doesn't do much in the way of background checks." Fangio hasn't moved, but something in his tone sets Lasadi's instincts blazing. A cold flush pulses between Lasadi's shoulder blades. He knows. Somehow, he knows.

"At least he didn't with Bryant, sounds like." Lasadi gives Fangio a bright smile and starts to stand; she needs to get away from this conversation. "I doubt he'd make the same mistake twice."

"Maybe not. For your sake I hope so, Lasadi Cazinho."

Lasadi breathes in sharp, muscles tensing to fight, to run; her crew is supposed to be here at the dockyard, but even if she calls for help, they won't get to her before Fangio makes his move. With Amani and Ryan here, she's outnumbered, even with the pistol Jay insisted she carry. And, she realizes with a sinking heart, it doesn't matter in the slightest if they let her walk away. One message to Francis Edan and the entire con is over.

"You were a hard woman to track down," Fangio says. He reaches for his metal coffee cup and relaxes back in his chair. Takes a sip. "And whoever faked your alias did an airtight job — but Finley has some ex-CLA friends who recognized your picture. Mercury Squadron, yeah? Impressive."

"Last I heard everyone in Mercury Squadron was dead," Las says.

"I heard that, too," Fangio says. "Your navigator, though, she's NMLF?" When Lasadi doesn't answer, he laughs. "It's obvious, only. The new recruits all have that look to them, it's in the eyes."

Amani nods agreement. "And the shoulders. They're always at attention. It's adorable, you can spot them a kilometer away."

"I'm doing the NMLF a favor," Lasadi says. Olds, let this work. Fangio's crew is from Durga's Belt, so they're not likely to be pro-Alliance — and they might keep quiet if they think the real secret won't affect their chances in the race. She can still spin this and keep Anton's name out of it. "I've been training their pilots; we figured this could be a good test run." She takes a deep breath, testing the currents. "Since you brought it up, the NMLF could use help from other pilots who believe in independence. We all know the Alliance isn't going to stop with Indira and Corusca."

Finlay Ryan's expression doesn't change, but their fingers tap sharp against their thigh. Nia Amani gives Lasadi an unreadable smile. And Peter Fangio tilts his head, studying Las with faint amusement.

"Alliance aren't in the Belt yet," Fangio finally says, setting his coffee cup back on the metal table with a gentle clink. "Theo'd've been rolling over in his grave to see an Alliance pilot like Bryant flying his ship. Keep it in one piece, will you."

"I will." Lasadi stands and inclines her head to the group. "Saints' path to you all, isn't that what they say here?"

"Saints' path," Ryan agrees.

"Keep sharp out there, Mercury," Fangio says. "Every race is a blank slate. The jungle doesn't care how well you flew last race — or last war."

"You too. And thank you."

Lasadi turns away, heart pounding, to find one of the gang of porter kids jogging her way. "Ms. James!" the boy says when he catches up with her. "Mr. Edan asked me to come find you. He's at the *Figment*."

Lasadi takes a deep breath and gins up a smile. No time to worry what Fangio and his crew might do with their new information, apparently. Or — olds be damned — how she's going to break the news to Anton.

She can already picture his disappointment. He won't say *I told you so*, but he had done in advance. He'd pointed out that this complicated plan was a risk, one she wasn't prepared to handle.

Another potentially disastrous move from an inexperienced captain, she can hear him saying: *I don't blame you, I blame myself for asking you to take this responsibility on.*

Lasadi follows the porter through the gates of the dockyard and back into the amphitheater, where the *Figment of the North* is still on display. It's weatherworn and marked by years of repeated damage and repairs. Theo had always scorned the flashier color schemes of some of his rivals, opting for a matte, mottled silver, the only adornment the script *Figment of the North* in bold blue on each side.

The ramp is down, an open invitation to her, and her alone; slow realization trickles through her. She did it. She got them access to this plane, and Anton? He can fuck off.

Jay trusts her. Ruby inexplicably does, she made that clear last night. Alex seems perfectly happy to follow her. Even Raj — that's what he was trying to say at dinner, wasn't it? Not that he didn't think Lasadi could handle pressure, but that he trusted her leadership.

The next breath Lasadi takes makes her feel lighter than she has in ages, like the atmosphere at Moie is rich with oxygen and life. She almost laughs in dizzy relief.

Anton can *fuck off.*

The amphitheater is near empty this time of morning, and one bored guard is standing outside the

*Figment*. He waves a hand to Lasadi when she reaches for her credentials with a "Welcome, Ms. James!"

"Thanks!" she says, bright. She drops a handful of joru in the porter boy's palm — she still hasn't worked out what the exchange rate is for credits, but he seems delighted — then heads for the open ramp.

"Mr. Edan?" she calls as she enters. The layout of the *Figment* is different from the *Green Lightning*. Instead of crew seats lining the walls, everything but the cockpit has been stripped to save weight and make room for Theo to stay on the plane. There's a hammock hung in one corner, along with a makeshift folding stove and dining table as ingeniously simplistic as one of the living pods in Ironfall.

She peers into the cockpit. "Mr. Edan?"

She hears the footfall a second before the attack comes, a shadow in the corner of her eye, and Lasadi flings her left hand up in front of her face as the garrote falls over her head. The cord tightens, biting into her wrist, but she can still breathe. Somehow, she barely registers that the *Figment*'s door has closed behind her.

Her attacker matches her in height, a man's grunts and the whiff of expensive hair gel cutting through the undercurrent of engine grease and rust. Lasadi shoves her weight back against him, boots slipping against the floor before her treads catch on some seam in the metal. Her right hand flails for a weapon, closes around something solid.

She yanks it up, bashing it back against her assailant's knee.

The man yelps and loosens his grip enough for Lasadi to push the cord back over her head and shove him away. She turns on him, panting, dropping the prybar she'd snatched up for the pistol tucked in the small of her back, under her jacket.

Sevi Bryant.

Lasadi switches on her earpiece. "Jay? Raj? Where are you?" She ducks as Bryant growls and flings a crate at her; it splinters against the wall to her left, spilling packaged rations over the floor. "If you're near the *Figment*, I need help."

"Come to claim your prize?" Bryant says. "I wouldn't fire. You know these old ships are notoriously prone to go up in flames."

And at that she identifies the other scent pinging for her attention. Not just grease from a half century of planes sitting in the yard, but something new and fresh. A leaking fuel cell, splashed near the tail of the plane where it would spread quick to the reactor that powers the thrusters. Another fuel cell is sitting beside the *Figment*'s door; Bryant rests his hand on it.

Lasadi doesn't drop her aim.

"Set that down." She takes slow, careful steps towards Bryant, keeping him in her sights.

Bryant glances at the pistol in her hand, and in his gaze is a question Lasadi doesn't have the answer to. The interior of these Garudas is bare metal, and Theo stripped the *Figment* of almost everything. Bryant's right: The chances she hits metal are high, and with the amount of fuel leaking out, any stray spark will send the ship up in flames.

And the coordinates with it.

Bryant clocks her hesitancy; he grins and flings the second fuel cell at her. It flies through the air, fuel spraying out in an arc that soaks through her sleeve even as she ducks the cell itself. Bryant charges, catching her off guard and slamming her back into the wall beside the door.

He's got her right arm in a death grip — not that she's going to pull the trigger anyway — and he aims a punch at her head. Lasadi ducks, coming up under his swing and bringing her left fist as hard as she can into his kidney. Bryant grunts in pain, but his grip on her right arm doesn't loosen.

He's got the advantage of weight, and of the fact he grew up on this planet with its stronger gravity, so when he whirls, she can't stop him from pulling her away from the wall with his momentum and sending her crashing against the floor near the *Figment*'s tail. She lands with a grunt, the air pushed from her lungs, and when she pants for breath she chokes on the fumes from the pool of fuel on the floor.

*The stench of electrical fire; she's pinned to the pilot's chair, pressure through her gut. She's been speared by something — she can taste iron maybe she can even taste that improbable metal through her core and when her hands touch it they come away slick with blood. It doesn't hurt but she can't move, and everything is a roar in her ears with Jay shouting her name and the flashing lights the reek of fuel and —*

Lasadi pushes the vision away, blinking to see Bryant's silhouette in the now-open doorway, morning light streaming in behind him. She can make out the white flash of his teeth when he grins. And a flame glimmering in his hand, the faintest spark against the darkness of his shadow.

Lasadi scrabbles to get to her feet, boots slipping in the spilled fuel.

The lighter burns bright and clear, wavering as it soars through the air in a perfect arc to land at her feet.

The fuel ignites around her in a blast of heat.

# CHAPTER 14
## RAJ

RAJ CAN SEE THE SMOKE BOILING INTO THE AIR WELL before he's in view of the *Figment of the North*. He sprints towards it, Jay on his heels, ducking under wings and skidding around corners, boots thudding on the hard-packed earth. Faintly in the back of his mind, Raj is aware of others shouting, an alarm bell ringing.

He tears through the dockyard gates and into the amphitheater, his heart sinking. Smoke is roiling out of the *Figment*'s open ramp door.

A lanky figure stumbles out of the black, glances over his shoulder. Sevi Bryant's eyes widen at Raj and Jay, and he starts running towards the dockyard gate.

Raj starts to give chase when another sound catches his attention from inside the *Figment*. A woman's grunt of pain.

Lasadi.

Someone's yelling behind him — he thinks it might be Jay — but Raj isn't processing that. The only thing he cares about is the black, smoky square of the *Figment*'s door, the dancing flames beyond, and the figure on the floor inside.

"Stop Bryant," he shouts at a stunned man in a guard's uniform, then turns to the ship. "Lasadi!" His boots slam on the ramp as he sprints inside, pulling his shirt up over his mouth and nose; he's barely aware of Jay at his back. His eyes water almost instantly, stinging in the smoke, he searches for her with tear-smeared vision. "Lasadi!"

"Here!" she calls. Somewhere to his left, closer to the flames. He feels his way towards her, choking on the smoke, expecting the worst: She's trapped under debris, unable to get away from the flames.

A blast of something humid and chemical cuts through the smoke as he approaches, and her figure appears in the gloom. She's not trapped — she's got the ship's fire extinguisher and is spraying fire suppressant foam on the blaze. It's working, but barely. Fire leaps, licks eagerly up her jacket sleeve. Lasadi drops the extinguisher, tearing off her jacket.

"Let's go!" Raj yells over the roar of the flames, but she shakes her head, coughing.

"No," she yells back. "Take the extinguisher." She throws her jacket to the ground and stamps out the flame, then disappears into the smoke.

Raj scoops up the extinguisher she dropped, targeting the base of the flames as well as he can. He's been through dozens of fire-extinguishing scenarios on ships, of course, and he assumes Lasadi and Jay have as well. But most of them practiced controlling a fire in a vacuum. There's no flipping a switch on the *Figment* and venting the oxygen. The upside is you don't have to burn with the ship if you can't get the fire out — but Lasadi's not leaving, so neither is he.

Something crashes behind him, and Lasadi is back, a wad of wet fabric in her arms. A hammock, by the flash of bright colors in the dull smoke. Together, she and Jay fling it over the fire, dropping to their knees to beat it back and smother the flame. White steam is beginning to replace the acrid black smoke, and with another strategic spray of suppressant chemical foam, the fire is finally out.

Raj drops the extinguisher and grabs Lasadi's arm; she's doubled over, coughing. "It's out," he says. "Let's go."

She lets him guide her towards the door and into the sweet, clean air outside, where she collapses on the foot of the ramp, panting. Raj drags in fresh air, hands on knees.

Jay's hand falls on his shoulder, squeezes. "Stay with her," the other man says. "I'm going after Bryant."

Raj nods; his teeth, his tongue, feel like he brushed with toxic ashes. He spits blackened phlegm, then turns to Lasadi.

Her face is streaked with soot and sweat but he doesn't see any blood. Her sleeve is blackened from the fire that had leapt up her arm — by the sharp tang of fuel emanating from her, her sleeve had been soaked in the stuff.

"Let me see," he murmurs, taking her hand and gingerly peeling back the sleeve. The shirt's ruined, but her arm doesn't look as bad as he feared. Her pale gold skin has been licked pink and angry, but it's not blistering. "Bryant did this?" he asks; he means the fire, he means her arm. He means putting her life in danger.

She nods and falls to coughing again. When she looks back up her jaw is set in fury. "Where is he?"

"Jay went after him. Give yourself a sec to — "

Someone shouts from inside the dockyard; a gunshot cracks through the humid morning air.

Raj jumps to his feet as Lasadi stumbles to hers — she pulls herself up with a wince that says she's hurt elsewhere, but she's obviously not going to sit still long enough for him to ask.

"Come on," she orders. "He'll head to his ship."

Lasadi seems sure of the direction, so Raj follows her, dashing through the forest of parked planes, emerging at the end of a row to see Sevi Bryant reach a squat Masali Viper, still almost fifty meters away. Raj bites back a curse. He'll be inside before they can reach him, and there won't be much they can do to stop him once he fires his engines.

Raj runs, leaving Lasadi behind him, lungs burning, leg muscles screaming after so much time spent off this world.

Bryant yanks open the door and hauls himself inside, turning back to pull the door shut after him. Even from this distance, Raj can see Bryant's sneer of triumph.

Raj charges. The door closes.

And then freezes to a grinding halt when a tall figure ducks under the Viper's wing, catching the edge of the door in his hands and wrenching it back open. Bryant's eyes widen in surprise as Peter Fangio grabs him by his collar and hauls him out of the doorway to his plane. Fangio decks him in the jaw.

Bryant collapses in a heap at Fangio's feet.

Raj pulls up short in his sprint, scooping up the pistol that's fallen from Bryant's outstretched hand and stepping back, covering the fallen pilot. Lasadi is behind him, but she doesn't stop short. She spits a curse at Bryant, aiming a sharp kick at his ribs. Bryant howls and curls protectively around himself.

Fangio lets her get a second kick in before holding out an arm. "We're golden," he says. "You don't need the assault charge, and he'll get what he deserves." Fangio stoops and closes a big fist around Bryant's arm, hauling him to his feet; Bryant shakes his head, blinking.

"What the hell is going on in my dockyard?"

The dockmaster has arrived, with Jay at her side. She strolls up as though in no hurry, then stops with arms crossed, taking in each of the disheveled folks in turn before zeroing in on Lasadi and Fangio. "James? Fangio? Care to explain? I've already spent the morning dealing with hassle from the owner of Moie Dreams Adventure Company, so this better be good."

"Smelled smoke," Fangio says. He shakes Bryant. "Saw this one running, heard Tita yelling for someone to stop him. So I did, didn't I."

"He set the *Figment* on fire," Lasadi says.

"We got it out," Raj says. "But you should double-check."

The dockmaster nods sharply, then stabs a finger at her gauntlet and raises it to her mouth. "Smoke's coming from the *Figment*," she says. "I need somebody there stat."

"I couldn't tell if anything major was damaged," Lasadi says, her voice hoarse. "But it wasn't burning too long."

"Are you all right?" Jay asks her.

"Fine. Despite some asshole dousing me with fuel and trying to set me on fire along with Theo's ship." Lasadi coughs into her sleeve, and all Raj can see is her trapped in the middle of those flames, the fire snaking up her arm — he can't chase it from his mind's eye. It takes all of Raj's self-control not to launch himself at Bryant and pummel that leer off his face.

"Arson?" The dockmaster lifts an eyebrow at Bryant. "A serious charge."

"It's not her ship," Bryant snarls.

"It's not yours, either," says the dockmaster. "But I would have gone with denying the charges. Because I don't care if you were torching the *Figment* on orders from Edan himself, that shit does not fly on my dock. Consider yourself banned from the Liluri Star Run, and every other race in this series once word gets out."

"The race board makes those decisions!"

The dockmaster laughs. "And who do you think is on the race board?"

"Some fucking mechanic?"

The dockmaster's smile turns sharp. "Some fucking mechanic is right. Fangio? Help me escort our friend Bryant here back to the sheriff?" She turns to Lasadi. "Any resources the dockyard has are at your disposal to help get the *Figment* flying by tomorrow. Any of my mechanics, too."

"That's very generous."

She shrugs. "Edan's good for it."

Fangio nods. "I'm sure Nia would be happy to help, too. She's already been over *Kalliope's Wager* a dozen times, and she causes trouble when she's bored."

"You'd help a competitor?" Lasadi asks.

"I was looking forward to racing against that ship," Fangio says. "Especially under the command of a captain who'll give me a run for my money." He ghosts Lasadi an overly familiar smile and she returns it with a shallow bow. Raj hadn't thought Lasadi knew Fangio before this race, but clearly something's shifted between the two since the pilot's orientation yesterday.

Jay clocks it, too; he gives Fangio a wary look. "Thank you both," he says. "I'll go check the damage and let you know if we need Nia's help."

Bryant may have been quick, but he's no match in strength to either Fangio or the dockmaster, and together they wrestle him easily towards the gate — and the gathering crowd of onlookers who've come to gawk at the *Figment*.

Raj, Jay, and Lasadi follow behind, more slowly.

"Everything good with you and Fangio?" Raj asks once the others have gotten out of earshot.

"He knows," Lasadi says. "He knows who I am."

Jay shakes his head. "Then we get the coordinates, and we get out of here before he tells anyone."

"He won't. He meant what he said back there, about looking forward to racing against the *Figment*. I gave him a line about how I'm helping train NMLF pilots, and this was part of a training mission. He and his crew bought it — or at least, they're happy enough with the story not to press any more." She stops, meeting each of their gazes in turn. "Anton doesn't need to know about Fangio."

"Understood," Jay says.

"Obviously," Raj says; the corner of Lasadi's mouth turns up. "And we'll keep a close eye on Fangio."

"Thank you."

She starts walking again, a wince at her first step.

"Don't worry about the *Figment*," Jay says. "We'll take care of everything there. You get to the clinic."

"I'm fine."

"You're never fine." Jay opens up a channel. "Alex? Qacha? Meet me at the *Figment* and bring every tool we have. Raj, make sure she goes to the clinic."

"You need all the help you can get with the *Figment*," Lasadi says, and holds up her hands to stop Jay from arguing. "I'm not saying I'll stay and help, I'm saying I'll go to the clinic on my own. I don't need an armed escort." Jay studies her suspiciously. "Do you want me to have the nurse call you when I get there as proof?"

"Yes, I do." They've reached the gate, and the *Figment of the North* has attracted a crowd of gawkers. None of the damage is visible from the outside, though sooty chemical foam has spilled down the ramp and steam is still trickling out of the door. Several of the dockyard's mechanics are yelling at people to stay back. "All right," Jay says. "Let's go check out that ship."

"Thank you," Lasadi says, then turns to Raj. "Thank you. For coming after me — and for staying to help." She's standing so close; Raj shoves his hands in his pockets to keep from pushing that strand of golden-brown hair behind her ear.

"Of course, Captain," he says. It comes out easy, professional. "Any time."

*Every time,* he thinks as she walks away. He'll be there every time she'll let him.

# CHAPTER 15
## LASADI

LASADI SHIFTS GINGERLY OFF HER HOTEL BED AT THE knock, setting her feet on the floor with a wince at her new aches. The doctor at the clinic had given her a burn salve for her right arm and told her there wouldn't be any scarring; she'd started laughing before he realized his faux pas. Any *more* scarring, he'd amended, with an apologetic grimace at the tapestry of burn scars on her bare left shoulder. And he hadn't even seen the worst of it.

No one has, since the doctors who put her back together, and she's been planning on keeping it that way.

She yanks open the door to her hotel room, stomach growling.

"Thanks," she says. "That was fast — oh."

Raj is standing a few steps back, hands shoved in his pockets. He's changed out of the grease-stained clothes she last saw him in at the dockyard and is wearing twill trousers and a loose cotton shirt in a rich green that brings out the warmth of his tawny skin. The sleeves are rolled up to display fine-toned forearms, sculpted muscle and sinew.

"You seem disappointed," Raj says, wry; Lasadi realizes with mortification she was probably ogling. "Expecting someone else?"

"Room service." Lasadi makes a show of looking past him, hoping he can't see the color rising in her cheeks. And, frankly, hoping to spot one of the staff heading her way with a tray of food. With the fight and planning, she'd forgotten about lunch, and now she wants nothing more than to eat her weight in fish and rice, then curl up for an early night's sleep before the big day tomorrow.

"I wanted to explain," Raj says. "For last night."

"You don't need to explain." Even if she did want an apology, she's not in the mood to talk about it now.

"I know you can fight your own battles." The quiet weight in his tone, the intensity in his eyes, Lasadi stills, studying him. "But last night wasn't just about you. Anton was trying to rattle you, and he was doing it in front of us to see if we cared enough to stop him. I needed him to know you had our respect."

Lasadi's surprise robs her of the easy *Don't worry about it* she'd planned in response. She'd been expecting a half-hearted *I got out of line.* A non-apology about how he was sorry she took it the wrong way. But Raj's explanation is simple, direct. And proof that he — like Ruby — sees and understands much more than she's given either of them credit for.

"You should cancel your room service," Raj says when she doesn't speak. He clears his throat. "The whole town is out at the race kickoff party, and I thought we could go have dinner and watch some of the festivities."

A spark flares in her chest before she realizes what he means — dinner with the crew. Another group dinner following rapid threads of conversation as they're flung across the table: Anton's veiled barbs and Ruby's teasing and Jay's inevitable preflight worrying and Alex's showboating to impress Qacha. She's exhausted thinking about it.

"We're going to spend plenty of time crammed together over the next few days," she says. "I'll pass on dinner with the group."

"Jay said you like to be alone before a big day. Said you like to study." He glances past her. She *had* been studying, poring over Theo's maps — which Jay and Alex had found in a secret compartment, and Qacha had deciphered quick based on Theo's journal and her own expert knowledge of the region. They have the coordinates, they have the plane, and now it's up to Lasadi's skill and preparation.

She's been trying to memorize the terrain, absorbing everything she can about handling a VTL-313 Garuda bush plane, watching accounts of older races to find anything that can help her settle the churn in her stomach. She set the room's holoprojector to play a series of interviews with race champions, who have been chattering quiet in the background while she studies maps and ship schematics. Now a pilot is describing her winning run five years ago, hands dipping out of view as she mimes her flight.

"Jay's right." Lasadi puts her hand on the door,

steeling herself to make her final excuses before Raj charms her into going out with the group anyway.

"The others all went out to dinner an hour ago," Raj says. "And I get it if you'd rather spend tonight neck-deep in books and weird talking heads, but . . ." Raj shrugs one shoulder with a faint smile. "But even if this is just another job, tonight this whole town's celebrating *you*. Come out and enjoy a bit of it."

Lasadi studies him. Is he asking her to *dinner*, dinner? Wearing that new shirt unbuttoned at the collar, running those fingers through his black hair while he waits for her answer — she gets the sudden, electric suspicion the gesture is hiding his own nerves.

Raj is maddening. From the moment they met, he's been a flame flickering on the edge of her vision. She's caught him watching her — but he hasn't made any overt gestures, not quite. Maybe he's holding back out of respect for her position, or maybe she's reading into his friendliness. He's this charming with everyone, she tells herself. From Qacha and Jay to the hotel staff, he gives everyone that same easy smile.

Now, though, that easy smile has been replaced by something more raw. Vulnerable. Raj catches his lower lip in his teeth; heat flickers in her belly.

"I'm not saying you need to put down a whole bottle of jienja and dance on the table," he says. "But don't eat dinner in your room."

"Is this a date?" Lasadi asks it before she can second-guess herself. She's not hoping for a yes — she doesn't dare to. The smart answer is no, and Raj is an intelligent man.

Color flares in Raj's cheeks. "I would like to get to know you. Outside of work."

It's neither denial nor affirmation — it's invitation. And it sounds so stiff and formal, like something out of an Arquellian period drama, that Lasadi laughs.

"Yes," she says, quick to stop that flash of hurt in Raj's eyes. She hadn't meant to laugh. "I would love to. But I've never been to dinner with an aristocrat. I don't know if I have the right evening wear packed."

Raj glances down at his own outfit. "I think in Moie, fancy dress means it doesn't have mud stains on it."

"Good, because that's as fancy as my dress ever gets." She powers down the holoprojector and slips her comm into her pocket. The worries that had plagued her evening vanish as she locks her door behind her. "Let's go get some food."

Lasadi had expected the party to be set up in the same amphitheater where she sat for the orientation, but the party's boundaries have spread to the entire town. Even though it's not late, the streets are filled with revelers who must've started drinking early, tourists and spectators out in the streets hoping for a glimpse of one of the more famous pilots competing in tomorrow's race.

Lasadi finds herself doing the same, she can't help but get caught up in the atmosphere of anticipation, knowing her idols are gathered in town tonight.

"That's Suli Charles," she whispers to Raj when she spots a tall, raven-haired person in their signature neon yellow flight jacket signing autographs outside a bar.

"They won three years in a row when I was younger. I can't believe they're still competing!"

"Do you want their autograph?" Raj asks.

Lasadi shakes her head quick. "I'm also competing," she points out. "I'm supposed to be playing it cool, not fangirling over — oh, gods. The man beside Suli? Arley Ng."

A nearby camera crew has noticed the pair, too, and a recording drone swoops in as the reporter — Joli Sainz, by the flame-red hair — exchanges good-natured banter with the pilots and peppers them with questions: "Any new improvements to your ship? It's been a few years since the town of Dakori was on the manifest like it was the year you won, Arley, do you think it'll show up again? Suli, last year you lost time in Howler Canyon — have you been working on your chicane moves?"

Raj nudges Lasadi with his elbow; she gets a faint whiff of citrus and sea salt. "Just think, maybe someday people will be clamoring for your autograph," he says. "Some little kid who watches this year's Star Run will spot you in the street and start yelling your name."

"Yelling my alias," she reminds him. He's slipped his hands in his pockets and stepped back a companionable distance, and she realizes she must have tensed up at his touch. If it bothers him, he doesn't show it.

"It's fun to dream, though," he says.

"Maybe dreams are dangerous."

His mischievous smile turns kind, and he tilts his head at a flag-draped alleyway. "C'mon. I spotted this place when I was exploring earlier today. It's quiet, and it smells divine."

The alley leads past a row of trinket shops and adventure guide operations, opening out into a charming plaza built on the roofs of the buildings below. A low balcony glowing with lamps faces the river, giving an incredible view over the south side of town, water tumbling over the rocks below. The sounds of revelry are hushed here, though they still drift up from the town in between sets from a trio of musicians in the corner of the little plaza.

As Lasadi suspected, the bulk of the event does seem to be down on the waterfront. Both sides of the river walk are decorated with bright flags and glimmering lights, and there's a light display over the river — hologram ships zipping under the bridges, scaled down slightly from the ships that will be launching tomorrow, but still big, and realistic enough that watching them bank around outcroppings and dive around the bridge supports is thrilling.

She has a flash of memory, sitting with her family, watching the pilots take off. Her grandmother shaking her head and asking who would be crazy enough to want to race this thing; Lasadi grinning, heart racing, thinking: *Me. I would be crazy enough.*

A pair of restaurants have staked out a claim on the little plaza, white tablecloths and red tablecloths respectively. Raj leads her to an empty red-clothed table near the musicians, with a view down the river. "The menu here looks amazing," he says, swiping a hand over the tabletop to activate it.

Lasadi leans in, frowning. "I don't recognize much."

"I love New Manilan food. We had a few amazing restaurants nearby when I was growing up."

"Didn't get a lot of it on Corusca," Lasadi says. "And even less of it in Ironfall."

"There's a great fried rice stand in Nestor's, by my place. I'll take you there next time work takes us back through Ironfall."

It's incredible, the way he simply assumes this little crew will be a permanent thing. Though why couldn't it be? Jay'd asked the others to come for her, and they'd done it without a second thought. The rest have become a crew already, she realizes with dizzying certainty. She's the one they're all still waiting for.

"What's wrong?" Raj asks, and Lasadi shakes her head, saved from having to explain her realization when a waiter arrives. She waves for Raj to go ahead and order off the unfamiliar menu, which he does with gusto.

He sits back when the wine comes, grinning. "Thanks for coming out," he says. "You needed to let someone celebrate you."

"For what?"

He raises his glass. "For getting us into such interesting messes."

She laughs. "I don't know why we're cheers-ing to that. This surely isn't what you signed up for." She tilts her head, remembering what Jay had said back in Icaba: *Raj said he'd been trying to get in touch with you, too, he's got this idea of us pulling some more jobs together.* "Speaking of, Jay said you had some jobs for us."

Raj sets his glass back down. "Not exactly. But you remember Lisbeth?"

"The little girl we found on Auburn Station, of

course I do." Her brow furrows as she tries to place how that fits.

"I took her back to her aunt and uncle. They said they had a job on the boards for months trying to find out what happened to Lisbeth and her dads, but the reward was too low. I figured we had a good thing going, as a crew. Maybe we could try working a few jobs together. Ruby was into it. Jay, too, but we needed to get you back, first."

"Oh."

"It's fine if you're not. I was just throwing the idea out."

"No — it's just." She can't figure out exactly how to phrase what's bothering her. "Even after Auburn Station, you wanted to work with me again?"

"I did."

"Huh." She takes another sip of wine as their food arrives, enjoying the secluded atmosphere. A few other diners are taking advantage of the relative quiet of this little plaza, and the musical trio are playing New Manilan waltzes that fade pleasant against the background.

She takes her first bite, stewed pork with papaya relish bursting over her tongue.

"This town has some of the best food I've ever eaten," she says, happy. She takes another bite, then slips her hand into her pocket. She's had enough of this fancy wine Raj ordered that she's ready to brave a confession of her own.

She pulls out Raj's cittern-string bracelet, the one he'd left on the *Nanshe* as an offering to the mixla, and lays it on the table between them.

"Oh, hey," Raj says. "I wondered what happened to that." He gives her a sly look, realizing. "Is that part of the mixla tradition? Like a lending library of jewelry that gets left behind?"

"No — I just . . . wanted something to remind me of home."

He lifts an eyebrow, and it's her turn to blush.

"Not home, but — " She clears her throat. "Some-one. Who I wanted to see again."

"Even after the Auburn Station job?"

Lasadi takes a deep breath. "Yes," she admits.

"Then keep it," Raj says. "I guess I started wearing it as a good luck charm, and you're probably the one who needs the most luck out of all of us."

"Thanks," she says, but she doesn't put it on; despite the wine, she can still hear distant warning bells. They've been talking about how well they work together, about their fledgling crew. They've both admitted they're attracted to each other, but that doesn't mean it's a good idea to act on those feelings, not if they want to keep working together.

She slips the bangle back into her pocket. "Do you play?" she asks.

"No," Raj says, too fast. "I mean, yeah. I do — but not recently. I used to be pretty good, but I got a little sidetracked by the military."

"So you have one, then," she asks. "You just don't play much."

He points to her pocket. "It needs new strings."

"They can't be that expensive."

"It's hard to find the time to practice." Raj smiles. "My parents made me take music lessons. It was supposed to be good for your brain and motor skills. You know, helping keep all those neural pathways elastic so you can be better at real subjects, like military strategy. I think they were a little bit scandalized when I actually started enjoying it."

It slowly occurs to Lasadi that the reason his voice sounds louder against the hush of the night is that the musicians have stopped playing. They're taking a break by the balcony. Her thumb brushes over the bracelet in her pocket.

"C'mon," she says, lifting her chin to the trio. "Go see if they'll let you give us a song."

A slow smile spreads over his face. "You want to watch me embarrass myself?"

"I believe in you."

And he laughs, takes another swig of wine, then pushes back from the table. Lasadi watches the casual swagger of his hips as he approaches the musicians, leans an elbow against the balcony and strikes up a conversation so natural-looking she'd assume he'd known them for years. Something he says makes all three laugh, and when he shoots a meaningful look at her, all three break into grins.

Lasadi's cheeks heat up. Olds, what did he tell them?

The woman who'd been playing the cittern leads him over to their abandoned chairs and hands over the elegant, teardrop-shaped instrument. He sits. Strums a few chords while they chat, adjusts the position of his knee.

And then he begins to play.

Raj Demetriou's voice is surprisingly sweet, if

untrained. He starts quiet, rasping faint around the edges of the words until he warms up to a rich baritone. He fumbles a chord badly and laughs, then strums a quick staccato and starts over.

This time, his fingers are more confident, his voice stronger, and one by one the others sitting in the little square turn. Lasadi doesn't recognize the song, but others apparently do, and she spots fingers tapping on thighs, heels rapping against the cobblestones. A few voices even join Raj's in the chorus — though the verses are melancholy, the chorus soars with nostalgia and hope. Something about waiting for a lover to return home from a voyage.

An older couple seated at the white tables rise up to dance, the leader whirling his partner with grace, both men stamping their feet at the chorus before Raj finishes with a flourish and they catch each other in an embrace, laughing.

Lasadi looks away from the dancing couple; Raj is smiling direct at her. It sears straight into her core. *This is a mistake,* she tells herself, but she can't turn away from his smile.

He makes to stand, but the dancing couple yell for another, and Raj obliges, slipping into something with a more upbeat rhythm that gets two more couples joining the men on the impromptu dance floor. This song is more familiar, like something Lasadi must have heard on an Indiran media show.

This one ends with an accelerando that has the dancers spinning and the crowd clapping, Lasadi joining them and whooping with delight when Raj plays his final chords.

"Keep going," says the citternist when Raj rises to hand back her instrument.

Raj laughs and shakes out his left hand. "It's been a while since I've had the calluses," he says. "My fingers are killing me."

Across the plaza, the first two men who were dancing lift their drinks to Raj in a toast, and he raises his hand to greet them, then rejoins Lasadi at their table.

"You didn't tell me you were impressive," she says.

He smiles. "I didn't want to get your hopes up. I'm rusty. I wasn't sure how it would go."

"Well, looks to me like you're a local celebrity."

"So much for our planned life of crime, I guess I'll be settling down in Moie to serenade tourists."

"I'll tell Jay to start hunting for a new grifter," she says, before she realizes she, too, has apparently bought into this shared dream of a crew. He makes it so easy.

Lasadi reaches for the wine bottle to refill both their glasses. She could bask in this glow forever — the mild buzz, the warm night, the pre-race jitters all but forgotten. But something tugs at the edge of her attention; a familiar red-haired woman's attention was also caught by Raj's playing.

Joli Sainz is wearing a vivid orange jacket tonight, her red hair in a perfect teased mane. She gives them both a perfect smile, her camera drone swooping towards their table.

"Joli Sainz, with the *Arquellian Star*," she says, dropping into an empty seat at their table. "Everyone's been wanting a word with you, Ms. James. How are you feeling about tomorrow?"

"Like we both need to get our rest," Raj says. He

swipes credits onto the table to cover their tab, then grabs the wine bottle by the neck and holds out his elbow for Lasadi. "Shall we?"

He steers them away from camera drone and Joli Sainz behind them, back down the alley to the main street.

"Bottle's not empty," he says when they're comfortably lost in the crowd and she's comfortably lost in the sensation of warm muscles moving against her arm, under her palm, through the thin fabric of his cotton shirt. "Want to head back to the hotel and away from prying eyes?"

But the prying eyes she's worried about are back at the hotel. Jay, Ruby, Alex, all watching her come back home with Raj and a bottle of wine, and wondering exactly what sort of mess their trusted captain is getting herself into. She and Raj spent time getting to know each other tonight, that's all. Whatever comes next can't be rushed, not if they want to give this fledgling crew a chance to come into its own.

"I should go back and get to sleep," she says. "Why don't you stay out, though? Enjoy yourself."

A crack in his easy smile; he understands immediately that she doesn't want to be seen walking back into the hotel with him. He covers it quick. "Makes sense," he says; they've come upon yet another little plaza with an amazing view across the river. He tilts the wine bottle at an empty stone bench. "I think I'll enjoy the view a while. I'll see you in the morning, Captain."

"Good night, Raj."

She's back in her room and locked the door before she realizes she hadn't thought of Anton at all tonight.

He's just a client in her mind, as he should have been from the beginning. She's happy to help him for the cause, but her crew is what matters now. Somehow, over the last day, she's slipped the inexorable pull of his gravity, and now she's free to make her own path.

She closes her eyes, but she sleeps fitful as her mind combs through tangles of excitement for the race the next day and worries at the thorny problem of what to do about Raj. She hears Qacha's voice sometime after midnight, giggling with Alex, though it's another hour before the girl slips into their hotel room and fumbles into bed while Lasadi pretends to sleep. And another hour later when the quiet padding gait of something not quite heavy as a human passes by her door, pausing to sniff at the door, let out a faint growl, and head on.

*Trust your gut,* Lasadi tells herself as the dawn light warms the cracks of the door. *It will show you the path.*

# CHAPTER 16
## RAJ

"So." Ruby leans a hip against the wall, arms folded. This morning she's ditched the sassy local sundresses she's been wearing for the past few days and is back in her usual slim black pants, practical boots, and red leather jacket. The morning light glints on the gold ink etched into her collarbones. "What did you do to piss off the captain this time?"

Raj finishes his double check of the rations crate, marks it off the list. They're down at the dockyard, finalizing the rest of the preparations. Jay and Alex are inside the *Figment* securing gear while Lasadi and Qacha attend the sendoff ceremony. Anton is here, too, but he's not helping. He's made himself comfortable inside the *Figment*, on a series of calls or reading messages this whole time, a scowl on his face. Raj has started to ignore him, like a hole in the floor that you know is dangerous, but you won't fall into it so long as you steer clear.

"I don't know what you're talking about."

"You took her out to dinner last night, and this morning she's barely looked at you. What'd you do?"

A flare of applause and cheers sounds from the amphitheater and Raj checks the time. It's twenty minutes from the first heat's liftoff, so the sendoff ceremony must be coming to a close. When the echo of fireworks and the onlookers' cheers die down, Raj turns to the next crate — medical supplies — and sighs.

"Dinner went fine."

"Did it."

Raj intends to keep it short and sweet, but one detail spins out into the next, and pretty soon he's sitting on the medical supply crate. They've still got time — Las and Qacha haven't arrived yet.

"So you spent an hour choosing between two shades of green shirt, bought her a meal she called the best she'd ever eaten, then serenaded her on a plaza," says Ruby once he's done recounting last night's events. "I can see why she's ignoring you now."

"I was trying to help her unwind," he says. "But seeing each other probably isn't the smartest idea — and I think she realized that before I did."

"So you'll both pretend you're not parched for each other and continue working side by side. Sound healthy, does it?"

"I'm not willing to risk what we're building," Raj says. "Especially if she's not."

"Take it slow, then. Figure out how to be friends first, there's no need to rush."

Raj laughs. "'Take it slow,' says Ruby Quiñones."

She throws a ration packet at his head; Raj ducks it with a grin, tosses it back at her. "Do as I say, only. Not as I do." She drops the ration packet back in the crate at her feet, then fastens the lid. "And remember we're all adults on this crew. Don't you dare use our precious feelings as an excuse if you're just scared pissless of rejection."

Another chorus of cheers sounds from the amphitheater, and a band starts playing. That'll be the end of the ceremony, which means Lasadi and Qacha and the rest of the pilots will be streaming back to their planes. To avoid collisions in the narrow Moie Valley, the race will be sent off in heats of two planes each, positions randomly assigned. All forty-some planes will be airborne in less than ten minutes; it will feel like eternity to the pilots in the last heats, but there's a clear benefit to going last, too. Every racer gets the list of checkpoints one minute before the first heat lifts off. The last heats have extra time to study the list and plot their optimal course.

"Something else came up last night," Raj says. He needs to get this out of the way, and wants to do it quickly, before Lasadi gets back. "That reporter of yours came by for an interview. I shut her down, but she might have gotten some footage of me. Have you been watching the bounty boards?"

"I'm doing my best," Ruby answers. "But deleting messages on the bounty boards is putting mousetraps on the kitchen floor while ignoring the nest in your pantry."

"But it's fixed the problem in spirit."

Ruby fixes him with a shrewd look. "It's nothing you need to tell the captain about, is what you mean."

"There's a lot going on right now."

"I'd let Lasadi worry about what she does and does not need to know, Raj. Give us a hand loading these in."

He takes the other end of the crate Ruby's been filling and helps load it into the *Figment*. Headhunters had been a bigger problem when he first deserted, but then he met Ruby, and she's been trying to clean up the bounty boards for him ever since. After that last brush with them in his neighborhood hub in Ironfall, she came up with a script to alert her the instant something new pops up. He knows that won't help them catch private messages, but at least it'll stop his father from blasting his name everywhere.

"You know you can shut this down any time," Ruby says quietly once they're back outside, and Raj flinches.

Talk to his father, she means.

That's not happening. He'd spoken up against his father's plans, and the man had him arrested, then planned for his "accidental" death to keep his secrets hidden. Raj hasn't said a word in these past three years that could incriminate his father for war crimes, because the risk was so great to himself. Occasional headhunters, he can handle. But if his father unsealed the court-martial records, where Raj himself was convicted of sparking the Battle of Tannis by destroying a neutral medical transport, he wouldn't have a single safe place to hide in the entire Durga System.

Though maybe his father isn't trying to kill him anymore. Maybe he's satisfied dragging his only son's name so deep through the mud it'll never come clean.

Maybe Ruby's right, and if Raj grovels, his father will finally let him stay in exile in peace.

"I'll take care of it."

Ruby straightens, surprised. "Really?"

"I'll talk to him as soon as we're done here."

"Great. Then I'll delete my scripts."

Raj's eyes widen. "Don't."

"If you're really going to talk to your dad, you don't need me scrubbing the boards for bounties, do you." She arches an eyebrow in challenge. "Or am I calling your bluff."

"You called my bluff. But I'll talk to him. Eventually. Just let me do it on my own terms."

"I'll follow up," Ruby says, then leans in. "I intercepted one of Anton's messages yesterday. He's meant to meet the NMLF leadership committee in Icaba once we get back."

"Seriously? I thought they never came out of hiding."

"Apparently whatever we're bringing home is flash enough. Should we tell the captain?"

Raj shakes his head. "We shouldn't distract her." And winces at Ruby's raised eyebrow. Dammit. That was a test. "I mean yes, because it's not up to us to decide what she needs to know. Still, I'd rather go to her when we have something solid."

"Use your best judgement," says Ruby drily.

Voices are approaching, Lasadi and Qacha, by the sound of it. Raj seals the medical crate. "What was the level on those water tanks?" he asks, hoisting it up to hand to Ruby.

"Ninety-eight percent."

"Perfect. Hey — since we're not keeping things from each other anymore, what was that note you got from the Ayalasi? You seemed upset. Is everything okay?"

Ruby's pinkie nail flicks against her thumb, her mouth going flat. "That's none of your damn business, is it." Ruby takes the medical crate, then turns on her heel and heads into the ship.

Raj shakes his head and grabs the last rations crate, straightening as Lasadi and Qacha come around the corner.

"Morning, Captain," he says.

"Everything good to go?" Lasadi asks. Her smile is polite and friendly. Nothing outwardly off about it, but Raj has seen the fire in Lasadi's soul through those smoky brown eyes, and he can tell when the shutters are firmly closed. It's the same perfectly inoffensive smile she gives to Anton, though Raj isn't sure the other man would notice.

"All accounted for. Did you two pick up any good intel on what the route might be?"

"Just speculation." Lasadi gestures for him to go ahead up the ramp with his crate. "A lot of people think it'll concentrate on the northern towns this year, but there's talk every year. No one ever really knows."

Ruby's right — Lasadi isn't exactly being cold to him, but she's slammed a polished, professional mask down over any spark of connection they'd had last night. It stings, but she must be thinking about the crew. It's the only reason he can think of for her not wanting to be seen walking back into the hotel with him last night.

There's no rush, Ruby had said. Everything that's meant to be will happen in its time.

Of course, there's probably another reason for her to keep her distance this morning — Anton. Raj has been enjoying the way the senator holed up out of sight all yesterday, and would love for him to stay behind in Moie, but Anton has made it clear he wants to be there himself when they reach the Arquellian test plane Theodor Usoro found in the jungle.

"We're in the fifth heat with Fangio," Lasadi says when everyone's gathered aboard. "Not bad, and it'll give us a chance to think through our route — especially since we've got a sixth stop no one else has to make."

"Fangio?" Jay asks. "I thought the draws were random."

"They claim to be," Lasadi says. "But somehow they also end up being the most dramatic match-ups."

"There's already chatter with the commenters," Qacha says. "Both offworld teams face-to-face, Peter Fangio's chance to finally beat the *Figment of the North*, that sort of thing."

Jay's had the main race feed running as he and Alex secured gear in the cargo hold, and Raj has caught bits of it. The commentators are the same every year, a married couple who'd met on the racing circuit as pilots before transitioning into announcers in their retirement. They're interspersing details about which pilots are up next with snippets of interviews and speculation about which stops might be on the manifest.

It's part of the fun, Qacha had told him. Not even the announcers know where the stops are until the final racer has been given their manifest.

Now the announcers are vamping to fill the time before the launch of the first heat — five minutes — and reminiscing about the crash five years ago between

Arley Ng and Noura Samson that took them both out of the race.

"Shut that off, please," Lasadi says. She takes a final look around the interior of the *Figment*. "And grab a seat. We're airborne in ten."

They've brought over the passenger seats from the *Green Lightning* to accommodate their little crew, and Raj takes the seat behind Lasadi's; Anton's already taken the one behind Qacha. Ruby straps herself in near the back, studying a tablet in her hand, and Jay and Alex take the seats across from her.

Raj can only see a sliver of Lasadi's profile when she turns to speak to Qacha, but the excitement in the curve of her lips and glitter in her eye is unmistakable. She's in her element. It's impossible not to be thrilled for her.

Collegially, of course.

The *Figment*'s radio crackles open. "Stand by for manifest," says the dockmaster.

Lasadi glances over her shoulder. "Alex?"

"On it."

The kid unbuckles as a dockworker arrives, banging on the *Figment*'s open door. "Five minutes, *Figment*," the dockworker says, handing Alex a sealed envelope. "And your manifest. Good luck out there."

Alex slams his hand on the button to close the door and sprints the short distance to the cockpit, grinning as Lasadi tears open the paper.

The radio crackles again. "Heat one is cleared for takeoff. Heat two in position." A few seconds later, the dull roar of nearby thrusters fills Raj's ears; by the sound of it, both planes headed east.

"Well, that's different," Lasadi says after a moment.

Raj cranes his neck to see. Pilots can hit the check-points in any order, but generally there's one way to do it that makes the most sense. Normally the five check-points surround Moie, forcing pilots to crisscross the mountains to hit all the points of the star.

Raj doesn't know any of the names on the list, but he can see what has Lasadi concerned as Qacha highlights them on her map.

This time four of the checkpoints are to the north, with a lone town marked in the south. The point they're going for is somewhere in the middle of the four northern checkpoints.

"We can hit Theo's coordinates most efficiently on this leg, or this leg," Qacha says, pointing. "But both of those mean ending up at the coordinates later, when we'd have barely an hour or so before dark."

"Ideally we want to hit it first thing now, or first thing tomorrow."

Qacha nods. The timer on the dashboard is counting down. Four minutes.

The radio crackles. "Heat two cleared for takeoff. Heat three in position."

"If we go north clockwise," Qacha says once the roar of heat two has died down, "we could hit three of the checkpoints and then land at the crash site. But it would be so inefficient, and I don't think we could get there by nightfall." She sighs in frustration. "Either we get to the crash site way too early, or we won't make it before nightfall."

Lasadi frowns at the map. "Why not head south to Navarro first? Then north, counterclockwise, ending in White Rock. If we push, we could hit four checkpoints and make it to Theo's coordinates by nightfall. Then we can explore the crash site in the morning, hit the final checkpoint, and have a fighting chance at beating anyone else to Moie."

"Because we're looking for the smartest way to get the job done," Anton says. "Not the flashiest."

"*Figment*, stand by for tow," someone says through the radio.

"Copy tow. Qacha?" Lasadi prompts, attention on the map as though Anton hadn't spoken; a muscle jumps in Anton's jaw. A second later the tow unit connects with the *Figment of the North*, tugging them forward towards the launch pad.

"Hold on," Qacha says. "I'm calculating the route."

Another roar of engines sounds, closer than before. Heat three is airborne; they head east as well.

"*Figment*, you're on deck," someone says through the radio.

"Copy on deck," Lasadi responds. She switches on the engines and the plane comes to life around them. The tow unit tugs them forward again, and now they're on the launch pad — nose to nose with the other ship from heat five: Peter Fangio's *Kalliope's Wager*.

Lasadi trades a salute with Fangio through the cockpit's window as the roar of heat four's engines engulfs them. When it dies down, she turns to Qacha. "No one's going south first — but even without our sixth stop, that route makes the most sense. Why?"

Qacha traces the route, then shares a look at Lasadi. "Because it means going through the Leopard's Maw."

"*Figment*, you're free to launch in ten. Nine. Eight . . ."

Lasadi grins at Qacha and hits the engine.

"Strap in, everyone!"

Raj's stomach drops through the floor of the plane as it leaps into the air, banking hard to the right where every other racer had gone straight, and he forces himself not to close his eyes as Lasadi races straight for the narrow cleft in the cliff.

Peter Fangio dives in behind them.

# CHAPTER 17
## LASADI

THEODOR USORO'S *FIGMENT OF THE NORTH* MAY BE nothing much to look at on the ground, but once in the air, it's a stunningly beautiful plane. More responsive than the *Green Lightning*, but still familiar in the easy, agile way it banks and turns at Lasadi's inputs.

Lasadi didn't expect running the Leopard's Maw to be any easier the second time, not when she's coming at it from reverse, in a different plane than before. But Qacha's quiet, confident instruction is spot on and Lasadi relaxes into the controls, trusting herself, Qacha, the plane as the ravine tears past them in a blur of emerald foliage and damp gray stone.

"Fangio's losing time on us," Qacha says. "And the ravine widens in eight hundred meters. You can push it."

"Copy. Increasing speed."

"Obstacle up ahead, port."

"I see it." Las dives them low to clear an overhang, then banks around the reaching branches of a lone kapok tree jutting out from the ravine floor below. "Are there multiple routes to Navarro?" Lasadi asks. "Or will we be fighting Fangio the whole way."

"There are two main options," Qacha answers, absorbing herself in the map now they're out of the trickiest part of the Leopard's Maw. She grins up at Lasadi. "But my dad showed me a third once."

"We need to lose Fangio or he'll follow us."

"Hold on."

Lasadi focuses on flying while Qacha shuffles paper in her lap. She's seen this scenery so many times, plugged into immersion feeds and holoplays, watching livecasts of the race, but nothing compares to being here, watching the rising mist spiral up from the jungle floor, the trickling waterfalls cascading like diamond necklaces through shrubs and vines and trees so lush they make Lasadi wonder if she's ever actually seen the color green before. She sweeps to starboard, wingtip brushing the glorious explosion of pink blossoms from the iypan tree clinging to the ravine wall.

"We'll let him pass," Qacha says. "Half speed and hard to port in five. Four. Three. Two — *now*."

Lasadi cuts the engines and banks hard to port, following close to the ravine wall as it opens into the valley below.

"Careful," says Qacha. "Take a wide arc around those rocks ahead, and we should be out of visual when they come through."

The outcropping of rocks seems small from a distance, but upon getting closer, Lasadi would guess the formation is a couple of kilometers long. It looks like a cluster of skyscrapers drawn by a child, crumbling columns jutting out from the jungle canopy below and pushing up against the sky. They're topped improbably with trees of their own, vine-like roots finding whatever perch they can in the stone.

"Not a lot of room," notes Lasadi. "Everyone hold on tight if you're not already." She soars behind the tower of rocks, keeping her speed as low as she dares to afford them the time without dropping from the sky. "Is he out?"

"Not yet." Qacha's gnawing on her lower lip, craning her neck to get a view.

"So I was too fast?"

"No such thing," Qacha replies. "He's too sl— Wait. There he is."

Lasadi ducks the plane under a low-hanging vine. "Did he spot us?"

"I don't think so. He wouldn't think we went this way." Qacha turns back to check. "He's gone — he took the western route, I think. We're good."

"Copy that." Lasadi lets out her breath and pushes the thrusters back to full power, soaring free of the narrow space behind the outcropping and out over the valley. Peter Fangio's ship is already out of sight beyond a plateau several kilometers away. Lasadi cracks her neck to relax her shoulders after that flight. "All good back there?" she asks.

Anton gives her a tight, unhappy smile. Raj looks a little green. Ruby's got her eyes squeezed shut and Alex is grinning. Jay gives her an easy thumbs-up.

"Great. Qacha, let's see this shortcut of your dad's."

✳

The shortcut gets them to Navarro ahead of Peter Fangio; he's not even on the control's radar by the time the *Figment* has checked in and been given the go-ahead to launch again. The Navarro dockyard is empty of spectators, which the dockmaster had apologized for.

"No one thought we'd see action today," he'd said, locking his seal onto the manifest and handing it back. "Saints' path to you."

Their advantage didn't hold, though. Qacha may know these mountains, but Fangio is a veteran of the Star Run, and by the third checkpoint — a tiny, ugly, industrial spaceport that bears no resemblance to the lovely iypan tree that is its namesake — Fangio is back on their tail. He beats them to the dockyard with seconds to spare.

"C'mon," Lasadi mutters, drumming her fingers on the controls while the dockmaster takes their time getting to the *Figment*. The northern checkpoints have been busier than Navarro, since all but Lasadi and Fangio started there and are working their way south. There's only one dockmaster to approve manifests, though, and they're making their way through the group in order.

The *Figment*'s radio crackles to life.

"Thought I lost you back there after the Maw," says Fangio. Lasadi can see the *Kalliope's Wager* parked a few dozen meters away, engines warm and ready for liftoff.

"Were you worried?" Lasadi asks.

"Course not," he says. "A pilot with your reputation?"

Lasadi's hands tighten on the controls. *Do not mention Mercury,* she wills him; she can sense Anton's attention on the conversation, cold interest emanating from him. "Turns out you're not so bad yourself," she says. "We'll see who makes it to White Rock first, though."

Fangio's laugh is rich, even through the radio. "We'll see. Saints' path to you."

"Saints' path."

His connection cuts out as the dockmaster steps down from the *Wager*'s open door, and her engines roar to life. Peter Fangio and his crew soar into the air; it's a full two minutes before Lasadi can follow.

Qacha leads her on what seems like the smartest route to White Rock, but even so, she can't catch *Kalliope's Wager*. It doesn't matter, Lasadi tells herself, because she's not racing the *Wager*. She's racing the sun.

A handful of racers — including Peter Fangio and his crew — are at the White Rock docks when Lasadi touches the *Figment* down, settling in to camp there for the night. White Rock is the easternmost checkpoint of the group, a lumber town nestled in a flat, wide valley ringed by chalky cliffs flaming rich gold in the setting sun. The dockmaster greets Lasadi with a friendly wave.

"Strange route you and Fangio took," he says, scrolling through his tablet for the *Figment*'s check-in history. "But it's working. You've got one checkpoint left before Moie — only a handful of others managed to hit four checkpoints today, but they've still got to get all the way to Navarro."

He squints up at her, shielding his eyes from the slanting rays of the sun as he points one leathery hand at a spot a few dozen meters away. "You can take that berth there. Do you want a hotel recommendation? Or are you and your crew sleeping on the ship?"

"We're not staying in White Rock." Lasadi cracks her neck, giving her shoulders a quick stretch, though it'll take a hot bath and a strong hand at massage to unknot her back after these last hours of constant tension and trick flying to navigate the Liluri Mountains without breaking any elevation rules.

The dockmaster shakes his head. "Sun's setting," he says. "There are no good touchdowns near here. You'll run out of light before you find a clearing in the jungle big enough to camp in."

"We've got a spot in mind," Lasadi says. She digs her fingertips into the back of her neck, working the screaming muscles along the ridge of her spine, then rolls her neck to loosen it. Just a little bit more today, and she can take a break.

"Well, I can't stop you, but I don't recommend it," says the dockmaster. He hands over his tablet for her signature. "Safe flying out there."

Lasadi's lower back protests as she slips back into the pilot's seat. Qacha's already in her co-pilot's seat, hunched over the map in her lap. Lasadi waves to the dockmaster through the window and buckles her harness.

"How far is it?" she asks Qacha.

"About forty-five minutes." Qacha cranes her neck to study the sky out the window. "We'll be cutting it close. And if these coordinates are wrong, who knows where it'll be safe to land."

Across the dockyard, Peter Fangio and his crew have a cookstove out and are cracking open beers with the crew of the ship next door. It's such a comfortable scene, but it's teeming with as much danger for Lasadi as a deeper run into the jungle. Fangio's been coy about not letting her real identity slip, but get those beers flowing and he might. Good thing they're not staying here.

Lasadi opens up the channel to the rest of the crew. "Jay?"

"All set back here," he says.

Lasadi takes a deep breath. "All right. Let's — "

The *Figment*'s radio crackles open. She's expecting the dockmaster, but it's Fangio's voice. She can see him through the cockpit's window, standing apart from his crew, talking into his comm but looking straight at her through the window.

"Join us for dinner, *Figment*," he says.

"Sorry, *Wager*," Lasadi replies. "We've got other plans."

Even at this distance, Lasadi can make out the surprise on Fangio's face. "Are you crazy?" he asks. "There's nowhere to park within hours of White Rock."

"We'll see," Lasadi says. She raises a hand to wave through the window. "And we'll see who gets to Moie first tomorrow."

Fangio raises his own hand in salute. "Don't crash that plane, Mercury," he says, and a trail of ice slips down her spine. "Or get yourself killed. I had a lot of fun today."

"See you in the air," Lasadi says. She doesn't let herself turn, doesn't let herself check if Anton noticed Fangio's comment. But she doesn't have to — she can feel the silent fury rolling off him in waves. She clears her throat, dries the palms of her hands on her thighs. "Let's do this, Qacha."

"Copy. Next stop, Theodor Usoro's mysterious coordinates."

The *Figment* soars into the air; Lasadi blinks against the dimming light as the valley around White Rock smears into daubs of colors, the chalky cliffs fading to ashen gray and casting dark shadows over the jungle below.

# CHAPTER 18
## LASADI

"WE'RE ABOUT FIVE HUNDRED METERS OUT," QACHA SAYS, when they reach a jungle mountain valley that's near identical to every other one they've passed today — even more so with Durga touching the horizon. Qacha points. "There's the canyon. Do you see it?"

Lasadi has to squint to make out what Qacha's pointing at. The valley runs east to west, the mountains sweeping together to create a tall peak in the west that blots out what's left of the sun, casting the entire valley in shadow. Maybe when the sun was overhead, the dark cleft in the canyon floor would be easy to spot, but right now it's next to impossible to make out against the dark green of the jungle foliage.

"Where are we supposed to land?" Lasadi asks. "Are you sure this is it?"

"What do you mean?" Anton asks sharp; Lasadi ignores him, and to her credit, Qacha does, too.

"The landing site is protected in the cleft," Qacha says. She peers nervous down at the dark gash in the forested mountainside below them. "Maybe. The coordinates are directly over the canyon, at least."

*And we trust the coordinates.* She smooths one hand, then the other, down her thigh to dry her palms.

"Lead me in."

Lasadi slows the *Figment of the North* to hover over the point Qacha directs her to, then engages the landing gear. The landing lights and camera come on automatic — all glitches from the fire gone, thanks to Qacha's electrical work — and she leans forward to study the screen. Nudges the *Figment* slow along the edge of the dark cleft until something catches her eye.

A glint of metal, shaped like a wing. And there, tangled in vines a few meters below, is the rest of the plane.

Qacha breaths in quick and whispers what sounds like a prayer.

"I think we found Theodor Usoro's final resting place," Lasadi says.

And she's found the spot where he was trying to land: a ledge, jutting out about fifteen meters down from the top of the cliff, about twice as wide as the *Figment* and three times as long. Shrouded in shadow.

Qacha gives Lasadi a nervous glance, then clears her throat and straightens, going into professional mode. "Landing gear check's good," she says. "The ledge appears to be clear of debris."

"Keep an eye on the side cameras," says Lasadi. "I want as much clearance as we can get without going over the edge."

"Copy that."

And Lasadi slowly eases the *Figment of the North* into

the cleft. Heart rate calm, breathing steady, all senses alive and bright as she steadies the plane to the slow, confident beat of Qacha's quiet voice ticking off their altitude.

Even Anton is silent as darkness swallows them.

And ever so gently, the *Figment*'s land gear touches solid stone. Lasadi's knuckles are white on the controls as she waits for Qacha's confirmation that their position is secure, then she lets out her breath and sinks back against the seat. Cuts the engine.

"We're at camp," Lasadi calls.

"Where is camp?" Ruby calls back.

"Let's go find out." Lasadi unbuckles her harness and slips out of her seat. Raj is smiling at her, Anton glaring; she ignores them both to find Jay at the controls to the ramp.

"Plenty of room," he says as it lowers. He plays a torch over the ledge, revealing uneven stone, mostly dry but for a few glassy puddles left from the afternoon's rainstorm. "Nice job, Las."

"Watch your step," she says, though nobody has made a move to leave the ship. "It's not a wide ledge and it looks like a long way down."

"Ladies first," says Jay.

But Alex pushes past them both. "Are we checking it out or what?" Alex grins at her and strolls down the ramp until his feet hit stone. He turns in a slow circle. "Wow, Cap. Nice landing job."

"Well, nothing ate Alex," Ruby says after a minute. "We might be safe."

Lasadi lets out a laugh she hadn't realized she was holding back, at the absurd reality that all the rest of them were indeed subconsciously waiting to see if something happened to the seventeen-year-old kid who'd volunteered as bait. She follows Alex down the ramp to survey their camp for herself.

It's not just a *nice* landing job — it's a perfect landing job, actually, equidistant from the canyon wall and the edge of the ledge. The ledge is bare stone, about the size of the plaza where she and Raj had dinner the night before. Lasadi could put two more planes the size of the Garuda down here if she had them. And didn't think the stress of trying to land in an even tighter area would kill her.

Here, the canyon is about thirty meters across, the stone pitted and craggy in the dim light.

"Granite," Raj says. He glances at Qacha for confirmation, and she nods. "There were river canyons like these in Granisa, where my family . . ." He trails off with a wince.

Ruby shoots him a look. "Were you going to say something obnoxious, like 'where my family had a summer home'?" she asks, dry.

"Yeah." Raj clears his throat. "Anyway, it's sturdy stuff, is what I was trying to say. We can feel good about camping here."

"Glad to hear it," Lasadi says. "Because we're not flying anywhere else this time of day." She looks to Jay, who's standing closer to the ledge than any of the rest of them have dared. "How far down does it go?"

Jay tosses a rock over; it echoes as it tumbles down. It's a long breath before it hits the bottom with a splash.

"A ways," Jay answers.

The sky above is washed a deep blue, the last rays of

the sun catching pink and gold in the clouds above. Something flashes overhead with a leathery slap of wings and a staccato of supersonic chirps. Beside Lasadi, Ruby looks up.

"Bats?" she asks.

Qacha nods. "They live in the cliffs. Now is their favorite time to hunt."

"This is just wild," Ruby says, grinning. "I can't believe you grew up with all this stuff."

"I suppose everything seems normal if you grow up with it," Qacha says.

"We're losing light fast," Lasadi points out. "Chat while we're setting up camp. Only bring out what you need from the ship — we don't want to waste a bunch of time repacking in the morning."

Ruby flips her a casual salute and turns to walk back up the ramp. Lasadi is about to follow her when a touch above her elbow stops her. She knows that calm, possessive hand, not quite circling her arm, definitely not letting her go.

She turns to meet Anton's gaze; the fading light has cast his eyes into shadow. "What is it?"

"Walk with me," he says.

There's nowhere to walk but the far edge of the ledge, not quite out of earshot from the others, though the sound of the river below offers them a touch of privacy. The rest of Lasadi's crew aren't trying to listen in, though, they're laughing with each other as they unload, their voices ringing off the walls.

Here, the ledge narrows to a point that isn't quite comfortable. The stone feels sturdy beneath Lasadi's boots, but she's not far from the edge, and the drop —

she's not going to think about the drop. She stops to face Anton.

"You were right about us being able to decipher Theo's journal once we had his maps," Lasadi says, attempting to take control of the conversation with naked flattery. "And the coordinates led us straight here. I'm eager to see what we find tomorrow."

"How long has Fangio known?" An angry muscle works in Anton's jaw.

"We don't have to worry about him. He — "

"How. Long." The words snap like ice.

Lasadi takes a deep breath. "I don't know how long. But he told me yesterday and I dealt with it."

"And you didn't come to me."

"I *dealt* with it, Anton."

"You didn't deal with it," Anton says, voice low and dangerous. "You ignored it, which will create an even bigger problem."

"I told him I was working to help train NMLF pilots — isn't that the story you wanted out? That Qacha and I are racing the Star Run as a publicity stunt for the NMLF?"

"That's classified," Anton says, as though he and Vasavada hadn't told her exactly that. Panic spikes her heart rate — maybe they'd changed their minds and she hadn't known — but she shoves the thought aside. She's not second-guessing herself with him anymore. She knows what Anton told her, she gave Fangio that story, and she's not going to let Anton knock cracks in her memory.

She doesn't grovel, doesn't rise to his bait.

"It worked," she says instead. "He's from the Belt, he has no love for the Alliance."

"You don't know that."

"I know plenty of Belt drifters like Fangio," she says. "I've lived with them for the past three years."

"Making you the expert?" he asks, sarcastic.

"More than you."

She's slashed too close to the line, she can tell by the way his gaze stills on hers, emotionless.

In the way he says, voice completely even, "Is this a game, Lasadi?"

She's always pushed his buttons, he's told her, forcing an issue to see how far she can go before he snaps. Though of course when the roles are reversed — and they often are — he's not pushing buttons, he's *testing*. When she breaks under that test it's because she's weak and emotional. When he snaps under her needling, it's because he's an exasperated leader who's at his limit with a foolish little girl.

She knows this precipitous place all too well, and it never ends without scars.

If Jay were here, he'd know how to disarm Anton. Offer an easy joke and an explanation Anton would actually accept. Olds, he'd probably claim *he* was the one who spoke with Fangio — he'd taken credit for Lasadi's decisions more than once during their Mercury days, when it seemed like Anton was going to tear a perfectly good decision apart simply because he was in a mood with Lasadi.

But Jay's not here, and Lasadi's not Mercury's captain — or sharing Anton's bed.

She no longer gives a shit about massaging Anton's ego.

"No," she says. Calm, cool. No weak emotion in sight. "It's not a game. I didn't come to you about Fangio because *you* asked *me* to do this job, and I'm doing it as I see fit. We got your coordinates, we're at the location, and Fangio's not a problem. So far we haven't failed to deliver, and if you have a problem with how I run my crew, we can talk about it tomorrow when we've got the goods in hand."

Anton tilts his head, studying her, and for a brief, terrifying moment she can sense how close the edge is, how far down the river. *The jungle eats pilots alive.*

Then he smiles. Genuinely smiles.

"I'm proud of you, Captain," he says. "I don't say that enough."

Lasadi studies him, uncertain.

"I won't lie. I had my doubts during the early days of Mercury Squadron, but you've grown into your own. You've proved your loyalty, too. After the Battle of Tannis you could have destroyed all the peace we had worked for, but you made the sacrifice to stay silent — and your country thanks you. But the true pleasure for me is to see how you rebuilt your life. To meet the people whose loyalty you earned. And to see how you've grown in your confidence."

Anton's smile turns wry. "You never would have stood up to me like that before," he says. "It makes me proud that you will now."

And like that, the storm of his anger has cleared to reveal the sun of his affection — only maybe that sun has always been there, and she's the one who hadn't been strong enough before to weather the storm. Anton's right, she's a completely different person from the girl he first gave command of Mercury. She'd been a capable pilot, of course, but she wasn't the most senior, and she'd had to fight like hell to earn the respect of Henri, Tania, Ana Mara — all the others who grumbled she was only there because she was sleeping with Anton.

She'd earned that in the end, and maybe making her fight for respect had been part of Anton's plan all along. He always had keenly understood the strengths of his people, and gave them tests to shore up their weaknesses. Years ago she'd passed the test of gaining Mercury Squadron's trust. And now?

"Thank you," she says. It's not relief washing through her, but something stronger. Peace. "For trusting me."

"I do, Lasadi. You've proven that I can." But Anton's smile fades. "And I respect you. Which is why I come to you with this advice."

"What is it?"

"The Arquellian."

"Raj," Lasadi says. "The Arquellian has a name."

"He was out well past midnight last night."

"So were Qacha and Alex," Lasadi points out.

"It would be one thing if this were a lover's tryst," Anton says, and despite their newfound understanding, an icy sliver sticks in her spine. Does he know Lasadi was out with Raj last night? "However, this morning I intercepted a signal going to an Alliance ship in orbit. The flagship. You know who his father is?"

"I do."

"Blood is thicker than loyalty to a cause, Lasadi. In the CLA, in the Senate — in your crew. Blood is thick."

"I trust him."

"I know. You're very trusting, it's one of the things I always loved about you." He gives her a kind smile. "We're at a dangerous time in history with the Limitations Act. Our enemies would do anything to keep it from passing."

"I wouldn't put that in jeopardy."

"Be careful." Anton tucks a strand of hair behind her ear. "I've taught you everything I can. I want to see the cause succeed, but I also want to see you happy. Even if it's not with me."

She acts before she can second-guess herself, stepping into him. His arms envelop her, and just like always, they carry strength, safety, *home*. He's changed his cologne, but beneath it he still smells like the Anton she fell in love with: sandalwood and cinnamon and heat.

Her skin devours the pressure of his touch, the way one broad hand covers her shoulder, the other searing pleasant warmth into her back, and for one wild moment she knows that if he of all people took her to bed and saw her scars, he wouldn't look away, he wouldn't pity her. He would know her as he always had. He would see her for the woman she is despite the burns.

She has to stop herself from burrowing her face into his neck and letting his hands linger over her touch-starved skin — she doesn't want *Anton*, not anymore. She wants to be known. And despite his flaws, despite their fraught history, he knows her better than anyone.

She breaks the hug before it's too late, ready to make her excuses and leave, when Ruby's voice cuts through her attention.

"Alex?" Ruby's standing at the ramp to the *Figment*. She whirls, scanning the small ledge. "Alex, where are you?"

Lasadi turns as well, but there's nowhere to hide in this little area.

Alex is gone.

# CHAPTER 19
## RAJ

ALEX IS GONE, VANISHED WITHOUT A TRACE — RUBY CALLS his name and it echoes down the canyon like the stone Jay threw. Like Alex's scream surely would have if he'd fallen. Raj spins, trying to spot where the kid could have gone in the small ledge.

"Alex!" Ruby calls again, the knife's edge of panic sharpening her brother's name.

"Here!" comes the echoing response. "Relax!"

Ruby's been peering fearfully over the edge of the ledge into darkness, but Alex's voice comes from above. In the twilight Raj catches a glimmer of motion: Alex has scaled the canyon wall to reach the crashed plane tangled in vines. He waves from the pilot's seat.

Ruby breathes a scathing curse. "Some warning, only, if you're going to scamper off!" She's trying to do miffed, but Raj catches the haunted look in her eyes before she turns away.

"What did you find up there?" Raj calls.

"Not much. If there was a name on the plane, it's

been rusted off. But they weren't transporting cargo, there's no personal luggage or anything inside."

"No body?"

"Nope. But it's definitely not going to fly, it's in a million pieces. Come on up, it's not a hard climb."

In the light, maybe it would be a cinch. But this twilight gloom is a different story. Raj glances at Jay. "We've got headlamps?"

It's quick work for Raj to scale the boulders with a headlamp, following Qacha as she nimbly picks her way up the wall. None of the other offworlders are interested in trying, and Raj doesn't blame them. He grew up rock climbing in this same gravity, but it's unfamiliar territory and he's been living at lower gravities for a few years now. Not to mention his paranoia about potential creepy-crawlies lurking in the jungle. Qacha doesn't seem to be worried as she reaches for handholds, and Alex didn't get stung by anything nasty, so Raj tries to push the thought out of his mind.

Whereas the ledge had smelled clean and cool from the bare stone and the water flowing by below, more of the rich decay of the jungle reaches him the farther up he climbs. Along with the sharp bite of rust and mildew — but not the reek of death one would expect to find at a crash site.

The plane is a small two-seater, one wing broken off and teetering above them on the cliff's edge, the body of the plane broken in half.

"The comms are fried," Alex says from inside the plane. He's still sitting in the pilot's seat, jabbing a finger at the controls. Raj joins Qacha crouched outside; she's intelligently hesitant to go in. "But there's still plenty of fuel in the cell. You think whoever crashed here got out on foot?"

"Maybe," Qacha says, but it doesn't sound like she believes it's possible. "But in that case I doubt we'd ever find them. There's not much in between here and White Rock, and you saw it while we were flying over."

"Maybe they followed the river."

"It has to have been Theo," Qacha says. "Who else would have come out here? The plane's not rusted enough to have been here longer than a year."

Alex shifts and the seat adjustment catch fails, sliding the seat back on rails. Alex lurches backwards with a cry of surprise, and one of the vines holding the plane in place snaps. The ship drops a meter before other vines catch, coming to a precipitous stop with a shriek of metal on stone. Raj throws up his arms as clumps of soil and debris pepper them from above. Some animal chatters nearby, irritated at having its sleep disturbed.

"Time to get out of here," Raj says. He holds out a hand to help Alex crawl through the missing windshield, then stops, tilting his head as his headlamp sweeps over something unexpected at Alex's feet. "Wait. What's that?"

Alex shines his own light down to find a battered journal wedged under the seat. He shifts to grab it and the plane jolts again. Raj catches his arm and carefully helps him climb out of the plane.

"Careful, kid," Raj says. "If I don't bring you down with me, your sister's going to kill me."

"Also I'm a valuable member of the crew," says

Alex, with a note of wounded pride. In the darkness Raj can't tell if he's actually insulted, or pretending.

"I'm way more scared of your sister than I am worried about how we're going to get past an alarm system," Raj says.

"An *alarm system*," Alex says, shaking his head. He leaps nimbly past Raj and starts the climb back down. "You'd have died on Auburn Station fifteen times if I hadn't been there. I am a master of my craft."

Qacha laughs and follows him, stopping to shine her light for Raj on the trickier places. The plane above seems to have settled again, and whatever animal was chattering at them has calmed down. Still, Raj doesn't relax until his feet hit the solid stone of the ledge and he's out from under the potential fall of Theo Usoro's plane.

The others have finished setting up camp, settling around a portable fire ring with rations. Ruby, sitting cross-legged on the far side of the ring between Qacha and Lasadi, gives Alex a frayed look he ignores. Raj takes the rations packet Jay hands him and finds a perch on one of the crates someone dragged out.

"It was Theo Usoro's plane, all right." Alex holds up the journal he's been skimming through. "And he definitely thought there were aliens here."

Ruby laughs. "Like, 'Dear Diary, today I got captured by aliens'?"

"No, but he wrote he was coming here to bring the alien artifacts back and prove he was right about them." He glances at Anton. "I thought you said he found an Alliance test plane."

"That's what he told me," Anton says. He seems

genuinely surprised by the strange turn Theodor Usoro's second journal has taken.

"Get this," Alex says. "He writes, 'I left them originally out of a profound sense of wonder for the creatures. I couldn't disturb that which should be revered, and turn it into a thing for the people of Moie to gawk at. Another spot for them to put on their tourist maps and trample with their guided tours.'"

Alex drifts off, tracing his finger down the page before flipping to the next one.

"What is it?" Raj asks.

"He actually goes off for a while about what an asshole the owner of Moie Dreams Adventure Company is." Alex flips another page. "And now he's burning on the mayor. Okay. Here's good stuff again. 'But everyone who mocked me will soon learn I was telling the truth. Something not of Earth landed on Indira, though it's impossible to tell if it was before or after humans came as refugees on our own ark. Tomorrow I will follow the River of Blood to their temple and clear my name.'"

Alex flips a page. "And then there are a lot of details about what he had for breakfast."

He sets the journal in Lasadi's outstretched hand; everyone sits in silence a minute as she pages through it. It's eerily peaceful, with insects chirping in the night, the trickle of water below. Some beast snarls in the distance; another snuffs through the underbrush along the opposite rim of the canyon.

"Why does he call it the river of blood?" Ruby finally asks.

Qacha shrugs. "Like how the Icaba River is muddy

with red silt? It might be something like that. Maybe the soil is very oxidized here."

Lasadi's paging through the book. "He doesn't say anything more about that," she says. "But he definitely had a way with words. 'The mayor crows at me like a white-tailed baboon, head full of his own wind.'"

"Theo was like that," Anton says. "Some of the letters he wrote me were quite colorful."

"Well, I can't wait to see what's down there," Alex says.

Ruby gives him a look. "Aliens at the end of the River of Blood isn't exactly what I signed up for."

Lasadi laughs. "Should be a piece of cake after getting possessed by ghosts on a haunted space station," Lasadi says to Ruby. She tilts her head back, braid slipping off her shoulder and falling down her back. "The stars are amazing here."

It's the most relaxed she's been in Anton's presence; whatever passed between them after she landed the *Figment* must have put her mind at ease. Raj saw her face in the moment after she and Anton hugged; she'd seemed profoundly at peace. Maybe Raj has had Anton pegged wrong this whole time.

Or maybe he's an even better con artist than Raj thought.

Raj cranes his neck, following her gaze to the slash of black sky visible directly above them. Someone — he doesn't note who — turns the fire ring down until it's barely flickering, and as his eyes adjust, the sky is set with diamonds. A glow paints the horizon to the east, one of Indira's moons cresting the low hills the ravine they're camped in opens into.

"Corusca," Jay says quietly, and heads turn to the glow. They eat the rest of their meal in silence, watching Corusca rise; Raj can't help but remember watching it as a young man, knowing the moon was inhabited but never thinking about it seriously until he was sent there to quell an uprising. He wonders if Lasadi ever stood and stared up at Indira the way he stared up at her homeworld. She must have.

When he looks down, Lasadi is watching him. He smiles at her, but her own smile is a touch too slow to come. When it does, her eyes remain troubled.

"Let's get some sleep," Lasadi says, getting to her feet. "I want to be packed up before dawn so we can head in at first light."

# CHAPTER 20
## RAJ

QACHA WHISTLES LOW WHEN SHE STEPS TO THE EDGE OF the ledge. "So that's why Theo called it the River of Blood."

Raj steps up beside her. His eyes go wide.

The first rays of the sun have set the morning mist glowing, illuminating the canyon and giving them their first view of the river about twenty meters below. While the upper part of the canyon is granite like the ledge they're standing on now, it transitions to dark jasper, knobby boulders worn smooth by centuries of water. The river fills the floor of the canyon, a few handspans of water flowing over a smooth stone base of blood-red jasper. Downstream, the jasper drops away in steps to form a shallow falls, water cascading white and lacy in stunning contrast to the red stone below.

"Incredible," Raj says. The rest of the crew have joined him and Qacha, staring down into the River of Blood below.

Lasadi is the one who breaks the spell. "We need to

get moving," she says. "Raj, Qacha, Alex — you three apparently like scrambling around on rocks, so you're in charge of getting us all to the bottom of the canyon. The rest of us will finish breaking camp."

"On it," says Raj. The view is gorgeous, but what's even more gorgeous is that unlike the sheer limestone-and-jasper cliffs on the far side of the canyon, the wall below this ledge is broken up and cracked, massive boulders and seams in the rock that will make the journey down — and back up — much more manageable.

"This top section looks like the tricky part," he says. "But if we rappel down to that boulder, the rest is a fairly easy climb." He expects confirmation from Qacha, but she's still staring at the river. "What is it?"

She glances between him and Alex, a line sketched between her brows. "It's nothing," she says. "Just a story my grandma used to tell me. A teaching tale, like if my brother and I were fighting over something and she wanted us to share?"

"What was the story?" asks Alex.

"About a village that went missing in this part of the Liluri Mountains. A century or so ago, someone found palladium and there was a rush in the area. A bunch of miners got really rich overnight, and the village of Tatzin sprouted out of nothing. But one day, a miner flew to Moie to get supplies, and when he flew back to Tatzin, it was gone."

"Gone?" asks Alex.

"He couldn't find it anywhere. He searched until he ran out of fuel, food. He finally found his way back to another town and said he'd found nothing where the village had been. My grandma always used to say the people of Tatzin fought because of their greed until all of them had been killed, and the mountains were upset with the greed of the people of Tatzin, and swallowed the village up. She'd say, 'There's a river in that part of the mountains that still flows red, it was stained so badly with their blood.' And that's why Temu and I should share whatever we were fighting over."

She frowns back down at the river. "But once, my father told me a different version. In his, the mountain didn't swallow the village. He says the people of Tatzin discovered an ancient cursed treasure, and they wanted to keep outsiders from discovering it and spreading the curse. So they hid the village themselves and now kill anyone who comes close. In his version, the blood that stains the river is from outsiders who come searching for them."

Raj shakes off the chill at the back of his neck, telling himself it's simply the cooler air drifting from the canyon below.

"Your dad was trying to scare you," he says. "C'mon. Let's get our line tied and test this route."

"Then you just unclip your harness at the bottom, and you can make your way down from there," Raj says. He's miming proper rappelling technique while the others watch with varying degrees of skepticism. "That first granite boulder has plenty of deep handholds, the smaller jasper ones below are a bit more slippery. It's not steep, though. Go slow and you'll be fine."

Lasadi's mouth is pressed in a flat line. Anton's frowning at Raj with arms crossed. Jay's scrubbing a hand over his jaw, Ruby's chewing on her lower lip.

"It's not as far down as it looks," Raj says.

"Some of us didn't grow up on Indira," Ruby shoots back.

Raj isn't sure that's an advantage at the moment, especially given how long it's been since he's done much scrambling up and down rocks. He's tested the route and now his arms ache from the effort. His muscles and frame may have been developed in this gravity, but in truth he's been living in Durga's Belt for the past three years and not pushing himself. When they're back on the *Nanshe* he'll have to join Jay in the gym.

"I'll carry you, sis," Alex says brightly; she swats at him.

"I didn't say I couldn't do it. I said I hope you all know how to tie some good knots, only. How do we keep our gear from getting wet?"

"Pretty sure we're all getting wet," Raj says. "But I think I saw a dry bag in the *Figment* that would work for any of your electronics. Give me a second. Alex, Qacha, start getting them down this cliff."

By the time he returns from rummaging through the gear already packed away in the *Figment of the North*, everyone but Ruby and Alex has made it down to the bigger boulder below. Ruby quickly stashes her gear and slings the bag over her shoulder, then slips over the edge of the cliff with a muttered prayer and surprising grace. Raj follows after.

He, Qacha, and Alex help the others pick good lines

and spot them through the tricky spots, and soon they're at the bottom of the canyon.

Raj's boots splash into the water, which comes up to midcalf. It's cold now, but it'll feel refreshing as the day heats up. The river fills the entire bottom of the canyon, the jasper beneath is a little slick, but the surface is relatively even and the going is easy.

As the sun rises, the blood river becomes even more dazzling. The sun's rays catch in the water to sparkle like cut glass, drawing out the many shades of brick, rust, umber, garnet, wine in the stone beneath. The canyon walls narrow as they walk to a choke point where the water tumbles over boulders in an airy veil; they scramble up and over, stone slippery under the soles of boots.

"I needed a shower," Raj says when he finally climbs to the top of the little waterfall, but no one answers — they're all staring at the sight ahead.

The walls of the canyon sweep out after the choke point, coming back together about twenty meters away, forming a near-perfect circle of placid water. At the far end, the river disappears into a cleft in the cliff face. The cleft is about three times Raj's height and three meters wide at the bottom, a dark gash breathing out cool air that seeps through Raj's damp clothes.

The ravine's end would be gorgeous on its own, but the truly stunning thing is the pair of tall columns framing the cave's entrance: a pair of vaguely humanoid figures, obviously carved by human hand.

"The colonists of Tatzin?" Alex asks Qacha.

She shakes her head. "That's a story."

"If this is out here," Ruby asks, "why doesn't anyone know about it?"

"Theo knew," points out Alex.

"The jungle hides many things," Qacha says. "Besides, look at the carvings. They're ancient. Whoever carved these is long gone."

Lasadi clears her throat. "And we need to be long gone, too. Let's move."

The closer they get to the statues, the less they seem human. They stretch up grotesquely, the lines morphing as the angle of view changes, turning the humanoid figures into slender, monstrous giants. A pair of hollowed-out stones are set at their feet like bowls for an offering; Raj tries not to think about the fact that each bowl is big enough to hold a human body.

A meter-wide flat ledge juts out from the wall of the cave, Raj realizes with relief. He hadn't been looking forward to fording the river in the dark. But before Lasadi can climb up onto it, Alex grabs her arm.

"Hold up, Cap," he says quietly. Lasadi's gaze follows Alex's finger as he points, tracing one strangely taut vine to where it disappears into a canopy of other trailing vines. And there, in between the green foliage, are a series of points. Sharpened sticks, aimed downward.

"This is the trigger," Alex says, pointing to a wide, flat rock flush with the rest of the stones at the entrance. It clearly isn't a natural part of the river, but Raj wouldn't have thought twice about stepping on it, especially given the pair of statues at the entrance. Humans made the statues, why wouldn't they have placed a few stones to make it easier to navigate the cave?

Looking at it more closely, though, Raj can tell where it's meant to slip under the weight of whoever steps unknowingly on it, releasing the vine it's holding taut.

"Want me to disarm it?" Alex asks.

"Leave it for now," Lasadi says. "If the person who set the trap is still around, we don't want to alert them."

"Somebody had a lot of time on their hands," says Qacha, leaning forward to examine it. "That can't have been easy to put together. But it's not fresh."

"Still," says Lasadi. "We go slowly and keep our eyes peeled. Alex?"

"On it, Cap."

Alex and Qacha take the lead as the group moves slowly into the cave. Raj plays his headlamp over the river, a sense of unease pricking the back of his neck at the enclosed space. It's larger than some of the tunnels in Ironfall or Artemis City, but somehow more claustrophobic. Perhaps because it's alive, the walls dripping with water and lichen, shadows rustling and lurching as his light hits rock formations.

At first, the chill increases along with the darkness. But it only takes a few minutes before Raj begins to feel a trickle of warmth again. Natural daylight glows at the far end of the cave, along with a rush of water that grows louder at every step.

Not long later, the tunnel opens back up into a circular sinkhole where the river broke through the upper layers of stone and collapsed the roof of a natural cave large enough the *Nanshe* could park snugly inside. The collapsed ceiling exposes a wide circle of sky, with a deep red-black pool in the middle of the chamber and a narrow ledge skirting the edge of the pool.

Water pours down from the far side in a silvery curtain, one main waterfall and a dozen smaller streams obscuring the back half of the chamber. The lip of the hole drips with languid hanging vines, their leaves glistening with water. Sunlight cuts through in wide beams, illuminating the center pool, and the statues.

The statues are similar to the ones flanking the entrance, though these are much smaller, under two meters each. Each also has a bowl at its feet; when Raj kneels to brush the debris out of one, it's stained black underneath.

"So this is why Theo called it a temple," Lasadi says.

"I'd love to know who built this," Raj says. He steps onto the ledge, squinting down into the pool as his eyes adjust to the light. There, glowing faintly in the beams of light spearing down from the open skylight above, is an angular shape very much out of place among the organic shapes of the chamber.

"Is that . . . ?" Raj kneels, trying to get a closer look. "What the hell kind of ship is that?"

# CHAPTER 21
## LASADI

LASADI STEPS UP BESIDE RAJ, FROWNING AT THE WATER. The silhouette deep in the pool is unmistakable: a spacecraft. But it's not like any ship she's ever seen before. "Anton said it was some sort of experimental plane the Arquellians were testing," she says. She glances back at him for confirmation. "Right?"

"Or aliens," says Alex.

"There's no such thing as aliens," Lasadi says. "But of course Arquellian covert tech would look strange."

"It's Arquellian," Anton says, firm. "Believe me. I didn't just rush here once I got Theo's journal. I did my research — the Arquellians have been testing tech in New Manila for some time."

"That's true," says Qacha. "My dad and I spotted an Arquellian ship once, out near Balazia. They weren't allowed to fly over New Manila even before we were forced into the Alliance, but that never stopped them."

"Okay." The slant of daylight into the pool has gotten steep, and Lasadi doesn't want to burn any more of it arguing. "We found the crashed ship Theo told you about. What exactly are we looking for here?"

"A cloaking device," Anton says; Lasadi gives him a surprised look. She hadn't actually expected him to reveal what the tech was. "According to Theodor's notes, it appears to be a sapphire about the size of your fist."

"Do we have to swim?" Alex asks. "We don't have environment suits."

"You don't need a suit," Qacha laughs. "It's just water."

Alex gives her skeptical side-eye, and Lasadi doesn't blame him. She can handle zero-G, she's been dealing with it her entire life. But submerging herself in water, with its strange currents and eddies and the drowning-choking-dying bit? She's not sure she wants to try it for the first time today.

"I'd love to watch Alex try to swim," Anton says. "But we don't need to. Theodor's journal says he already pulled out the cloaking device and secured it in this cavern. We just have to find it."

Ruby shrugs. "I mean, we could still push Alex in and find out what happens."

"Ha, ha." Alex shoots her an irritated look.

"We split up," Lasadi says before Ruby keeps needling her brother. "Jay, Qacha — take the left side of the pool. Anton and Ruby, to the right. Raj and Alex, we'll head around to the far side."

Lasadi spares a glance at the statues ringing the chamber as they pass, but doesn't stop to examine them close; behind her, Ruby and Anton have begun to study the first one. While the statues are similar to the pair outside the cavern, they don't seem to have been carved by the same person. Each is carved with different levels of skill, and the farther back in the chamber they go, the older the statues appear. They also become less humanoid, more like a twirling, winged dancer. Or a flickering flame.

"Someone's been here recent," Lasadi says, stooping in front of the last statue in the row; there's sodden ash in the bowl, the charred remains of a bundle of leaves. Beyond this, the path disappears behind the waterfalls and into darkness.

"Why leave an offering at this statue in particular?" Raj asks. He runs his fingers over the smooth stone, then goes still, his hand gentle on the statue's waist. "Alex? Can you take a look at this?"

Alex flicks on his headlamp and wedges a shoulder against the wall to get a good angle on whatever Raj found. "Oh, hey. That's definitely a lock."

"Do we need to find the key?" Las asks.

"Nope," Alex says. "I am a key. A valued member of the team." He fishes a set of lockpicks out of his backpack.

"You are," Lasadi says. "What's going on with you and Ruby, anyway?"

"I think she's over having me around."

"That's not true at all," says Raj. He's moved back to explore the previous statue, shifting the bowl at its feet to see what's underneath. "This one seems like it's solid stone."

"She doesn't have to be responsible for me." Alex's tongue darts between his lips as his fingers work the picks. "I can handle myself."

"I don't think that's it," Raj says.

"Of course it is. She doesn't want to be responsible for anybody but herself. Even when the ayas ask her — okay, got it."

He sits back, a triumphant grin on his face, and gently pries the front half of the statue open. It swings out, the hidden hinge mechanism perfectly flush with the stone.

"Even when the ayas ask what?" Raj asks.

"Nothing," says Alex. "Forget I said anything, she's already mad at me."

Lasadi leans in for a better look, but doesn't touch anything until Alex examines it. The statue is hollow, the back half set into the cave to make room for a larger chamber. A metal box is wedged inside.

"Nothing high-tech about this," Alex finally says. "And it doesn't seem to be boobytrapped."

Lasadi reaches for the box, fingertips closing over the rusted metal. It's wedged in, but a bit of pressure pulls it loose. She opens it, heart pounding with anticipation.

It's empty but for a scrap of paper.

Lasadi unrolls it, careful not to smudge the ink. A single sentence is written in the same script as the rest of Theo's journals: *Come get it if you dare.*

"I'm starting to think he actually was crazy," Raj says.

"The aliens scrambled his brain."

Lasadi ignores them both, dropping the scrap of paper back in the box. Raj takes it from her, turning it over in his hands one last time before reaching to place it back in the statue. He stops halfway, leaning in to shine his light. "Wait. Look at this."

Hidden at the back of the hollow is a carved stone rod about the length of Raj's hand — it's familiar, but Lasadi doesn't quite place it.

"That totem you and I stole from the collector on Artemis?" Raj says, prodding her memory.

"I think *I* officially stole it," says Lasadi, but she takes it from him, studying the stone. It's cold and black as obsidian, carved in the shape of a bird. A heron, maybe. "This does look like that totem. I thought you said it was some cult from an asteroid."

"The Tisare cult," Raj says. "That's what the buyers told me, anyway. This isn't part of what we need to return to Anton, is it?" When Lasadi shakes her head, he slips the little totem into his bag and then closes up the statue. "Then we can run it by my buyers once we get back out to Durga's Belt."

"We?"

"They'll like you," he says with a wink.

"Does it matter if your buyers like me?" Lasadi asks.

"Vash and Gracie are special," Raj says. He elbows Alex. "You're going to love Vash, she'll have a trick or two to teach you."

"Well?" Lasadi stands, brushing her hands off and turning to face the rest of the narrow ledge as it sweeps around into darkness behind the veil of waterfalls. "Let's dare to go get it."

She lets Alex walk in front of her, a responsibility he takes seriously despite his penchant for joking. He steps careful, shining his headlamp over every inch of the path before continuing on. Qacha and Jay must have finished their exploration of the left-hand side of the pool, because she can see their headlamps playing over the wall from the opposite side.

Once her eyes adjust, it's not as dark as she had thought behind the waterfalls — and she can easily see there's nothing back here.

Lasadi bites back a curse, shining a light over the far wall and illuminating nothing but a pile of rubbish — human-made debris, she'd guess. They don't have time for this. She's about to turn back when Jay's headlamp hits the pile of rubbish at the exact same time hers does; even over the rush of the waterfall she hears Qacha's gasp.

Where before there had seemed to be nothing but a pile of rubbish, when both lights hit at once, a figure emerges from the shadows. A man, sitting directly behind the widest part of the waterfall, cross-legged on top of the pile as though in meditation — although it's not exactly a temporary meditation: The man's cheeks and eyes are sunken, the flesh decaying off sharp cheek-bones and showing dull yellow teeth.

He's wearing a tattered flight jumpsuit and a yellow-and-black jacket Lasadi would recognize anywhere after years of seeing it on the top step of the Liluri Star Run podium.

"Usoro," she says. May the old ones know his soul.

Jay looks down, and the figure vanishes.

"Keep your light trained on him." Lasadi steps closer; Qacha's approaching from the other side. His skeletal hands are clutched around a ragged bundle, blue light glimmering through the wrappings. The "jewel" they're seeking: a sphere the size of her fist, blue as a sapphire. If it was a sapphire it would be worth a fortune — but since it's not, it's worth even more. An entire country's independence, maybe. Intricate webs of wires and nanochips pulse inside the translucent sapphire case.

"So that's the cloaking device?" Qacha asks. "How does it work?"

"Anton said Theo's journals talk about how it works," Lasadi says. Usoro has a strange, ethereal quality to him even when they're standing this close. When Jay's light hits at the right angle, she can see him clear as day. But the parts of his face and body still in shadow aren't just darkened. They practically vanish from view, refracting the light somehow into a camouflage of the stone behind him. "It's incredible."

"Don't touch him," Alex says, and she's about to respond that it's only a dead body when he barks, louder. "Captain! Don't *touch* him. Look."

Usoro seems to be sitting on a pile of rubbish, but when Lasadi follows Alex's finger, it's not random trash. Usoro is seated on crates of what appear to be explosives, his arms wrapped in the wires.

"'Come get it if you dare,'" Lasadi quotes. She sits back on her heels, studying Usoro; his face flickers in grotesque patches, a flash of jawbone, a flit of toothy grin. "Alex?"

"I think I have an idea," he says. "Qacha, I'm going to need your help — the rest of you might want to stand back."

"Don't bring the whole temple down," Lasadi says.

"Don't worry, Cap. I probably won't." Alex flashes

her a smile, then steps careful around Usoro to confer with Qacha.

Lasadi straightens, giving them space.

"Anton?" she calls; she hasn't heard his or Ruby's voice for a minute, but that's not much of a surprise given they've been behind the waterfall. She picks her way out, playing her light over the rest of the cavern. A pair of headlamps flicker near the entrance to the tunnel that led them here. "Anton, we've got it."

"Good," answers a voice from the tunnel, and it's neither Anton nor Ruby. Lasadi's blood runs cold as a shadow detaches itself from the wall and steps forward, dragging another figure with him.

It's Sevi Bryant, his hand clamped over Anton's mouth, pistol to his temple. He's flanked by a trio of toughs, one of whom has his arm around Ruby's neck.

"Because we've got the rest of your crew," Bryant says. "Hand over the jewel, and no one gets hurt."

# CHAPTER 22
## RAJ

SEVI BRYANT DROPS HIS HAND FROM ANTON'S MOUTH, BUT leaves the gun pressed to his temple. He's got a trio of vicious-looking mercs with him, two men and a woman; the man and woman to his right have plasma carbines raised to cover Raj, Lasadi, and Jay. The scar-faced man on Bryant's left has his arm around Ruby's throat; her boots scrabble for purchase against the wet stones.

Bryant lifts his chin to Scar, who drops Ruby and shoves her forward to splash in the shallow water washing over the edge of the pool. Scar wrenches her arm behind her back and she cries out, murder in her eyes, as he shifts the barrel of his pistol against the base of her skull.

Raj's hand itches to pull the gun on his hip, but the woman in blue's plasma carbine swings his way, the barrel pointed straight at his chest. If Blue loses concentration, Raj might be fast enough to draw before she can fire — but he can't take her out and also keep Ruby from getting a bullet in the head.

"The jewel," Bryant growls. "Your friend doesn't have all day."

Anton struggles in Bryant's grip. "I'm a Coruscan senator," he says. "If you hurt me — "

"Yeah?" Bryant laughs. "Anybody know you're out here in the jungle? Seems to me you've been hiding the fact you're even in New Manila, so I can't imagine someone will come searching for your body here."

"We don't have it," Lasadi says, holding her empty hands up.

"Bullshit."

"*Yet*," she finishes. "We're trying to work out a way to get it."

"Then work fast." Bryant gives her a vicious smile. "Tell you what, I'll even give you an incentive. There's what, five of you? Get me the jewel in the next two minutes and all five walk out. Take two minutes longer, and it'll be four of you. I don't suppose I need to spell it out further, they *do* teach math on your backwards little moon."

Raj catches the flash of a look Lasadi sends his way. Bryant only counted five of them, which means Qacha and Alex — wherever they are — have an advantage.

"Wait," Lasadi says. "Let me see what I can do."

She starts to step backwards, back around the veil of waterfalls, when Bryant barks for her to stop. "Where the fuck do you think you're going?"

"To get it!" She throws her hands up. "Isn't that what you want?"

Bryant studies her suspiciously, then nods for the

woman in blue and the man with the ocular implant to go with her. Blue and Cyclops pick their way carefully on the narrow path.

"Captain," Raj says quietly. "Let me get it."

"No. It's too dangerous."

"Exactly," Raj says, putting all the urgency he can into his voice. She needs to understand this. "If something happens to me, you can get us out. If something happens to you . . ."

Lasadi takes a sharp breath, realizing what he's saying.

"Adorable," Bryant calls. "I thought you were a bunch of offworlders, but you've got yourself an Arquellian boyfriend, Tita." His teeth catch the light as he smiles. "Or Lasadi, or whatever it is they've been calling you."

A flicker of movement above Bryant's head catches Raj's attention, and it takes all he has to not immediately look. He risks a glance when Bryant's attention is on Lasadi, schooling the surprise off his face. There's a ledge about three meters off the ground by the entrance to the tunnel; Raj hadn't noticed it before because the dark stone blended in with everything around it. But now he can make out a person crouched on the ledge.

Qacha waves to him and Raj blinks his acknowledgement. She points down — from her position, she's almost directly above and behind the woman with the plasma carbine — then makes a motion like grabbing a person's throat. Raises a thumb and her eyebrow.

Raj nods slowly. Stretches out a hand hidden behind his thigh: *Wait.*

"I should be demonstrating better fraternity," Bryant

is saying. "Tell you what. Hand the jewel to your Arquellian boyfriend, and he can come with me as a hostage. Your crew will be free to go — and if you're lucky, maybe I'll do you a favor and take this one off your hands for good."

"He's part of my crew, too," Lasadi says, voice dangerously sharp.

"Is he?" Bryant gives her a sideways smile. "How do you think I found you?"

"You planted a tracker," Lasadi says, confident. "Before you attacked me on the *Figment*."

"Before I tried to *destroy* the *Figment*?" Bryant asks. "Doesn't make any sense. And the race officials would have noticed it before you left. The Arquellian turned it on this morning before you came down here."

"Fuck you, Bryant," Raj says, but there's a flicker of uncertainty on Lasadi's face, the briefest of hesitations that sticks in his soul like shrapnel. It suddenly hits him, all those sideways glances and odd looks she's been shooting him since last night. Since her heart-to-heart with Anton. Anton hadn't just made up with Lasadi like Raj had thought, he'd said something to her about Raj, something that shook Lasadi's fragile faith in him.

Anton can go to hell, but Raj can use Lasadi's indecision to their advantage now.

"It's fine." Raj brushes the backs of his fingers over her arm. "I'll go."

Lasadi shakes her head. "Raj. You don't have to do this."

"I do." He shifts closer to her, drops his voice. "Pretend to kiss me," he whispers, and she blinks at him, then tilts her head. Lifts her chin, and for a brief, shining moment he thinks she may actually do it. But her lips stop short — of course they do.

"Don't look yet," he murmurs. "Qacha's on the ledge above Bryant." Lasadi's nostrils flare, but otherwise she doesn't react. "She'll get the drop on the woman. Let me handle Bryant. Help Ruby."

"Enough!" Bryant yells.

Raj breaks the false kiss, lingering to tuck a strand of Lasadi's hair behind her ear. She's watching him with a curious expression, but he doesn't have time to analyze what she's thinking. He lets his fingers complete the gesture, but his gaze cuts to Jay over Lasadi's shoulder. Raj motions with his eyes to his left, indicating Scar, who still has his gun to Ruby's head. Jay nods faintly.

Raj turns away, trying not to wonder why Lasadi's touch lingers on his sleeve — adding some realism to the con, he imagines; she's a better actor than he initially gave her credit for. He kneels in front of the last statue before the waterfall, makes a show of trying to unlock it, then finally swings the face open and reaches into the hollow to grab the metal box.

He cracks it open as though checking what's inside, then gets back to his feet. Edges past Lasadi without touching her, walks past Ruby without decking Scar, passes by Blue and underneath the ledge Qacha is waiting on. He holds out the box to Bryant.

"Here's what you want," he says.

"Open it," growls Bryant. "Show me."

Raj looks back as Scar hauls Ruby back to her feet, turning them both to watch Raj open the box. He searches Ruby's face — she's angry, scared. And ready to fight. *Wait,* he tries to tell her, not willing to risk trying to signal to her. *Wait until I act.*

Scar seems to sense Ruby's intention to fight back, though, and he yanks her back; she stumbles, precipitously close to falling in the pool. "Can you swim?" he asks with a wry grin.

She wrenches herself away from him. "Get your fucking hands off me," she snarls, and Scar laughs.

"All right," he says, and shoves. Swings his pistol from her to Lasadi as Ruby tilts back, arms windmilling, falling to the pool.

And everything happens at once.

Ruby splashes into the water as Qacha crashes into the woman in blue with a wild howl that sweeps through the cavern, seeming to come from everywhere. A blast of plasma from Blue's carbine scorches one of the statues and catches Cyclops's shoulder. He screams, dropping his own weapon. A bullet from Lasadi's gun takes Scar between the eyes.

Raj pivots and drops the box as Bryant fires, ducking for cover with ears ringing. By the time he's turned back with his own gun in hand Bryant has scooped up the metal box and disappeared into the shadow of the tunnel, dragging Anton with him.

Raj spins back to the rest of the fight. Qacha is standing over Blue, whose neck is at an impossible angle. Jay has finished off Cyclops, and Scar is sprawled on the rocks, his blood threading its way into the river which seems already stained that color from the jasper.

Lasadi is sprawled on the stones, too — but she's not injured. She's lying flat on her belly, hand outstretched for Ruby. Raj kneels beside her, catching

Ruby's flailing hand in his own, and together they haul the dripping hacker out of the pool.

"We have to go," Qacha shouts. "We have to go *now*."

"We have to get the jewel," Lasadi says, but Qacha shakes her head.

"Run!" she shouts again.

Raj scrambles to his feet with Ruby's arm over his shoulder, his body following Qacha's frantic direction while his mind slowly begins to understand why. Somewhere beyond the rush of the waterfall he can hear someone whooping — Alex? — followed by the rumble of thunder.

Not thunder.

Explosives.

Raj wraps his arm around Ruby's waist, and together they run for the cave entrance, the rest of the crew on their tail. He remembers the trick stone at the entrance in time to sidestep it, but only because Jay yells his name. He splashes down into the pool outside the cleft in the cliff, Ruby's arm still tight around his neck; Jay and Lasadi jump down beside him.

The rumbling inside the chamber has become a dull roar, getting louder by the second

Qacha pauses at the entrance to the cleft, pulling out a utility knife. "Get back," she calls, then severs the vine and presses herself flat against the canyon wall. There's a sharp crack as the vines above the cave entrance shiver, the lattice of sharp stakes crashing to the ground along with a tumble of rocks. Raj doesn't understand why at first, not until the debris and shrapnel from the explosion inside the chamber crash into the new avalanche of sticks and boulders in the entryway, slowing its force enough to keep it from blasting over the small group in the pool outside.

The roar dies, fades to a murmur of clattering stones, settling earth, and trickling water as the river finds a route through the new debris cluttering the entrance to the chamber. The crystal clear water they're standing in begins to cloud with mud.

"Alex!" Ruby turns on Qacha, half in anguish, half in fury. "My brother is in there!"

"It's okay!" But it's not Qacha who answers. The voice floats down from the cliffs above. Raj cranes his neck to spot Alex perched among the foliage, waving his arm. He holds up a blue jewel. "I got it!"

"We couldn't figure out a way to get the device without blowing up the whole chamber," Qacha says. "So we went with this."

Lasadi frowns up at Alex, who's still grinning. "And what was . . . this?"

"A rudimentary pulley, with a weight set to release the instant Alex grabbed the jewel — it yanked him up and out of the blast." Qacha looks apologetic. "We were going to tell you the plan, but then Bryant showed up."

"And he still has Anton," Lasadi says. Her gaze sweeps around the little group, inscrutable when it lands on Raj. He can't tell if she's upset at his earlier ruse with the false kiss, or if she does actually believe the suspicion Bryant tried to cast his way. Yesterday he wouldn't have thought it possible, but Anton's been ferreting out the weaknesses in Raj's position with the crew since the very first day. And apparently it's started working on Lasadi.

"Let's go," she orders, turning away from Raj. "Alex! Meet us at the ship." He waves and vanishes into the jungle above.

"I'm going to murder that kid," Ruby mutters to Raj.

"He just got us our payday," Raj points out. "Surely that's worth a stay of execution. You all right?"

"I'm good." Ruby wipes her hands ineffectually on her soaking wet clothes, scraping back the curls that have escaped from her ponytail and plastered themselves to her cheeks. "But I'm done with water and caves. I'd rather take a spacewalk, and saints in hell I hate spacewalks."

"Swimming's fun, if you know how."

"You can keep it, arkie."

She means the slur in jest, he knows it. Doesn't keep it from slicing straight through the widening chinks in his armor.

The little crew splashes down the River of Blood, helping each other over the small drops and rapids, no longer caring how wet they get or marveling at the gorgeous jasper in the brighter sun of midmorning. Raj breathes a sigh of relief when they get to the ledge where the *Figment of the North* is parked and their rope is still in place.

He watches the others carefully as they climb. No one seems to be injured, and the day's adventure has made even the offworlders less tentative about the scramble back up the boulders. He gives Jay a boost up a particularly steep section, then turns to find Lasadi waiting for him.

His heart lurches at her mixed expression. They're standing on a small ledge, and she's as close to him now as she'd been in the cavern. And so much farther away.

Raj clears his throat. "About before," he says, then falters at how to phrase the next part.

"It was an act, I understand," Lasadi says before he can finish. Her expression is so stony he can't tell if the idea relieves or upsets her. "All part of the con."

"If you want it to be," he says, and her lips part in surprise. "Lasadi — "

But someone yells her name from above; Ruby's voice with an edge of panic.

"We can talk about this later," she says, and Raj gives her a carefree smile — so easy after a lifetime's practice pretending he doesn't mind being dismissed by the ones he wishes loved him.

"Okay, Cap," he says, boosting her the rest of the way. He finds his own handholds, muscles and uncalloused fingertips screaming, though not as loud as his own thoughts. For some reason Anton's words back in Icaba keep swirling in his mind: "They'll see through you in a heartbeat if they haven't already."

Lasadi clearly has. In the past, he'd have considered that his cue to move on. But now? Nothing says he can't make himself the kind of person who's worth knowing once you take off the masks.

The murmur of panicked voices cuts through his thoughts when he reaches the top, and no one's waiting to help haul him over the edge once he arrives. He wrenches himself up and over the ledge, getting gingerly into a crouch and dusting off his hands.

The *Figment of the North*, still parked where they left it, has been joined by a second plane, which must be

Bryant's. Bryant's body is lying facedown in the open door to his plane, and by the way Jay has his back to the body, they must not need to worry about him anymore.

The others are all gathered in a cluster around the ramp to the *Figment*, and the figure lying there with blood streaming down his face.

Anton.

# CHAPTER 23
## LASADI

LASADI DROPS TO HER KNEES BESIDE ANTON'S PRONE FORM, heart lurching in panic. His skin is ashen, the right side of his face sheeted in blood, his neck at what must be a painful angle. But his hand is still warm, his pulse faint. His breath so shallow it barely moves his chest.

He's injured, but he's alive; relief washes through her.

"Get me the medkit," she says to Qacha. She smooths a thumb over Anton's cheek, takes the wad of gauze Qacha hands her to daub blood away from the wound on his temple. There's so much blood, but at least the cut is shallow, and it hasn't yet started to swell. She presses the gauze there, holding Anton's face as his eyelids begin to flutter, as his breath catches, his mouth working unconscious syllables — her name, she realizes with a start — before he finally opens his eyes.

Anton blinks at her. "Lasadi?" He reaches a shaky hand to stroke her cheek. "Oh, thank the old ones you're all right."

"Careful." His wound must be bad, she's never heard him invoke the old ones. "You've had a nasty blow to the head."

"I'll be okay." He takes over pressing the gauze against his temple, giving her fingers a quick squeeze of thanks. He struggles upright, and for a split second she considers ordering him to stay lying down, but she's seen him injured before. His pride will be as wounded as his head, and he won't welcome her trying to mother him. He winces as he sits up, hand going to his ribs.

"What happened?" she asks.

"Bryant didn't open the box until we got back," Anton says. He closes his eyes a moment; Lasadi puts a hand on his shoulder to steady him. He coughs into his handkerchief, wipes away blood, and Lasadi's heart lurches again. He must be more badly hurt than he's letting on. "But when he saw Theo's note inside he lost it. He had been planning to take me hostage, I think, but he turned on me then. I fought back, and . . . well."

"He's dead," Jay confirms, though there hadn't been much question given the amount of blood.

"I tried to get to the *Figment* to stop my own bleeding," says Anton. "But he must have hit me harder than I thought. I'll be fine." He turns a look of pure worry on Lasadi. "I heard an explosion and feared the worst."

"We're all right," she says. "And Alex got the device."

"Fuck that thing," Anton says. "Fuck Theo and his tricks. If you'd been hurt — "

"I'm fine." Lasadi sits back on her heels, suddenly exhausted. "How did Bryant know to come after us?"

"He'd spent time on the *Figment*," Ruby says. "And

BLOOD RIVER BLUES   233

he'd've known Theo. Maybe he had an idea what Theo found out here, then overheard us talking about it."

"Maybe," Lasadi says. She doesn't like that possibility, but she likes the alternative even less: one of them told Bryant. No one here has a reason to betray Anton and the NMLF. Even with what Anton said about Raj yesterday — that he was searching for a way to get back to his family? Lasadi understands how strong that pull can be. But she can't see it. Not Raj.

"Even if he knew, it still doesn't answer how he found us here," Qacha says. "He might have seen Theodor's maps on the *Figment*, but he didn't have the journal we had to decipher them. And he definitely didn't follow us."

"Bryant said there was a beacon."

"I scanned the whole ship before we left," Jay says. "So did the race officials. It wasn't there when we left, which means . . ." Jay obviously doesn't want to voice the alternative.

"He found us somehow," Lasadi says. "Figure it out."

"On it," says Ruby. She's stripped off her soaked jacket and dragged her hair into a ponytail to try to tame it, but stray curls are already trying to escape as they dry. She pulls a scanner out of her dry bag and switches it on, walking around the far side of the hull.

"Qacha, Jay, check over the systems to make sure Bryant didn't do anything to our ship. Alex? Go put that device in the safest place you can find. Raj, make sure we're wrapped up here, we need to get airborne."

Anton's trying to stand now, hand pressed to the cut on his scalp. Lasadi helps support him, his arm heavy warmth on her shoulders, his breath ragged against her cheek.

"Ruby!" Jay calls from inside the *Figment*, and Ruby rushes up the ramp past them. A moment later, she curses.

"Found the tracker." Ruby appears in the door, a round device in the center of her palm. "It was hidden in the hold. Alliance tech."

"It was *in* the ship? How?" Lasadi studies Jay, who's also emerged from the *Figment*. His expression is cold; he knows exactly what this means. It wasn't slapped on the hull at one of the checkpoints — it was inside. The problem is every person who's been in this ship since Jay and the race officials scanned it back in Moie is standing on this ledge. And Lasadi trusts each and every one of them with her life.

"And how did Bryant get Alliance tech?" Anton asks.

Lasadi glances at Raj without meaning to, and the pure hurt in his expression knifes through her.

"It wasn't me," Raj says. "I know what Bryant said back there, but he was messing with us."

"You didn't set the beacon this morning?"

"When would I have?" Raj says, sharp.

"You were alone in the ship while the rest of us were climbing down the cliff," Anton says. "You could have activated the beacon then."

"And what — get my own crew killed?" Color blazes in Raj's cheeks. "I think we all know who we don't trust here: the man with the failing senatorial campaign who's been receiving huge donations from an anonymous source. Ruby, tell them what we found."

"We've found the donations," Ruby says with a nervous glance at Raj. "I haven't been able to trace where they're from, only. They're encrypted."

"They're from the NMLF," Anton says. "I'll admit, I don't have the luxury to help them for free even though we fight for the same cause. I'm in the middle of a hard campaign, and they want me to retain my seat as much as anyone. Vasavada will verify it when we arrive back at Icaba." He turns to Lasadi. "Are you really taking the word of this deserter over mine? He'd do anything to make things better with his father."

"I'm not taking anyone's word yet," Lasadi says.

Anton lifts an eyebrow. "Perhaps you don't know Raj's father has been putting his name on the bounty boards."

Lasadi frowns at Raj. "Is that true?"

"Of course not," Raj snaps, then shakes his head. "I mean, yes, my father's put my name on the bounty boards. Yes, I need to make things right with him. But I wouldn't sell you out to do it." He turns to the others. "Maybe you all remember how Bryant was about to murder me back there?"

"He wasn't going to murder you," Alex points out. "He was about to take you with him and strand the rest of us."

"Alex!" Ruby gasps.

Alex's eyes widen as he realizes how that came off. "Sorry, Raj. I mean, I don't think you did it. But that's what happened." He looks at his sister. "He didn't," he says, but it sounds like a question. "It's Raj, everybody."

It's Raj, yes. And Lasadi can't believe he would

endanger them all, but the evidence is clear: one of them planted the beacon and set it off this morning. She's been playing her memories of the morning through while the rest of them talk; any of them had an opportunity alone in the *Figment* to turn on the beacon. The fact it's Alliance tech probably rules out Qacha — what tech the NMLF aren't manufacturing themselves they've been getting from non-Alliance countries like Teguça and New Sarjun. She also can't imagine Qacha acting outside of orders, and Lasadi doesn't see the advantage to the NMLF in ordering the double-cross and murder of a Coruscan senator.

Jay's obviously not the traitor, she trusts him with her life. Ruby's face in the cave said she truly thought she might die — she's a good actress, but Lasadi can't think of a single motive she'd have to sell them out. And unless Alex is hiding a serious mastermind under that happy-go-lucky facade, she can rule him out, too.

Leaving Anton and Raj. She's fond of Raj. She's attracted to him. And that doesn't matter, because now is the time to think with her brain rather than being swayed by her heart. Raj is Arquellian, like Bryant. He's a deserter who has every reason to want to get back in the good graces of his father — and to stop the attempts on his life. Anton, on the other hand, is a Coruscan hero of the people. A man of pure conviction. A man who will do anything — absolutely anything — if it's in service to the cause.

Lasadi doesn't know Raj as well as she wishes she did. But she knows Anton better than she knows her own mind.

She turns to Jay, tilting her chin at Raj. "Cuff him."

Jay goes still. "Las."

"That was an order," she says. "You remember Jerez City."

"Lasadi — " But Jay cuts himself off, realization dawning on his face at the reference. When he turns back to Raj his dark eyes are flint. He holds out his hand.

"Your gun, man."

"Are you fucking serious right now." Raj isn't talking to Jay, though; Lasadi forces herself to look him in the eye, steeling herself against the storm of confusion and hurt brewing there.

"Don't make this worse for yourself," she says. Her jaw aches from clenching it. "Or for the rest of us. Someone here called Bryant, and there's no one else it could possibly be."

Some bright spark flares out between them, leaving a chill colder than the blast of air that had rushed from the cave after the explosion, and a silence just as deafening. The expression on Raj's face isn't anger. It's betrayal, so pure and wounded it breaks her heart.

"Raj," she says. "Give Jay your gun."

And she turns away, unable to watch Jay cuff him. She stalks up the ramp and drops into the pilot's seat. "Everybody strap in," she yells back, counting her breaths, calling up her checklists, ignoring Qacha's concern. Losing herself in the process of flight before she loses herself to the flood of emotion that threatens to overwhelm her.

She fires up the engine as soon as Jay gives her the all clear, certainty in her decision rising as does the *Figment of the North.*

# CHAPTER 24
## LASADI

Lifting off the ledge in the bright morning light is far easier than landing in the dark had been, though Sevi Bryant's ship on the ledge makes it a bit harder to maneuver. As does the torment racing through Lasadi's mind.

"Head due west, towards that mountain with the bald patch," Qacha says once they've evened out. Her voice is strained. "We'll head to the south of it. Our next checkpoint is about an hour's flight. Captain?" The younger woman's lips are drawn in a tight line.

"What is it?"

"I apologize for letting the beacon be placed in the ship."

"We all did," Lasadi says. "That's the nature of traitors, they masquerade as your friend until the moment comes to sink a knife in your back."

"Then who do you trust?" Qacha asks.

"Yourself. And your gut." And Lasadi's gut says this whole situation is very, very wrong. Sevi Bryant showing up to steal the cloaking device out from under them is one part of the betrayal, but somehow she can't keep from thinking it's only the whiskers of the mouse. "Did you and Jay find anything out of the ordinary when you checked through the systems?"

Qacha shakes her head. "Bryant didn't mess with our ship — at least not that I can tell."

"He probably figured they'd kill us all and take it home with them. Did you check comms?"

"Hold on." Qacha calls up the screen. "All good. Just — oh."

Lasadi double-checks their connection to make sure they're alone on this channel. No one is in the seats directly behind them. Anton has cleaned himself up and is conferring with Jay near the back; Ruby and Alex are sitting nearby in uncomfortable silence. Raj has been cuffed and strapped into a seat, Jay keeping watch on them all with a gun laid on his thigh.

Lasadi's mind is racing. Jay will follow her lead, as will Qacha. She obviously doesn't have to worry about Anton having a change of heart when it comes to Raj. But Ruby and Alex are a problem. Raj was their friend first, which makes them wild cards. She'll need to talk to them before they do something stupid.

"What did you find?" Lasadi asks Qacha.

"There was a call put out, through our main system, while we were gone. Through a guest login."

"If it was Bryant, why wouldn't he use his own ship's comms?"

"The *Figment*'s comm is more powerful than your standard bush plane," Qacha says. "And whoever sent this message wasn't pinging locally — this was a private communication on a tightbeam to someone in orbit."

"To who?"

Qacha shakes her head, and Lasadi opens the group channel. "Ruby, come up here a sec."

Ruby startles — Lasadi caught her deep in worry — but slips off her harness and heads to the front. Lasadi half listens to Qacha's next set of instructions as they glide past the mountain with the bald patch and find the next landmark to guide them to the final checkpoint before they return to Moie.

Ruby slips into the seat behind Qacha's. "Las — Captain. About Raj — "

"Qacha found an outgoing communication I didn't authorize," she says, cutting Ruby off. "Potentially a private beam to orbit. Can you see who the recipient was? And keep this quiet until we know what's going on."

Ruby gives her a long, dark look, then grabs her tablet and starts typing. The *Figment*'s nav panel chimes to let Lasadi know Ruby's logged into the system.

"Okay," Ruby says after a moment. "It definitely was sent to a location in orbit. I'm cross-referencing with the flight paths of any registered ships that could have been in that location. I'll work on decrypting the message, too. But it could have been triggered to send while we were out." Ruby looks up. "Any one of us could have done."

"Only one of us did," says Lasadi. "Figure out when it was sent, and who it went to."

Lasadi pushes her speed as she flies, the jungle slipping beneath her, but her mind is no longer on the race.

They've set a course for the final checkpoint before returning to Moie — as they'd planned to this morning before Anton accused Raj of betraying them all and everything she knew about the world imploded — but she doesn't care about the Star Run anymore.

Everything has gone so, so wrong with this job, and cracks are splintering this barely formed team at the suspicion that one of their own had betrayed them. "Trust your gut," she'd told Qacha. But now the whole fate of this mission — of this crew — rests on Lasadi Cazinho's warped sense of who to trust, dismantled so many times over the years, she barely trusts herself.

She's startled out of her thoughts by Ruby's low whistle. "The call went to the flagship of the Alliance navy."

"Raj's father's ship," Qacha says.

"He defected," snaps Ruby.

Lasadi glances back at her. "Anton told me he intercepted a message Raj sent yesterday morning, to that same ship. To his father."

"Yesterday morning?" Ruby looks puzzled, but not surprised.

"You knew about it?"

"We talked yesterday morning," Ruby says. "He promised me he'd call his dad, but I didn't think he had. But it wasn't to sell us out, Captain. Anton was right, Raj's had headhunters after him. I've been helping keep his name off the boards, but it'll not stop until he talks to his father."

Lasadi keeps her gaze on the horizon, keeps the *Figment* level as her thoughts despite the jagged uneven hills, the soaring peaks, the vast and verdant canyons. "Did you decode the message?"

"Got it, Captain." She holds the tablet out, and Lasadi glances down at the words on the screen. Tonight — followed by a set of coordinates for a location on Indira.

A chill touches the back of Lasadi's neck.

"Where is that?" Qacha asks. She's scouring her maps, but Lasadi knows those coordinates already — they're only a few numbers off from the ones Anton gave her when she was flying down in the *Nanshe*'s shuttle.

"Icaba," says Lasadi.

"Exactly," says Ruby. "Which is where Anton has gotten the leaders of the NMLF to meet him tonight in order to hand over the device."

"How do you know that?" Lasadi looks back in surprise; Ruby's gnawing on her lower lip.

"I intercepted Anton's messages," she says.

"On your own?"

"Raj asked me to. But Captain."

Lasadi returns her attention to the horizon, willing the pieces to fall into place faster. "Which means Raj knew about the meeting, too."

"*Captain*," Ruby hisses. "Lasadi. You have to listen to me. Raj wouldn't."

"Back in the bar at the *Golden Macaw*," Lasadi says. "You remember? You called me a hopeless romantic?"

Ruby nods, slow.

"Prove me right."

Ruby's lips part, but she doesn't answer. She understands, Lasadi thinks — or at least Lasadi has made her angry enough she'll find the answers Lasadi needs out of spite. Ruby presses herself back against her seat with a scowl of concentration, calling up a new screen on her tablet.

"We have to warn them," Qacha says a moment later. "If the Alliance is on their way to Icaba, we have to tell Commander Vasavada."

"Get word to her. Tell her we need a new secure meeting point."

"Yes, Captain." Qacha starts to open a channel, then stills.

"What is it?"

"Icaba," Qacha says simply. "Even if the leadership committee isn't there, the Alliance is still coming."

"I know," Lasadi says; it's all she's been able to think about since she realized a message had gone out to the Alliance flagship. "I saw what they did to Tannis, and I won't let them destroy Icaba. Let me think."

She keeps flying while Qacha receives the new coordinates from Vasavada, homing in on the fifth and final checkpoint of the Liluri Star Run. They're surely out of the running after how much time they spent in the jungle — Peter Fangio was their closest rival, but he must be well past this final checkpoint now. That's the farthest thing from Lasadi's mind at the moment, though. The race doesn't matter. The cloaking device doesn't matter. The traitor in her hold doesn't matter.

What matters now is keeping the Alliance from razing the town of Icaba the way they rained down fire on Tannis. She couldn't stop them then, but she can do something now.

A new ping from the comms captures Lasadi's attention. She's expecting the dockmaster at the fifth check-point — they're close enough — but instead it's Peter Fangio.

"*Figment*, it's good to see you," he says, cheerful voice streaked faint with static. "I was rallying them to send out a search party."

She frowns at the incoming town through the cockpit window, trying to make out Fangio's ship among the others at the distant dockyard. "Why aren't you well on your way to Moie, *Wager*?"

"Bum thruster cost us time this morning in White Rock, so we figured you'd've beat us here by hours. A bit worried when you hadn't — get lost in the jungle, did you?"

"Something like that."

Another channel opens — this time it is the dock-master. "*Figment of the North*, we've got you in view. You're cleared to land."

Qacha reaches for the comms button to respond, but Lasadi holds out a hand.

"Plot the fastest course to Icaba."

"But we're almost there," Qacha says. "If we don't land, it'll cause all sorts of red flags. They'll ask questions."

"We want them to." Lasadi tilts her head at Qacha; the little town is approaching, the dock-master pinging them again to request a response. "Do you want to be a hero for New Manila?" Qacha's eyes widen. "Then get in touch with a reporter called Joli Sainz. She's back in Moie right now covering the race." Lasadi hits the comms button on the dash. "Thank you, Dockmaster, but

*Figment* declines to land. Something more important has come up."

Fangio's channel pings once more. "What the hell are you doing, Mercury?"

"There are more important things out there than winning races, Fangio," Lasadi says. "Do me a favor, yeah? Get yourself a podium in Moie, and while you're up there, tell the world what the Alliance is about to do to the town of Icaba."

# CHAPTER 25
## RAJ

Raj thought he was going to die at the hands of the NMLF once before; now he's sure of it.

When Jay snapped cuffs around Raj's wrists back at the River of Blood, Raj hadn't struggled — in part because he'd been so surprised at the sudden turn of suspicion, in part because he assumed it was part of some plan he hadn't been let in on yet.

Nowhere in his mind did he think he'd be entering a nightmare scenario where his crew — where *Lasadi* — actually *did* suspect him of putting a beacon on their own ship. Of working with Sevi Bryant and trying to get them all killed.

Maybe Anton's wormed his way into Lasadi's mind, into Jay's mind, pushed them into viewing him as the enemy they fought together and not the friend he's become. But Ruby? Alex? The kid was watching Raj the whole flight like he wanted to help but wasn't sure who to believe. And Ruby went up to talk to Lasadi and

Qacha early in the trip and hasn't spared him another glance since.

The *Figment of the North* touches down with a jolt, the ramp opening to reveal not the town of Icaba, but a shady emerald clearing in the middle of the jungle. Tall, thick-trunked trees stretch sinewy into the canopy, dripping with vines; a blast of humid air slaps Raj across the face. A handful of small aircraft are here already, and a dozen NMLF soldiers in fatigues wait for them outside, rifles in their hands. Commander Vasavada stands slightly apart from them, speaking with three older soldiers.

"C'mon," Jay murmurs; he might be about to say something else, but Anton's watching them, a self-satisfied smile on his face. Raj ignores the asshole politician, focuses on the man he thought was his friend.

"Jay," Raj says. "Listen to me. You know me."

Jay's mouth sets in a thin line, hands stilling on the buckle at the center of Raj's chest. But it's Anton who answers. "I think we all know you, Mr. Demetriou. You're a cliché. An Arquellian coward who deserted his crew once before, and was willing to do it again in a heartbeat. What did Bryant offer you? A better buyer? Or were you just using Bryant to dispose of your own crew so you could take the device back to the Alliance?"

"I wasn't working with Bryant," Raj says through clenched teeth.

A smile curls the corner of Anton's lip. "A play to get your father to take you back?"

"Anton," Lasadi snaps before Raj can answer; she's waiting for them by the ramp. "I'll do the talking."

Raj straightens. "Las."

Something flickers over her face — grief at his betrayal? Or simply resolve. "Bring him," she tells Jay.

"Lasadi. You have to fucking listen to me."

"I *said*, I'll do the talking," she says, then turns her back. "Gag him if he's not going to keep his mouth shut," she calls over her shoulder.

Raj surges against the harness, but it holds; Jay flinches back. "You better gag me, Kamiya," Raj snarls. Willing the other man to give a shit about what's about to happen. Willing him to remember they're crew. "Because I'm sure as hell not going quietly."

Anton grabs a wad of gauze from the med kit. "I've heard enough of that accent," he says, shoving the cloth into Raj's mouth and tying it roughly with a strip of fabric. A muscle jumps in Jay's jaw, but he doesn't stop Anton. When Anton's done, Jay releases Raj's harness and helps Anton haul Raj to his feet.

Raj fights them down the ramp — until a dozen rifles lift. Raj freezes, his blood still boiling but the certainty settling in.

He's going to die in New Manila, and he's worn so many masks that the people he thought were crew act like they don't even know him anymore. Maybe they don't. Maybe they never did. Either way, he's been too scared to reveal his true self, and he's going to die without a last chance.

He's been so focused on Jay that it takes him a moment to realize the three figures in NMLF fatigues near Vasavada aren't lowly soldiers. They're wearing the same uniform as the rest, but their faces are covered by red scarves. One man tall and thin, one short and stocky, and an older woman with silver threaded through her black braids. Raj knows that trio of figures. He knows their noms de guerre, though he's never seen their faces — no one has. The secretive leadership committee of the NMLF, commanders Abi, Beram, and Cael.

In his anger and confusion he'd almost forgotten: Anton had arranged to meet them in Icaba to give them the device in person. Given the fact that their meeting has changed locations, they must have realized the danger in time.

His relief is short-lived; understanding sinks through him like a stone.

Raj will no longer be under suspicion just for trying to steal the device. They'll assume he intended to kill the NMLF leadership committee, as well.

"Welcome back," Vasavada says to Anton and Lasadi. "I take it you were successful?"

"We were, Commander," Anton answers. He turns to the committee, holds out the device to the woman — Commander Abi. It glimmers blue in the palm of her hand. "Anton Kato. It's a pleasure to meet you all in person."

"This device could change the course of the war," Abi says. "It seemed worth the risk to meet."

Anton gives her a bright smile. "Getting it was a fascinating tale. I look forward to telling you over dinner.

"We shouldn't linger," says the tall man, Commander Beram. "It's good you got here sooner than expected."

"That was my decision," says Lasadi. "Once we realized the original meeting was compromised."

"A sound decision," Anton says before he turns back to the committee. "I'm glad the change in plans didn't disrupt your schedule. Still. We still have much to discuss about the future partnership between our two causes. I hoped we could spend some time in conversation."

"We'll discuss it," says the stocky man. Commander Cael's voice is raspy and familiar; it's he who most often voices their announcements and manifestos. He turns to Raj, piercing him with blue eyes. "It seems you had trouble." Those eyes are stony, impassive. The look of someone who would execute him in cold blood and sit down to an unbothered breakfast.

It's the same look his father had given him, right before he'd ordered Raj be thrown in the brig for threatening to tell the world the Alliance was about to bomb civilians at Tannis. Raj will never forget that expression: calm, unworried. Almost disinterested in his son's fate. Had his father known then that he would order his own son killed? Had he already made the calculation that winning the war was more important in the end? Did he already have a story in mind to tell Raj's mother?

Raj won't get a chance to ask him, now.

"There was a traitor in our midst," Anton says to the committee. "An Arquellian. Trying to steal the device for the Alliance instead."

Raj growls at him, frustrated by his inability to speak for himself; a half-dozen rifles swing to his chest and he stills.

"He has connections," says Vasavada. "His father's an admiral."

"His death would send a message," says Abi.

"Or escalate the Alliance's response before we're ready," says Beram. "He would make a valuable hostage."

"Or a complicated one," points out Cael. "Why would we treat him different from any other traitor?"

"If you'll excuse me, Commanders." Lasadi has stepped forward, and whether it's intentional or not, she's shielding Raj from the raised rifles. "The reason I made the decision to return early was because I feared even if we secured the committee's safety, the Alliance might still act against Icaba like they did Tannis. We have an idea of how to stop them."

Lasadi glances at Raj, and he didn't think it was possible to feel even more betrayed. But she has one more arrow she can use against him, doesn't she? She knows what's in his sealed court-martial records — that he was found guilty in absentia of destroying the medical transport that sparked the Battle of Tannis — and she's going to use it to seal his fate.

"What is it, soldier?" Abi asks.

"We need to deal with the traitor first," Lasadi says. She turns back to Raj, reaching to untie the gag. Where Anton had been rough, Lasadi's fingers are careful as they disentangle the knot from strands of his hair. The gentleness ends in her fingers, though — her expression is still hard, her jaw is set firm.

Raj spits the gag onto the ground, working saliva back over his tongue and waiting for her to speak.

She doesn't.

"You know me, Las," he finally says.

"Do I?" Her eyes flash pain. "We've just met. And Anton, I've known him since I was twenty. You're a grifter and a deserter. He's a war hero and a senator. Which one of you should I trust?"

Raj could shout this — gods he wants to. But he keeps his voice pitched low. This is for her, only. "I know I haven't told you everything," he murmurs. "I know I haven't been completely open with you. But you know one thing about me: I would never hurt you. I would never hurt Jay. Ruby. Alex. Any of you. If I haven't shown you that, then I deserve what comes next."

She studies his face a moment, then leans in. "I do know that," she says — or he thinks she says, it's so quiet he's not sure he heard her.

She turns away, and he realizes with a sinking heart that he most definitely misheard. Because what she says to the committee is:

"We have an Alliance traitor to make an example of."

The rifles rise again, pointing at Raj, and he can't remember how to breathe. This is it, his final moment, and he can't think of any of the prayers his mother used to hide from his father. The gag's gone, but he doesn't have any last words — or know why it would matter to speak them, since the only people who will hear are former friends who now apparently believe beyond doubt he's the kind of man who would betray them.

He straightens his spine, ready to meet his death with dignity. The fear will be worse, he tells himself. The fear will be harder to weather than the hail of bullets about to tear into him.

*Do it*, he wills the soldiers, *Make it fast.*

Lasadi glances his way, so brief and cold his heart

would break if it wasn't in pieces at her feet already. And she turns to Anton, like she was always going to in the end. The asshole is smiling at her with a possessive gleam in his eyes, like he knows he won, like she's some prize instead of the complicated, razor-sharp woman Raj missed his chance to be good enough for.

Lasadi raises a single finger to brush against Anton's chest.

"You," she says, and his smile falters. "The traitor is you."

# CHAPTER 26
## LASADI

SHE DOESN'T BOTHER TO SEE HOW ANYONE ELSE TAKES THE revelation — all Lasadi wants is to enjoy the wash of shock, fear, and fury over Anton's face as he processes what she's said.

"What fantasy is this?" he asks.

"It's the truth, Anton," she says. "You've been working with the Alliance this whole time."

His eyes narrow. "I want you to be very, very clear you're choosing an Arquellian defector's word over mine."

"I'm extremely clear." She takes a step back, but she doesn't let down her guard. "Ruby? Tell them what you found."

Ruby clears her throat. "Anton's been receiving large, anonymous campaign donations. I couldn't trace them at first, but he told us they're from the NMLF." She turns to Commander Vasavada. "And that you'd confirm it."

Vasavada shares a look with the three members of the NMLF leadership committee, but doesn't answer.

"I got the key I needed to trace the deposits about an hour ago," Ruby says. "They're from the Alliance."

"Lies." Anton laughs like he's in complete shock at the absurdity of the accusations.

"Qacha?" Lasadi prompts.

The NMLF soldier steps forward, saluting Vasavada and the committee. "Commanders," she says, voice clear and spine straight. "When we returned to the *Figment*, we discovered a coded transmission had been sent to a vessel in orbit — the Alliance flagship. The message contained two pieces of information: the coordinates to Icaba, and a time. Tonight. I traced the time of the message, and it was sent right before we all returned." She turns to Anton, apologetic. "While you were alone at the *Figment*."

"I was unconscious!" Anton says.

"You weren't," Lasadi says. "The cut on your temple came from a knife, not a blow. When you realized the device wasn't in the box, you killed Bryant so he couldn't talk, then made it seem like you'd been injured."

For the first time, Anton's expression shifts into uncertainty; it shivers through Lasadi like an earthquake, leaving cracks in the foundation of her world. Some part of her had expected him to have an explanation, she realizes, some secret master plan he hadn't let her in on yet. But no. There's a glimmer of real fear simmering beneath his anger. All the facts she and Ruby and Qacha are laying out amount to the naked truth. He betrayed them, nothing more complicated or honorable about it.

"Anton Kato laid a trap for you," Lasadi says, turning to meet the gazes of the three NMLF committee members. "He found something so valuable it would lure you out of hiding to meet with him in person, and then he tipped the Alliance off to where you'd be, and when."

"We agreed to contribute to his campaign, but after the device was delivered," says Commander Cael.

"He was insistent we stay for dinner," notes Beram.

Abi lifts her chin, dark eyes glittering. "Is all this true, Senator Kato?"

"Of course not!" Anton gives Lasadi a withering look, then turns back to Commander Abi. "I'm the most anti-Alliance senator in Corusca. I don't know how the Arquellian found out about our meeting, but he's the one who sent the message."

"I'm the one who found out about the meeting," Ruby says. "Because I hacked into your messages. Even after I traced the donation to the Alliance I couldn't figure out why — it's a lot of risk for some money, only. But then I found this." She flicks on the mini holoprojector in her palm, and a bust flickers into view. Lasadi doesn't recognize the old woman with the shaved head, gold hoop earrings, and piercing blue eyes, but she knows the name when Ruby says, "Felice Evander, Alliance ambassador to Corusca. You need to do more than delete a message from your comm if you want it to disappear forever."

"I don't know whose bed you crawled into, Kato," Evander is saying, her voice rough-edged with static and age, her figure flickering in the humid jungle air. "But whatever you offered the gold stars back home must be pretty valuable. I've been authorized to provide you with the support you need to pass the Limitations Act. We'll discuss details once you've returned from your trip."

"You'd do anything for the cause," Lasadi says to Anton. "But your cause stops at Corusca's borders, doesn't it?"

Lasadi's been waiting for the moment when the realization kicks in, when Anton understands this isn't a joke. And there it is — the sharp intake of breath, his nostrils flaring. He reaches for his gun with one hand, for her arm with the other, but she's faster.

She whirls into him, left hand held like a blade and snapping into his wrist as he raises the gun to her head — it goes flying out of his grip, and she breaks his hold on her arm easily and steps back, her own pistol in her hands and aimed between his eyes.

"It's over, Anton," she says, quiet.

Vasavada raises her chin to two of the soldiers on her left, and they step forward to cuff Anton's hands behind his back.

"We'll deal with him," says Abi.

"You should go immediately," Lasadi says. She holsters her weapon and glances back at her crew. Jay has uncuffed Raj, and she can't bear the wounded look he gives her: *You didn't trust me enough to let me know what was going on?*

She had trusted him. But she hadn't trusted herself to convince Anton to play along, not unless she put her all into the ruse. If Anton had suspected, he could have contacted the Alliance again and changed the plan, and the NMLF leadership committee could have been caught by them anyway.

She'd done the only thing she thought would work at the time. Doesn't mean it was the right thing.

"Icaba office to Commander Vasavada."

A voice from Vasavada's gauntlet cuts through Lasadi's thoughts.

"Vasavada here."

"Someone's requesting permission to land in Icaba," says the voice. "She says she's a reporter."

Qacha grins. "She came!" And at Vasavada's lifted eyebrow, Qacha straightens her spine again. "We knew we needed to come straight here to warn the committee the Alliance are on their way, but even if they got out in time, the captain and I worried what they might do to Icaba."

"It wouldn't be the first time they'd shelled civilians to make an example of what happens if you harbor guerrillas," Lasadi says, and she can't help but turn to Anton again, trying to find the man she used to know beneath. Hadn't he been as horrified as she was at how the Alliance leveled Tannis? All those lives lost, simply because the CLA had chosen to make their base in the Tannis Valley. Though, maybe those lives were just another step on his way to power, sacrificed as easily as he'd tried to sacrifice Lasadi and her crew today.

She wants to be shocked, but she's been through this before — along with everyone under her command on Mercury Squadron. She'd told herself back then it was for the good of the cause. But had it been? Or has everything actually been just for the good of Anton?

The Limitations Act would loosen the Alliance's noose around Corusca, but is it worth it if it comes at the expense of New Manila's freedom? She knows what the Anton she'd fallen in love with as a young woman would have said — she still has his early speeches memorized. *Where one group suffers under Alliance rule, we all do.*

Had he ever believed the lofty ideals she'd idolized him for? Or had his rhetoric always been a path to power?

Lasadi doesn't have it in her to care; her loyalty now is to her crew, the crew she's shattered to make her own point. A hollow ache eats at her gut. Maybe she's learned more from Anton than she thought.

She forces away the thought, turning back to the committee. "We knew people would wonder what happened if we left the race abruptly. A reporter had been trying to interview me back in Moie, so I had Qacha call her and explain the situation."

"I told her I was a member of the NMLF Committee for Community in Icaba," Qacha says. "Racing in the Star Run to demonstrate a more unified New Manila. I said the Alliance was going to make an example of Icaba, and I had to leave the race to warn my people, and I invited her to see the community projects we've built here for herself. I apologize, Commander, if I overstepped."

Vasavada lifts a hand. "Let her land," she says over the radio. "And let's give her the best tour we can. She can broadcast it live, we have nothing to hide. Let the Alliance know there are eyes on what they're about to do in Icaba."

"And we'll be on our way out," says Abi. She holds out a hand to Lasadi. "Thank you for your heroism."

Lasadi shakes her head. "I'm just flying these days. The real heroes are here fighting."

"You should go as well," Vasavada says once Commanders Abi, Beram, and Cael head across the clearing to their separate planes. A handful of soldiers are accompanying them, marching Anton along. "Your presence might cause distracting questions. I'll have someone take you to your shuttles."

"I'll do it," says Qacha quick, with a glance at Alex. "That is — "

Vasavada follows Qacha's gaze with a faint smile. "Hurry back," she says, kind. "You have a reporter to talk with."

Lasadi is glad for the excuse to leave — she wants to put as much distance as she can between this place and herself. It's not New Manila she wants to run from, though. It's the person she knows she's wounded. Raj will be returning with her to the *Nanshe*, and she doesn't know the first thing about how to make amends.

To all of them, not just him. Two nights ago she was worried about harming their newfound bond by going out to a simple dinner with Raj; today she may have shattered the fledgling crew beyond repair.

She may not be able to make this right, but she has to try. No more running away.

Lasadi shakes Vasavada's hand. "Thank you for your hospitality, Commander. And best of luck."

"Luck to you all." Vasavada nods at each member of

the crew individually, giving an extra bow of respect to Raj before turning to her own plane.

Lasadi turns to Qacha. "Can we stop in town before we go to the shuttle? I need some supplies."

It's going to be a difficult conversation regardless, but she can at least start with a peace offering.

# CHAPTER 27
## RAJ

RAJ HAS NEVER BEEN HAPPIER TO SEE INDIRA'S CLOUDS swirling below him, a veil over the brilliant blues, emerald greens, snowy whites of the planet's surface. Last time he left Indira was on a troop transport; he'd craned his neck to make out the outline of his homeland. Today his attention is captured by the bright speck above them, growing brighter and larger by the minute in the screen of the shuttle he and Jay are sharing.

The *Nanshe*, waiting in orbit for them all to return home.

Lasadi and the others have already docked. Now a prompt on the controls asks if they want to engage the auto-docking systems, and Jay hits Y and leans back in his seat. Takes a deep breath.

"I'm sorry." Jay glances at Raj, then back to monitor the controls. "About the ruse back there. That was pretty shitty."

"You're both better actors than I gave you credit

for," Raj says. "I legitimately thought you were handing me over to the NMLF to die."

Jay winces.

"I meant that as a compliment."

"I want you to know I never suspected you for a minute."

"Thanks, man. Lasadi did, though."

Jay rubs his jaw as he considers. "She would have considered all the possibilities," he finally says. "But by the time she told me to cuff you she'd made up her mind it was Anton."

"How do you know? Ah — wait. Jerez City." Raj has been there. It's hardly worth the name *city*, it's a crime-infested junk pit bored into the core of Artemis. "You weren't going to cuff me until she said 'remember Jerez City.'"

Jay smiles. "Job we pulled for Nico about a year ago. He'd sent us there to escort one of his business partners back with a shipment. It was clear pretty quick the partner was going to double-cross Nico, so Lasadi tried to get out ahead of it. Confronted him. The guy rabbited before we could pin him down, and even though we made it back with the goods, it was six months before the guy came back to the surface — and when he did he took out a couple of Nico's people. Nobody we knew personally, but I don't think Lasadi's forgiven herself."

"If you'd gotten the guy back to Nico without tipping your hand, Nico would have handled him."

"Yep." Jay leans forward to answer a prompt from the auto-docking system.

"Are you okay?"

"What?"

"Anton," Raj says. "You have a lot of history there."

Jay frowns as though it hasn't occurred to him to think about how to feel. "I wish I was surprised," he finally says. "He was a powerful man to follow. So intoxicated by himself that it was hard not to be, too, you know? Like there's still a part of me that thinks *I'm* the one who's wrong for questioning him."

He's quiet a long time, and Raj lets him sit with his thoughts, both of them watching the *Nanshe* fill the screen.

"Blind faith feels good," Jay finally says. "I miss believing in something so strong — the cause, and the man who represented the cause. I guess part of me wanted that again."

"I get that," Raj says.

Jay looks at him sidelong. "Did you believe in your cause? During the war?"

Raj considers his response to the unexploded mine in front of him, a dozen answers on the tip of his tongue and all of them lies he's tossed off over the last few years. None of those lies come easily now, though. Even if they did, he's going to tell Jay the truth.

"Wholeheartedly," Raj says. "Until I realized how wrong I was to believe in any cause without questioning it."

Jay smiles faintly. "Fucking Alliance scum."

"You lost your chance to turn me in to Vasavada."

"She'd've had to step over my dead body for you." Jay reaches for the controls. "Hold on. The docking arm on this side is janky, I haven't had a chance to fix it."

The shuttle catches with a sharp lurch that sends

Raj's stomach reeling before they settle into the docking bay. "Holy shit, Jay."

Jay raises his hands — *I warned you, didn't I?* — then unbuckles his harness. "It was next on the to-fix list before Las took the *Nanshe* and went traipsing off across the system. But now we're home, safe and sound."

Raj engages his magboots and stands, following Jay to the shuttle's exit; Jay stops short of the airlock door. He turns back to Raj and holds out a tentative hand. "We good?"

"We're good." Raj ignores the hand, hauling Jay into an embrace. The other man squeezes him hard before letting go.

"Glad to hear it," Jay says. "Now go tell Las or she'll lock herself on the bridge and not come out until we're back at Ironfall."

Raj hesitates — he knows the conversation needs to happen, but he'd wanted to give her time to sort her thoughts. And take the time to sit with his own.

"Yeah," Jay says, waving away Raj's hesitation. "I'm not living on this boat for the next five days with the two of you avoiding each other. Go sort out your shit and meet the rest of us in the galley for dinner."

The bridge hatch is open, which he takes as a good sign.

Raj makes noise as he climbs the ladder, knocks as he pulls himself through. Lasadi stiffens when she glances over her shoulder, then turns back to silently plotting their course on a complicated stream of graphics on her screen.

He settles in the co-pilot's chair and waits, watching her without being obvious about it, trying not to break her concentration any more than he already has. Her eyes are bloodshot, rimmed in red like she's been crying — or trying not to. Her cheek is smudged with dirt — they're all filthy, still — and her lips are bloodless and chapped.

The little Coruscan house god, the mixla, catches his attention from its nook on the dash. She's put his cittern-string bracelet back in the stasis field at its feet, and he wonders if he should take it back. He'd left it there when they went to Auburn Station, a nod to Coruscan tradition to keep the wearer of the offering safe on their trip. He considers leaving it — not to tether himself to the *Nanshe* anymore, more as a way of tethering her to him. Even if it can only be as captain and crew.

He winces internally as he articulates the impulse to himself. Leaving something in Lasadi's view to remind her of him every time she sits down to do her damn job — now there's an arrogant thought.

Raj plucks the bracelet out of the stasis field, saying a silent, self-conscious prayer of thanks to the mixla for keeping them all safe this time around, then slips it back around his wrist. A muscle in Lasadi's cheek jumps at the gesture, but she doesn't comment, doesn't look at him until she enters her last command and the *Nanshe*'s autopilot engages. The stars on the screen begin to glide smoothly as the thrusters fire to burn them out of orbit and start the long haul back up the gravity well to Durga's Belt.

Lasadi leans back in her seat, watching the screen a

while before she finally turns to him, lips parting to speak.

"I wanted to apologize," Raj says as she breathes out: "I'm sorry."

"I'll go first," he says; her jaw is clenched tight. "I haven't been completely honest with you from the beginning. I didn't tell you who my father was at first, and I should have told you he was posting bounties on me. It's more or less been taken care of, but I understand it endangers anyone near me."

"You apologized for that already," she points out.

"But I wanted to make sure you knew it was real this time."

"Okay." She takes a deep breath. "What do you mean it's been taken care of."

"Ruby's got a script running to take the posts down. And I'll deal with my father. I just . . ." He wants to say something reassuring and confident: *I'll call him up, I'll do it when we get back to Ironfall.* "I don't know how," he finally says.

"It's okay. I'm not — " Lasadi looks down at her hands as though trying to figure out how to word it. "I'm not worried about the danger. If we're going to be a crew, we can figure it out together. But I can't keep us out of danger if I don't know what to watch for."

His heart sings at *us*, but they're a long way from things being all right. "Fair. I was deciding what information you needed to know, and that's not my call."

That seems to surprise her. "Thank you."

"I'm used to keeping people out, not letting them in. I've had a hard time breaking the habit, and I'm sorry."

"You barely knew me," Lasadi says. "But I'll do

better to prove worthy of that trust."

He starts to correct her — that's not what he meant at all — but she holds up a hand.

"I'm sorry for what I put you through," she says. "I couldn't let Anton know I suspected him, which meant I had to almost believe it myself. It was . . . excruciating. But I'm sure it was worse for you."

"Maybe next time I can be in on the joke," Raj says — it's meant for a laugh, to lighten the mood, and at the flinch in the corner of Lasadi's mouth, it's the wrong thing to say. He swallows, hard. Forces himself to tell her the truth. "It was devastating."

Lasadi's staring fixedly out at the stars.

"I was angry at you for not believing me. But I was angriest at myself that I was going to die without ever being completely honest with you. And Jay, and everyone. But mostly you." She finally meets his gaze. "And maybe next time I can be in on it, because I'll have proven you can trust me."

"I did," she says quickly. "I do. And I want to keep working together." Lasadi reaches into her pocket. "I got you something in Icaba. I noticed these in the corner store before we left for Moie, and he still had them. You said you needed new ones."

She holds out a package of cittern strings, and he takes them; their fingers don't quite touch. Raj turns them over in his hand, a smile spreading over his face.

"You sure you want me making a ruckus on the ship?"

"I would like that," Lasadi says. "And I think the others would, too."

"Well, thank you. I'll grab my cittern when we get

back to Ironfall."

"Raj." Lasadi takes a deep, slow breath. "Will you forgive me?"

Raj blinks at her, almost ready to brush the question off with another joke; he can't think of a time someone asked forgiveness from him, and he's not sure what it entails. A healing of some wound in himself, he suspects. Not a simple papering over, not a simple forgetting or ignoring.

"Yes," he says. "But I need to know that in the future you'll always be straight with me. If you have a problem with me, tell me." He gives her a gentle smile. "I can't keep guessing where I stand with you, I go straight to the worst-case scenario."

"I will," she says, and something unclenches deep in his core; he feels at once exhausted and light. And starving. Ruby's laugh drifts through the open hatch, along with the savory aroma of dinner from the galley. Raj's stomach rumbles loudly; Lasadi laughs. A touch of color has come back to her cheeks, the live current of tension has eased in her shoulders. They're back on firmer ground, and Raj should probably leave it that way — but they've agreed to be on the level with each other.

"Jay said to meet him in the galley for dinner," Raj says. "But I thought I was going to die back there, and one of my deepest regrets was not saying this when I had the chance." Raj clears his throat and forces himself to continue despite every terrified fiber of his being screaming at him to stop before he bares his soul beyond retreat. "I admire you. I respect you as our captain. I am also deeply attracted to you, and I think you feel the same way — but I can't actually tell, so I apologize if I've made things awkward. If the feelings aren't mutual, I understand and respect that. But I need to know."

And he'll live with it, though he can't think of how he possibly could. It'll be fine, he tells himself. He'll scratch the itch with a fling next time they're in port, and forget all about the woman who's become a magnet so strong she's begun to realign the core fibers of his soul.

"You make me want to be a better person," he says when she doesn't answer. "And that won't change whether you're my captain, or — " He doesn't dare put a word to that faint wisp of a dream. "We don't have to talk about this now," he says. "But I'm done lying to myself and you."

"No, it's fine," she says. "But I'm sorry, Raj. I don't know *how* to know what I feel about you."

He frowns, trying to parse the sentiment.

"Anton . . ."

He braces himself for the inevitable, ready to hear how she still has feelings for Anton, how wrecked she is by his betrayal. How no Arquellian deserter could compare to the dashing revolutionary hero.

"Anton — what a fucking bastard." She drags in a shaky breath. "I used to trust myself before I met him. It's like that part of me is broken, and I can't tell what pieces are real anymore."

There's so much he could say: *You know he broke you on purpose. You can't blame yourself. A partner is someone who helps you become more yourself, not less.* But any of those feel presumptuous, and he's not sure either of them are up for the emotional nuance those conversations might require.

"He did a number on you," Raj finally says. "But you won in the end."

"Yeah." She sighs. "Raj. I'll be honest. I want to tell you I share your feelings. But what I need right now is dinner, and a shower, and to sleep for three days. Until I get those things I'm in no state to parse what I feel."

It's not a yes, but his heart soars that it's not a no.

"Take your time," he says. "You know what I want, and if that matches what you want, great. If not, also fine." He's proud of how casual he sounds, of his easy posture and the nonchalant way he stands. "I'll see you down in the galley. Oh, and Las?"

Curiosity softens her features.

"From what I saw the last few days, you know exactly how to trust yourself. Your instinct saved all of our asses down there, more than once."

She frowns at his smile, returns his salute with surprise as he disappears down the ladder.

Jay, Ruby, and Alex go silent in the galley when he enters. Jay pauses at the rehydrator door, oven mitt on his hand. Ruby's gnawing her lower lip, worry in her eyes. Alex's leg is bouncing like mad.

"I have some bad news for you all," Raj says solemnly, then winks and slips the package of cittern strings out of his pocket, waves them at the group. "The captain authorized me to grab my cittern once we're back in port. I hope you like to sing."

He ducks the empty drink bulb Ruby flings his way, catches it laughing as it ricochets off the wall, and turns to help the rest of his crew prepare dinner.

# CHAPTER 28
## LASADI

SHE CAN HEAR THEIR LAUGHTER DRIFTING UP THE LADDER from the mess, but she's told herself she needs to check a few more things before she can join them. Verify their course, run some quick diagnostics, see to a few incoming messages.

Instead she's staring out the window, watching the stars through the *Nanshe*'s familiar screen, feeling Anton's weight and obligation to the cause and Indira's gravity falling away from her as she thinks about what Raj said.

She knew Raj had been hiding things before, but she doesn't begrudge him. He had every reason not to tell her about his father, his court-martial record, the head-hunters. He barely knew her, and anyway, she's got no room to be upset. If anyone understands building up walls to keep someone from getting too close, it's her.

She'd had close friends in the CLA — Henri among them; she still doesn't know if Anton was telling the truth about him being alive, but she owes it to his memory to find out. Anton had been grooming her for leadership early, though, and he hadn't approved of how friendly she'd been with people under her command. He taught her that leaders need walls and healthy distance. He taught her that leaders don't show scars or weaknesses. He taught her to keep the vulnerable parts her soul so far under lock and key that she's not even sure how to access them anymore.

He taught her to draw a line, knowing someday she'd need to put her friendships secondary to the cause.

The line's still there between herself and Jay, she realizes. She's appreciated that he doesn't press her when she doesn't want to open up, but what has silence gotten them? She still hasn't had a chance to ask what happened between him and Chiara, and before meeting Raj and Ruby and Alex, she might have assumed he didn't want to talk about it. But she can hear Jay joking with the rest of the crew in the galley, and she realizes with a jolt he's been as starved for companionship as she's been. Everyone else probably knows what happened with Chiara already. It isn't that Jay doesn't want to talk, he's just been respecting the line she never bothered erasing.

What she'd told Raj is true. She's starving, exhausted, and reeling from everything — the last thing she needs to do is make a rash decision in her current state. She needs time and space from the emotional turmoil of the last few days, and time and space from Anton before she'll be clearheaded enough to understand what she really feels about Raj.

And that had been completely fine with him.

His simple acceptance of her need for space almost tore down her last meager defenses and had her dragging him to bed — forget about the rest of the crew waiting in the galley.

Except that the one thing she is certain of right now is that the rest of the crew are relying on them both to make a smart decision.

She closes her eyes and takes a deep breath — whatever Jay and the others have put together smells divine, and she hasn't had more today than a ration bar while they were flying from the River of Blood to Icaba. She doesn't have to make any decisions now. All she has to do is eat, shower, and sleep until the autopilot tells her they've reached Ironfall in five days.

She opens her eyes, ready to head down, when a new message pops onto her screen.

Lasadi's heart catches in her throat as she sees the name: Evora Faye Cazinho.

Her sister.

Lasadi's fingers are ice as she swipes open the message.


Las,

I'm sure this message will bounce right back. Or maybe not, I guess — I've never written to a dead person. Does your address expire? Amit would say this is just another clue that I'm losing my mind. But here I am. Writing anyway.

Do you remember how we all used to watch races together? You probably do — you always said you'd be racing someday, and I believed you even though Amit made fun of you. The Star Run was this week, and you would have loved it — especially the bit at the end when the third-place winner, Peter Fangio, got all political about the Alliance and New Manila. They cut the feed, but it wasn't fast enough.

Amit and I still get together every year to watch it — we started again the year you died. Like some sort of memorial, I guess. Neither of us mentioned it, but I saw he put a little folded paper plane in your part of the family altar yesterday. Grandma says your name more in the prayers this time of year — almost as much as around your birthday or the anniversary of your — I'm not going to say it. Olds, I still can't believe you have a place in the altar, that's for grandparents, isn't it? Not for sisters.

I wouldn't admit this to Serious Big Brother Amit, but every year when we watch the race, I'm looking for you. I suppose I can tell you — I mean, I wouldn't tell you in real life, you and Amit both would make fun of me. You two always agreed on at least one thing: superstition and afterlife and all that stuff is nonsense. But I can tell you anything I want now you're dead, haha, and you have to listen.

I'm sorry, I'm rambling.

What I want to say is that this year I saw you. At the pilot orientation, when they were scanning the pilots, I swear I saw you. They never spend any time on the newcomers, you know that, so it was the briefest glimpse — but I recorded it and saved it so at least I can pretend you're still out there somewhere.

I just want to say how proud of you I am and how much I miss you.

I love you.

Evvi Faye

The words swim together as Lasadi fiercely blinks back tears.

She doesn't know which part of Evvi's letter was the biggest punch in the gut. The fact that her family made a place for her on the altar, that her grandmother speaks her name in prayers, or that her younger siblings get together to honor her memory every year.

They hadn't held banishing for her after all.

She's been an idiot.

An idiot not to reach out earlier, but also an idiot not to think Evvi and Amit might be watching the Star Run. If her sister recognized her, who else might have? Lasadi is supposed to be dead. Can she even reply to her sister without putting them all in danger?

She swipes the message away without rereading it, heart pounding.

This is another decision she needs to make after dinner, a shower, and sleep. She shoves the message out of her mind, scraping a thumbnail along her lash line to catch a traitorous drop of moisture there, then unbuckles from her chair and pushes herself into the galley where the others are waiting.

Jay spots her first, smile faltering — she must look as awful as she feels.

"I don't know about you all, but I'm beat to hell,"

she says, to get ahead of the questions. She slips into the open space beside Jay. "I'm going to sleep for three days."

"And you deserve it." Jay throws an arm around her shoulders in a hug, then reaches for the enchilada casserole bake to serve her up first.

"We all deserve a break. And you all deserve an apology."

"We're good, Cap." Ruby squeezes Lasadi's hand. "That was some fast thinking, and the rest of us will get the cues faster once we've worked with each other more."

Lasadi isn't afraid to meet Raj's gaze across the table anymore; when she does he smiles at her, encouraging. And happy — he seems genuinely happy even after the hell she just put him through. Maybe that's the thread of warmth Lasadi still has coiled in her core from Ruby's touch on her hand, from Jay's arm around her shoulder. Happiness.

"Have you seen the news?" Alex asks, voice tinged with excitement and pride. "Qacha gave an amazing interview, and Fangio went completely off, it was flash."

"And we got a message from Vasavada saying an Alliance transport was spotted in the area," says Jay. "But they're not moving in. The story's catching like fire — I think your plan worked."

"There's some good news, at least," Las says. She catches the hot sauce Alex nudges her way with her first real smile in ages. Since she watched Raj play the cittern in the square in Moie, maybe.

"See," Alex says to his sister. "People feel good when they help others."

"Shut it, Alex."

"It's good for your soul."

"Alex."

Lasadi's seen Ruby's annoyance when she bickers with her brother, but now her expression holds a knife's edge of warning. And his holds a calm defiance that makes him seem far older than seventeen.

"All right, Ruby," Lasadi says, floating the hot sauce back across the table to Alex. "Something's going on, and whatever it is, we're in it together." She smiles at Jay, wry. "Believe me. You can try to go deal with it on your own, but these assholes will apparently track you all the way across the Durga System. So you might as well save yourself the trouble and let us help from the beginning."

Ruby's mouth quirks up at that. "Fair point to you."

"You're stuck with us," says Jay. "So spit it out."

Lasadi knows that storm of doubt warring across Ruby's face all too well; when Ruby's gaze meets hers and the other woman decides to let the wall crumble down, Lasadi feels it like an electric jolt through her soul. Something fundamental and irreversible shifts in the room, and despite her exhaustion Lasadi knows one thing for certain. She'll fight like hell to protect every single person at this table — even if that fight is against her own fear.

"Okay," Ruby says. "So. You all know, I think, that Alex and I were raised by the Aymaya Apostles in Artemis City? Left at the doorstep — he was just a baby, and I was twelve. I left when I turned eighteen, and Alex . . ."

"Got kicked out," Raj says.

"The ayas still love me," Alex says around a bite of enchilada casserole. "They love me more when I'm not there, only."

Ruby rolls her eyes. "We still — *I* still give them money. It was to help with Alex, but now I guess . . . it's a tithe? I mean, they're good people. They do a lot to help others."

"And now they need help," Alex says. "They asked Ruby, but she doesn't want to."

"I didn't want to involve you all," Ruby says.

"We're already involved," Lasadi points out.

"We're crew," Jay adds.

"And we're happy to do a good deed for some monastics," Raj says. "It'll be a nice break after almost dying a bunch of times in the jungle."

Ruby takes a deep breath. "Okay," she finally says. "Only you may change your mind once I'm done telling you the story of the cursed relics of Saint Alixhi."

The adventure continues in the next book, *Cursed Saint Caper*.

Want more of Raj and Lasadi's story? Don't miss the free Nanshe Chronicles prequel novella, *Artemis City Shuffle*.

Head to jessiekwak.com/nanshe for more.

# ABOUT JESSIE KWAK

Jessie Kwak has always lived in imaginary lands, from Arrakis and Ankh-Morpork to Earthsea, Tatooine, and now Portland, Oregon. As a writer, she sends readers on their own journeys to immersive worlds filled with fascinating characters, gunfights, explosions, and dinner parties.

When she's not raving about her latest favorite sci-fi series to her friends, she can be found sewing, mountain biking, or out exploring new worlds both at home and abroad.

*(Author photo by Robert Kittilson.)*

*Connect with me:*
www.jessiekwak.com
jessie@jessiekwak.com

facebook.com/JessieKwak

twitter.com/jkwak

instagram.com/kwakjessie

# THE BULARI SAGA

**With stakes this high, humanity doesn't need a hero. They need someone who can win.**

\*\*Complete 5-book series + 3 prequel novellas + bonus short stories = over 500,000 words of adventure.\*\*

Willem Jaantzen didn't ask to be a hero. He just wants to keep his family safe in the shifting sands of Bulari's underground — and to get the city's upper crust to acknowledge just how far he's come since his days as an orphaned street kid. With his businesses thriving and his dark past swept into the annals of history, it looks like he has everything he could ever ask for. Until, that is, his oldest rival turns up murdered and the blame — and champagne — begins to flow.

It turns out Thala Coeur died as she lived: sowing chaos. And when a mysterious package bearing her call sign shows up on Jaantzen's doorstep, he and his family are quickly swallowed up in a web of lies, betrayals, and interplanetary politics. It'll only take one stray spark to start another civil war in the underworld, and Jaantzen's going to have to pull out every play from his notorious past if he wants to keep his city from going up in flames.

Jaantzen never wanted to be a hero, but that might just be a good thing. Because a hero could never stop the trouble that's heading humanity's way.

The Bulari Saga is a five-book series featuring gunfights, dinner parties, explosions, motorcycle chases, underworld intrigue, and a fiercely plucky found family who have each other's backs at every step. Perfect for fans of The Expanse, Firefly, and The Godfather.

**Start the adventure today at** jessiekwak.com/bulari-saga

# DID YOU LIKE THE BOOK?

As a reader, I rely on book recommendations to help me pick what to read next.

As a writer, book recommendations are the most powerful way for me to get the word out to new readers.

If you liked this book, please leave a review on the platform of your choice — or tell a friend! It's the easiest way to help authors you enjoy keep producing great work.

Cheers!

Jessie

Made in the USA
Middletown, DE
29 August 2022

71813908R00166